Before he had even quite realised he was doing it, his thumb was stroking over that plump lower lip and he was watching it tremble beneath his touch.

His breath came fast, matching the accelerated beat of his heart. It would be so easy to lose himself. The lust firing his blood wanted to claim her. It was that part that took charge as he leaned down to her.

His hand moved from her chin so his fingers stroked her neck, revelling in her heat and the rapid beat of her pulse under them. Her scent overpowered him. *Just one taste of her*, the demon within him urged. Just one taste and it would be enough. He breathed her in as his head lowered to her. His eyes fastened on her coral mouth.

When his lips were just a breath from touching hers she turned her head. He stopped just short of colliding with her cheek and paused, his breath harsh against her skin as he struggled for control.

Harper St George was raised in rural Alabama and along the tranquil coast of northwest Florida. It was this setting, filled with stories of the old days, that instilled in her a love of history, romance and adventure. At high school she discovered the romance novel, which combined all of those elements into one perfect package. She lives in Atlanta, Georgia, with her husband and two young children. Visit her website: www.harperstgeorge.com

Digital short stories by Harper St George

His Abductor's Desire
Her Forbidden Gunslinger

This is Harper St George's
powerful debut novel
for Mills & Boon® Historical Romance!

Visit the author profile page
at millsandboon.co.uk

ENSLAVED
BY THE VIKING

Harper St George

First published in Great Britain 2015
by Mills & Boon, an imprint of Harlequin (UK) Limited,
Large Print edition 2015
Harlequin (UK) Limited, Eton House, 18-24 Paradise Road,
Richmond, Surrey TW9 1SR

ISBN: 978-0-263-25561-4

Harlequin (UK) Limited's policy is to use papers that are natural,
renewable and recyclable products and made from wood grown in
sustainable forests. The logging and manufacturing processes conform
to the legal environmental regulations of the country of origin.

Printed and bound in Great Britain
by CPI Antony Rowe, Chippenham, Wiltshire

ENSLAVED
BY THE VIKING

For my family.

Thank you to Kathryn Cheshire,
my wonderful editor, for all of her insightful
advice and her willingness to help guide
me. I'd also like to thank Linda Fildew
for her support. Thank you to my agent,
Nicole Resciniti, for her enthusiasm and
encouragement. A huge thank you to my
amazing critique partners Erin Moore and
Tara Wyatt. This story would not have been
finished without them. Thank you to
Jessica Brace, Andrea R. Cooper,
Rachel Ezzo, Brandee Frost and
Nathan Jerpe for reading, offering advice
and commiserating with me!

Chapter One

Northumbria—AD 865

Eirik had never taken a captive before, but the idea that she could be his was nearly overpowering. He closed his eyes in an attempt to fight back the dark thought, but when he opened them and she still hadn't seen their boats, his heartbeat quickened. The longing sent his blood thrumming through his body so that it roared in his ears and blocked out almost everything else except his awareness of her.

For two years he'd been the leader of this fleet of longships. Even before that, he'd travelled under his father's command to far-reaching ends of the world. He'd become adept at reading signs, at picking up on cues that would go unnoticed by most, at trusting his instincts. It was why his men trusted him so explicitly. And now his instincts were telling him to take her.

She should have noticed them by now—after all, he could see her through the fog, so she should be able to see them. But she twirled in the dark mist as if she hadn't a care in her world. Perhaps the gods had left her there just for him. He blinked and banished the thought, his warrior's instinct taking over. There were no signal fires along the beach. Either the guards were asleep or there were no guards. Someone should be out walking with the girl, but she danced alone, a gift to be plucked from the desolate shores and taken home.

Eirik looked up and down the beach, searching for signs of an ambush, some shape that would emerge from the gloom and reveal itself to be an army of Saxons. Perhaps the girl had been planted as an enticement. Or perhaps something more sinister was at play. He'd heard tales of sirens who lured men to their deaths. They usually inhabited mythical islands that the sea swallowed up again, but it was possible the Northumbrian coast offered its own sirens. But the beach was empty and a quick look at the men rowing assured him that no one else had been enthralled by her as he had. Perhaps she was his own personal siren.

Her lithe form swayed as she twirled, luxuriating in abandon and unrestraint. The spell she wove pulled at him, promising freedom from the bonds of duty and the shadows of his past that had always held him in such rigid control. He wanted to join her and was struck by the absurdity of the thought. She was just a girl, like any other he'd seen in his travels, but he could name the exact moment she'd picked his shape out of the dense fog. Her gaze ignited small flares of awareness, and when it met his, he was struck by a strange shock of recognition. He'd never seen her before, never been this far north on these shores, but the feeling that she was his was there all the same.

The fleet's approach had been planned to coincide with the veil of the approaching dawn and his men were carefully trained in the art of stealth. It would be easy to take her. The terrible anticipation clenched tight in his gut. But he pushed it away and reminded himself that their journey up the coast was a scouting mission. There would be no captives.

Finally understanding the danger coming towards her, she turned to run. Blood rushed through him, powered by the need to stop her before she warned everyone. His booted feet splashed in the water and his men followed, dropping their oars and disembarking to pull the ship onto the shore.

* * *

It had stormed the previous night, but that didn't stop Merewyn from her morning ritual of walking on the beach. If her older brother's repeated threats on the matter hadn't deterred her, a little rain wasn't going to stand in her way. She lived for her mornings away from the manor, when she could be alone with the sunrise. It was probably silly, but in those brief moments she felt like anything was possible. That with the new day, the drudgery of her life *could* become something more than caring for her brother's children and being relegated to performing the household tasks of a servant.

She loved the children dearly, but they weren't hers. Blythe made sure that she remembered who had borne them, who was really in charge of the household. And she was right. As his wife, she should be in charge, but Merewyn couldn't help feeling slighted. On the beach, though, all of that fell away. She was free. She was happy. Her life was her own.

She smiled as she twirled in the mist, letting the moisture collect like tiny diamonds shining in the dark strands of her hair. Despite the cold, she put her arms up high and held the fur wrap aloft to catch the breeze. The salty wind made her think of freedom. She adored it.

But in the next moment, she saw the ship cutting through the surf, saw the wooden dragon's head set atop the prow and knew that freedom would never be hers again. The beast was so close she could have counted each of his pointed teeth where they protruded from the curve of his grotesque smile, promising death and suffering. She could have if she hadn't already noticed the other ships accompanying the first one, each drawing her attention as they emerged from the shroud of mist. The boats spread out wide before her, creating the illusion of dark wings, like a giant beast taking flight in search of its prey.

The beach was a long, flat stretch of sand that gave way to gentle, rolling grassland. Her figure standing at the sea's edge was surely as conspicuous as was that of the Northman standing in that first ship. The others blended into one mass of muscled humanity bending and rowing, but he stood tall with one foot resting on the gunwale as he stared directly at her. She had been spotted. He was coming for her.

Alfred had been right. He'd warned her all along to keep close to the manor while he was gone, that the Northmen were growing bolder, but she'd disregarded him as an overly protective older brother. But he'd been right, and now nothing could save her from them. Every story she'd ever heard of the horrible things they did to their captives sped through her mind in an instant. The terror was enough to paralyse her.

But she forcefully pushed her fear away and made herself move. At first in slow, wobbling steps backwards and then, after a half turn, in wider, faster strides that took her towards the grass. She had trouble tearing her gaze from that giant on the first boat. He moved, arms uncrossing from his chest, lord of all he set his eyes upon as he readied to jump from the boat.

The horrible certainty that he would catch her made her sprint faster towards the manor. It stood on a gentle slope about a half mile inland. It was too far away to reach before the boats touched the beach, but maybe she had a chance to warn everyone of the invaders. They wouldn't see the monsters coming without her warning. Even knowing where the fortress stood, she could hardly make out a light through the heavy fog.

Her legs pumped, toes digging deep into the sandy shore as she struggled to run, her blood prickling and settling heavy in her calves. She already had a painful stitch in her side, but Merewyn forced herself to keep going. She imagined she heard the wind striking the leather of a Northman's cloak. It spurred her to move faster and sooner than she had imagined possible she was running through the open gates of her home.

'Close the gates! The Northmen have come!' She barely managed to get the words out before she collapsed in a heap, struggling to catch her breath while her lungs constricted painfully in her chest.

Someone grabbed her arm and yanked her to her feet as the gates swung closed.

'How many?' a voice called out. She had no idea who had spoken in the chaos.

'Five ships, perhaps more.' She shook her head in frustration. She'd been too frightened to count and unable to see them clearly. There could have been more hiding in the fog.

'Dear God, they'll overrun us!'

A low roar filled her ears, and she realised it was the sound of the beasts just outside the gates. Their battle cries were fierce and almost inhuman. Her knees trembled and her blood ran cold. The horde had been so close on her heels it was a miracle she'd made it within the walls before they caught her. She immediately offered up a prayer of thanks and tried to remember what Alfred had told them to do if they were attacked while he was gone.

'Merewyn! What in God's name have you done?'

Merewyn turned to see Alfred's wife, Blythe, approaching. There was no denying the censure in the woman's eyes. 'The Danes are here—'

'How dare you lead them to us? This is what comes of your morning walks. Didn't Alfred forbid them?'

'They were coming straight for the beach. They already knew where the manor was.'

The blow was so unexpected, Merewyn staggered. The imprint of Blythe's hand burned hot on her cheek and her eyes stung with tears.

'Get below. I'll have to deal with this.' Blythe was already looking past her to the gates.

'Wh-what of the children?'

'Alythe has them all except Annis and Geoff. They just ran to your chamber. Take them with you.'

Merewyn ran to find her brother's youngest children. She was thankful she never allowed them to follow her to the beach in the mornings. Already she could hear the banging at the gates and the wood groaning as it struggled to withstand the assault. The hollow echo of the initial chop of an axe splitting into the gate reverberated through her and made her stomach clench with the knowledge that it was only a matter of time before the wood gave way.

Eirik used the thick hilt of his sword to bash through another door. Another empty chamber. He bit back the sour disappointment and stalked to the great hall. It, too, had been abandoned by the Saxons, but was now filling with his men. The lady of Wexbrough Manor stood glaring at him from her place in the far corner. Her guard had been disarmed and knelt, tethered, at the other end of the room. The servants and workmen had been gathered in the yard. Only young boys, women and old men—none capable of putting up much of a fight. That only left the family members, who were conspicuously absent. He knew they were hiding.

It shouldn't matter. They weren't here for captives. This was merely a scouting trip. The location was prime for a command post for the spring invasion and it hadn't yet been thoroughly assessed. Eirik would send men to report to his uncle, who was wintering to the south, and then leave to spend the winter at home, a place he hadn't seen in almost two years. Taking the girl wasn't part of that plan, and he assured himself it wasn't why he hoped to find her. He wanted to see her up close to understand what it was that drew him to her. To appease his curiosity.

His sharp gaze took in every shadow in the hall, searching for a glimpse of the blue gown she wore or a tendril of the dark hair that had streamed out behind her as she'd run. She would be hidden with the rest of the family, wherever that was. They didn't have time to search. The hair on his neck stood upright, a warning that they needed to make haste and had already spent enough time at the manor. Whether the lack of an adequate guard was a reflection of its lord's arrogance or its king's desperation in calling all the able-bodied men to him, Eirik didn't know. But the possibility that someone had escaped from the manor to summon nearby warriors to their aid was very real. Every instinct insisted they leave now.

The need to find her pressed tight on his chest and threatened to squeeze the air from his lungs. It was madness, sheer and utter madness. Eirik recognised it and kept a tight rein on it, refusing to give up control.

He stepped over bowls and tankards, all signs of

an interrupted breakfast, and stopped when he stood before the lady. Two chests of tribute, *danegeld* the lady had called it, were spilled on the floor between them. 'This is all you offer? You've already told me of your household's relation to your king. Doesn't your lord husband rank high enough to deserve more generosity from his king?' He kicked a gilded tankard so it came to rest at her feet.

If the woman had been shocked that he spoke her language, she never revealed it. Even now, she regarded him with the contempt he assumed she reserved for the lowest slaves.

'What more do you want from us, dog? Your hounds are already tearing apart the chapel.' Her words were punctuated by a loud crash coming from the general direction of that building.

'If you have nothing else to offer, we'll take your grain.' The tribute was no more than what she should pay. The lord of the manor had led a particularly brutal offensive against his uncle's men to the south just months ago. It didn't bother him at all that the loss of the grain meant she and her lord would face a particularly harsh winter. He repeated the words in his own tongue and they were greeted with sounds of disgust. Gold was exceedingly preferable to grain. Eirik smiled and raised his hand to a group of men who stood nearby awaiting his command. It was the signal to carry out his threat.

'Nay!' she yelled when the group moved to leave for the granary.

Almost at the same time, a shrill scream pierced the still morning air. The smile dropped from his mouth and his heart picked up speed in his chest. It was the girl. Eirik knew it without even knowing how he could be so sure. His feet were leaden, but moved faster as he followed the sound through the wide doorway that led to a pantry.

Shelves stacked with sacks of foodstuff lined the walls. Oak barrels had been stowed three deep against the wall, but a portion of them were pushed aside revealing a hidden chamber in the floor. A door that led to the underground chamber was thrown wide, leaving a yawning black hole in the earth.

His half-brother, Gunnar, had just ascended the steps inside. A figure was slung over his shoulder, struggling to be released.

'What have you found?' Eirik lowered his sword and took in the sight of the slender girl in the dark blue gown thrown over his brother's shoulder. Her chestnut hair spilled down his back and her fists beat futilely against him. Possessiveness, hot and fierce, rose up within him.

'There's nothing down there but children and old women.' Gunnar smiled. 'This is the only treasure.' His hand moved over her buttocks in a rough caress.

'Put her down.' The command was so harsh and forceful that even the girl stopped fighting to raise her head and look at him. Her dark eyes widened, and he watched the ivory column of her throat move as she swallowed. She recognised him. The pull he'd felt on the beach was stronger now. Eirik gritted his teeth and demanded control as he stowed his sword in the sheath strapped diagonally across his back.

'I found her.' Gunnar's voice was almost a growl. 'You have Kadlin.' Despite his harsh words, he was gentle as he allowed her to slide slowly from his grasp to land on her feet.

'Leave her to me, Gunnar.'

'Ah, finally, brother...' His brother's gaze was fierce, but clearly amused as if he held the secret to some jest that Eirik had yet to share. But the girl wasn't fighting now. She watched Eirik with those fathomless eyes.

Gunnar opened his mouth, no doubt to taunt him

again, but was interrupted before he could even start.

'Take her!' The voice was clear and steady as the manor's lady entered the pantry.

All eyes turned to her. Eirik was sure he heard a gasp come from the girl.

'Take her instead, and leave the grain,' the woman urged.

'I could take both,' Eirik countered as he wondered what the woman was about.

'Aye, but you don't have time for both.' Her clever eyes seized his before she turned them on the girl. The gaze was hard and assessing as it travelled her length. 'She's unmarried and unmarred from childbirth. She could fetch you a price worth more than a winter's worth of grain. Take her and go while you still can.'

Eirik didn't have time to weigh her words. In the next instant, the girl found her legs and surprised them all by running out the back way.

His blood thundered again, pounding through him and demanding he catch her.

Chapter Two

Merewyn ran even though she knew it was futile. Even though every figure she passed was a Northman and the only way out was through the front gates. She ran because she couldn't stand the idea of allowing them to take her. She ran to outpace the betrayal of those two words so bitterly spoken.

Take her! The words repeated themselves over and over in her head until they were meaningless. A chant. A curse. Words that she would remember for ever. But, most of all, she ran because she knew she would be taken.

She'd heard the stories of the Northmen often repeated in reverent voices by travellers around the fire in the great hall. They made slaves of their enemies and raped the women. She couldn't bear the thought. And if they didn't keep her after they finished, there were Eastern cities with whole markets devoted to the trade of humans where they could sell her. Merewyn couldn't let that happen. She couldn't live as a slave.

He was coming to get her. In her mind's eye, she saw the golden giant from the dragon ship following behind her. She knew it would be he who would give chase. Though she hadn't understood his words, she knew that he'd laid some sort of claim to her. She had felt it on the beach. His eyes had claimed her as surely as his hands would if he caught her.

His footsteps were hard on the ground and getting closer, no matter how fast she ran. His heavy gaze bore into her, touching her with its power. It crawled up her back like fingers clawing at her gown and reached for her neck. As he drew nearer, the visceral potency of his scrutiny made her heart leap into her throat and left her knees weak. When she couldn't take it another moment, when she was sure he would grab her, she ducked around the safety of the forge. But he was there, already rounding the opposite corner of the massive stone hearth to block her path. There would be no hiding from him.

He stood tall and wide before her, bent slightly at the knees, hands ready to grab her. He was larger than any of the men she knew; she was small and slight next to him. His eyes blazed with his intention to have her and she realised there was nothing left to do but fight him. She would long for death eventually if he took her; it was better to have it meted out to her now. She held no illusions of walking away from the fight. He would smite her out as easily as he would an insect. With that realisation, Merewyn's heart stopped its frenzied beating and a cold certainty descended over her body, bringing with it a calmness she had never experienced.

Her decision made, Merewyn's fingers closed around the hilt of the *seax* she kept in the belt at her waist and pulled it from its leather sheath. The long, thin blade would be useless against the chain mail he wore on his torso, so she'd have to aim low…or go for his throat. Just as she debated, he reached out for her, taking the choice from her by making her slash at his arm. She was rewarded with his low grunt of pain. Merewyn immediately pulled back to try again, but he recovered and lunged for her.

She swung blindly, only to have him grab her wrist and twist her arm behind her back. He yanked the knife from her before his other hand grabbed her free wrist and held it pressed to the stone hearth at her back. It happened too fast. Before she knew it, she was staring up into his face, so close that it left her breathless.

Death didn't seem to be an immediate option. The relentless pound of her heartbeat returned to send the blood whooshing through her ears. It rushed through her so fast and hard, it urged her body to action, but she was stuck, forced to await his judgement. As his gaze raked her, she couldn't shake the feeling that he was somehow appraising her worth, perhaps wondering how much she might fetch him in the slave market, or if he should just kill her now.

But then she met his eyes, and she realised it was neither of those. The look of fiery possession was unmistakable, and it seared her where it touched. It licked across her face and down her neck, a living flame, burning her up as though she was fuel for the fire. She'd never seen someone look so focused, so resolute. He meant to keep her for himself. He meant to own her...to violate her. She closed her eyes tight against the knowledge.

He didn't move.

Inches separated his broad chest from hers, but he made no attempt to touch her further. His breath brushed her cheek, calm and steady—not erratic like hers—and she observed it smelled of winter, cool and mild. It was foreign and uninvited, but not repugnant. The hands that held her were firm, but not hard. Nothing was happening as she'd imagined it might.

Confused by his inaction, she chanced opening her eyes to see the sun had finally found an opening in the clouds and was glinting along the knit mesh on his shoulder. Her gaze followed along the corded muscle of his neck, noting absurdly that it was clean shaven. Weren't the Norse barbarians supposed to be unkempt?

She followed the bearded curve of his strong chin to the hard, straight line of his mouth and upwards over the bizarrely graceful curve of his cheekbones. The man could have been a Viking god. The small lump at the bridge of his nose was his only flaw. She took a deep breath and found the courage to meet his eyes. The blue was vivid in its intensity. It made her stomach twist in fear, but at the same time she realised there was no rage in those eyes. She couldn't quite identify the emotion that burned there.

He wasn't a god, she had to remind herself. The small creases around his eyes had been put there from years of squinting into the sun, or maybe it was possible someone had made him laugh enough to create those lines. Merewyn took another long, deep breath and felt his warm breath fill her lungs. It shifted something within her. Faster than her heart went from one beat to the next, she was no longer overwhelmed by her fear. He was real. No longer just the monster sent to tear her world apart. Maybe he would listen.

'You don't have to take me. You can leave me here. I haven't been trained in any skill, so I won't be of any use to you.' The words tumbled out before she could get a grasp on them to make them into something compelling. She tried to keep her voice steady as she reasoned with him, but it still trembled near the end. And when his gaze left her face to flick downwards over her body, she knew without a doubt the skill for which he was assessing her. Another pang of terror shot through her, but she forced herself to stay calm and focused her gaze straight ahead. It landed on his hair where she studied the contrast of a single sun-bleached strand against the dark wheat of the rest of it, still damp from the morning's mist.

'You would choose to stay with your family when they would give you away?'

He looked to the bruise she knew had formed along her cheekbone. His voice was low, not mocking as she might have imagined it, and the words were his first spoken solely for her ears. The rough texture of it awakened something inside her, and she had no idea what it was. Only that its sound seeped in through her skin and warmed her in the pit of her stomach, claiming some part that hadn't been given, leaving her startled and disturbed.

She closed her eyes to force it out, but that only made Blythe's words sound louder in her head. *Take her!* They hadn't been forgotten in her fight with the Northman. They still echoed in her mind. What would it mean to stay with her family? Could she stay, knowing that she was expendable to them? Today's blow wasn't the first from Blythe. It wouldn't be the last. But how could she go…willingly? How could she leave Alfred and everything she had ever known and loved? She wouldn't. She couldn't submit to being owned by him. Couldn't resign herself to a fate where she was nothing. Whatever it meant to stay, it would be preferable to the uncertainty of belonging to him.

'I would stay with my family rather than go with a Dane.' This time, she made sure her voice was strong.

He was silent as he looked her over, his gaze touching every feature of her face, lingering on the bruise. Merewyn shifted so her hair partially covered it, hating that he could see it. His eyes settled on hers again. She would have sworn he saw deep inside her to that place he had awakened. It didn't seem fair that he could see so much of her when his face was stoic and closed.

'If you stay, you will be given away again. To a Dane, to a Saxon. You won't know until it's happened.' He sounded so certain. She hated him for that above all other things.

The words created a fissure in the, until now, pristine tapestry of her mind. Madness lazed in that tiny abyss. She resisted the pull in that direction and tried to shut out his words, to convince herself that he was lying, but there was a profound and underlying truth to them that she couldn't deny. If someone had told her yesterday that Blythe would utter those hated words, she wouldn't have believed it. But they had been said. Was it a stretch of the imagination to think she might offer her again?

Nay! Alfred wouldn't allow it.

But Alfred wasn't here, came the answer in her mind. She jerked her wrists to try to break free and when that didn't work she kicked him in his booted shin. It was a fruitless attempt, but she struck out at him as much to deny his words as to get away from him.

His grip tightened and he twisted her around so that her crossed wrists were held tight against her belly and his arms held her within their prison. His chest pressed solidly against her back, holding her front pinned to the forge. The rough stones pressed into her cheek. It was useless to struggle; he completely engulfed her with his size.

'Deny what you will, but you know I speak the truth.' The words were harsh against her ear, rustling the hair at her temple. 'I won't harm you. That's something you can't trust from your family.'

Merewyn bit her lip to stifle the sob that begged to come out. He wasn't right, damn him! He wasn't. One last futile push back against him caused him to squeeze her tight and made his hips push her forward so she was flush against the stones, held immobile by his body. Her mind rushed to find a way out of it, to figure out some way to make him leave so her life could go back to the way it was before her walk on the beach that morning. But it wouldn't be the same, even if he left her. Those horrible words would always be there, eating her alive.

Blythe hated her. It would happen again. Merewyn knew that he would take her with or without her cooperation. If she could somehow buy some time, maybe she could figure out a way to get away from him before anything horrible happened. But even as she contemplated the possibility, she recognised that there was a strange sense of security in the prison of his arms. He was so stoic and candid that she couldn't help but believe his promise of safety.

'Do you vow it? Can you promise I won't be harmed?' Even if he was a barbarian, she wanted to hear him say it.

Eirik could feel her heart fluttering beneath her ribs like the wings of a small bird locked in a cage. It beat beneath the wrist he held over her chest, and he would have sworn he felt it through the chain mail that covered his own. She was so small and fragile pressed against him. He could feel the delicacy of her bones beneath her flesh, and the softness of her body evoked indescribable visions of comfort and a need to protect her.

He'd known the rush of fear and anticipation when facing down an enemy. He'd known the triumph of vanquishing that enemy. But he'd never known anything like what he was feeling now. The triumph was there. It rushed through him, a roaring in his ears. But the fear was there, too. It wasn't anything like the fear of a battleaxe splitting open his skull. It wasn't like the fear of ordering a command that would result in the death of the men he led. It was the unknown fear of what she would do to him and why he wanted to have her. He wanted her in ways he couldn't even begin to comprehend, ways that went beyond the physical comfort she could offer him.

He'd been shocked and furious when he discovered her face marred by the bruise. His first thought was that Gunnar had put it there when he'd retrieved her in the cellar, but it was already a purple stain marring the ivory of her skin. Too dark to have been placed there moments ago. And although Gunnar was fierce in battle, he'd never known his brother to physically harm a woman. The lady at the manor had done it. There was no doubt in his mind. There was no denying the fierce need he felt to protect her from her own family.

Eirik's hands reflexively gripped the fabric of her gown as they sought the heat emanating from beneath, before he pushed away from her. He fought for the control that had been struggling to slip from his grasp the moment his gaze had found her on the beach. The need to touch her, to possess her, to make her know that she belonged to him, was strong. But it was enough now that she *was* his. There would be time later. Now he needed to focus on getting the men back on the boats before more Saxons arrived. They sailed for home today. Once there, he would decide the future of his pretty slave.

'You won't be harmed in my care. From this day forward, you are mine.'

Chapter Three

Merewyn tried to make her mind cooperate and think of some way out of her captivity. It wouldn't accept what had happened, even though she sat in the back of the boat, her gown sodden with sea-water and her hands bound before her. There was nothing she could do short of throwing herself over the side. Froth formed as the oars churned the blue-grey water, each stroke taking her farther into the unknown, but a watery grave held no appeal. So she gave up looking at the water and sat with her knees drawn up to her chest and her face buried against her bound and shaking hands. Anything to stop herself from looking at *him*.

She hated her growing fascination with the man who had taken her, and had been stunned when she realised she'd done nothing but watch him from the time he put her in the boat. He was the clear leader of these men; even the men in the other boats seemed to obey him. He stalked gracefully up and down the centre aisle between them as they rowed, shouting commands, heedless of the treacherous sway of the boat as it rode the waves. Power clung to him like the crimson cloak that flapped in the breeze with his every turn. Even with her eyes closed tight, she saw him. She could still feel the press of his chest at her back.

The crew gave a shout and she opened her eyes to the dark red sail rising above them. The sail flapped in the breeze until it was fully extended and caught the wind, causing the ship to lurch as if an invisible string had been picked up and was pulling them along. They were out on the open sea now; the land had long faded to a tiny blight on the horizon. The old string, the one that connected her to home, had been broken.

Merewyn turned and took one last look towards the land, but it was impossible to make out. She was lost. For the first time in her life she was set adrift on her own, moving away from everything she had known and the people who cared for her. Blythe had refused to look at her when the Northman had brought her back inside. The others had followed her lead and turned their eyes away, but in sadness and shame more than disdain. It was as if she had already been cut from their lives.

She hadn't even been able to say goodbye to Sempa, her old nursemaid, who had been out in the forest. If only Alfred hadn't been called away. He would have protected her. But she couldn't stop herself from wondering if he would be angry with his wife or if he would agree with her actions. Yesterday she would have thought he'd feel sorrow, but now that her world had been turned on its head, she didn't know what to think. He had seen the bruises left from Blythe's blows before and done nothing.

For the thousandth time she wondered what could have made the woman so quick to give her away. Had the loss of grain really meant starvation? Nay, it would be more than the grain. A sick thought, one that she had tried to banish, bloomed inside her and began to twist its bitter roots through her heart. Alythe was approaching the age of betrothal. Getting rid of Merewyn would eliminate competition, would make it that much easier to ensure she had the pick of bridegrooms and a sizeable dowry. Just before he'd left, Alfred had promised to see Merewyn married in the New Year. Had Blythe been so desperate to secure her daughter's future? Had she been such an impediment to that plan?

A bitter laugh threatened to escape, but it brought about tears that she forced herself to blink back. Despite Alfred's intention, Merewyn didn't care about finding a match that would see her in the king's company. She didn't want that life. She wanted the quiet life of running a manor; she wanted the care of an attentive husband and the time to devote to her family. Blythe would have known that if she hadn't spent her days thinking up ways to make life miserable for her.

A shrill whistle drew her attention across the water until it fell on the red-haired Northman who had carried her from the cellar. He was hard to miss standing near the prow of his ship, with his hair glistening in the sun. He was staring at her with a furrowed brow and sharp eyes. Though he was at least the width of five ships away with no hope of immediately reaching her, those eyes still had the power to ignite a chill within her. She remembered how he'd looked at her when he'd pulled her out of the cellar.

She jerked her face away before anyone could see the tear that had slipped down her cheek. She refused to cry before these heathens, no matter how much they frightened her. Her gaze landed directly on the giant who had taken her, the one the men called Eirik. The chain mail he'd worn was gone now, but his size hadn't diminished for the lack of it. His was a brawny strength, not the sinewy slimness she was used to in the men of her acquaintance.

Eirik's eyes narrowed, and he glared at her as he made his way down the narrow aisle between the men on his way to her. Her heart threatened to thrum out of her chest, and with the fear came anger. What had she done to deserve such a look? Why had she gone with him so easily?

Eirik dropped into a squat in front of the girl. Her eyes were seething with anger as she watched him, but her cheeks were pale from fear. He was glad to see it. That terror would do her well on their journey. It would make her less likely to fight or do something equally stupid. He'd learned from his years of fighting that fear was the finest binding, far more effective than hemp or sealskin. It kept men in their place and he assumed it would work on women. The girl needed to hang on to a healthy dose of it in order to stay safe on the crossing.

'What is your name, girl?' He slipped into her native Northumbrian tongue.

She spat in his face instead of answering.

It was an admirable and unexpected gesture. A corner of his mouth twitched up in what might have become a smile of appreciation had he not been so irritated at her exchange with Gunnar. His brother had been a rival since birth, and he knew the whole ship speculated that a fight between them was imminent. But it would happen after their father's death, when the next jarl would be decided. Eirik refused to allow it to happen over something as paltry as a woman, and a slave at that.

He let her stew while he wiped the spittle away with the back of his hand. She chewed her bottom lip, possibly regretting her impulsive response. The girl should be reprimanded for her disrespect, but Eirik knew it for the distress it was. There would be time for punishment if she didn't come to heel on her own. 'Without a name, I'll have to call you slave.'

'You could return me and we wouldn't have to bother with social niceties.'

He had to swallow back the urge to smile again. Amazing, given that just moments ago he'd been ready to toss her back to shore with the strength of his anger. If only Gunnar didn't want her, too. She was too pretty. She had the delicate face of a woman who had been taken care of. Her skin wasn't creased or roughened from working in the sun or the dry, winter wind. Her brow was finely formed above eyes as wide and dark as chestnuts. Ivory skin was smooth over defined cheekbones and a narrow chin. But it was her lips that ultimately held his gaze. Whether they were red from the cold or if it was their natural colour, he didn't know. But they were lush and soft and he had the peculiar urge to know their taste.

He took a deep breath and forced his mind away from such thoughts. His instincts had won on land, but on the sea, he had to maintain control. He grabbed her bound wrists harsher than he intended, but she only winced without muttering a sound.

'My brother is the lord of that manor. He'll pay you for me if you take me back now.'

He'd guessed that she was of noble blood, given her hiding spot with the family and the clothes she wore. The dark blue gown was of a fine-spun wool no peasant could afford, and he guessed the amber piping along the hem of the sleeve and shoulder to be silken velvet. It was no surprise her brother was lord.

'And what would he buy you back with, slave? I've taken everything.' Eirik didn't even bother to point out that if the man's own wife had given her away, he'd be unlikely to bargain for her.

He didn't have to. The doubt was written clearly on her face. Just before she looked away, Eirik got a glimpse into those deep eyes and saw just how hurt and alone she felt. The knowledge twisted something deep inside him and made him angry in a way he couldn't grasp. He cursed it as he withdrew his knife from the sheath at his boot. She gasped then and tried to pull away, but his fingers tightened and held her immobile.

'The sea is there.' He pointed with the knife. 'And Gunnar is there.' Her wide eyes darted in his brother's direction before settling again on Eirik. 'If the water or a sea monster doesn't claim you first, he will.' He paused, allowing the significance of those words to sink in before continuing, 'If you attempt to harm one of the men, you'll be at their mercy. Do you understand? There is no escape.'

'Aye.' The word came out harsh between her clenched teeth. Eirik welcomed the fire that had returned to burn fierce in her eyes. *Her* anger, he could understand.

When her hands relaxed, he set the knife to the hemp binding and began to saw through it. His pace was fast and efficient, because already her close proximity was beginning to weaken him. The air was being squeezed from his chest, causing his breaths to become more frequent, and his limbs felt wrong. Heavy near the ends and alive with sensation. She unbalanced him—a dangerous state for a warrior—and it made him angry that someone so insignificant could hold so much power over him.

He was Eirik, son of the jarl Hegard. He had amassed a fortune raiding and trading while leading his men to victories in the lands south of the North Sea. He would one day be called jarl in place of his father. When the day came that he, too, went to take his place in Asgard, the skalds would write verses of his heroic deeds.

Who was this girl? She was no one. She'd probably never been more than two leagues from her home and knew only the coarse words of her own Northumbrian tongue. She had no right to have any effect on him.

When the bindings fell away, he threw them into the water and meant to leave her there in the stern of the boat. He would have, except that when he moved to rise, the red welts the rope had left on her wrists caught his attention. And when he looked at her face, he noted the ivory skin and knew from experience that it wouldn't stay that way with the sun and wind beating down on it.

He left her to return to his chest at the bow of

the boat. Some of his men watched him, but he ignored them and their speculative looks as he dug through the chest for the ointment. He refused to ponder why he cared so much about her welfare. Leather pouch in hand, he returned to once again kneel before her. She regarded him suspiciously as he untied the opening and dipped his fingers inside. The moment he withdrew his hand with his two fingers piled high with the oily, fishy-smelling goo, she pulled back in disgust.

'Ugh! What is that?'

Eirik ignored her and grabbed her hand in his. He couldn't help but notice how soft her skin was compared to his callused palm. He wanted to stroke it, to luxuriate in the satin texture, but he forced the thought out of his mind and rubbed the ointment on the scrapes, first one wrist and then the other. When he grabbed her chin to repeat the process on her face, she wasn't so docile. Her arms came up to knock him aside and even managed to loosen his grip. She grabbed his forearm and would have forcibly pushed him away, except that he lurched forward and wrapped his hand in her hair to pull her across his lap.

The brief skirmish ended to the cheers of the men nearest them when his arm closed around her, holding her chest tight to his. Eirik's breath came harsh and fast as he looked into the dark depths of her eyes. He tried to tell himself that it was from the fight, but he was a seasoned warrior who didn't wind easily. Besides, a tightness had begun in his groin. It was her. The darkness in him that had been appeased by her capture was awake again, bringing with it a desire that he despised.

'Take me back,' she whispered, her eyes wide and pleading. She must have felt the tension within him, because she sat stone still atop him.

'You are mine!' The words ripped from him with such vehemence, she startled. 'Even if your lord brother sent two boats laden with gold, I would not sell you back.'

The words shocked her into silence. She didn't protest when he rubbed a coat of the ointment over her face, just stared at him with those too-big eyes that made him want to reassure her. To stop the things she was making him feel, Eirik needed to get away from her. He moved to his feet so fast that he dumped her none too gently on the deck and didn't bother to look back as he made his way to the bow of the boat. The girl was dangerous to him. He vowed to stay away from her lest she weaken him.

Chapter Four

There came a time, over the next several days, when Merewyn would have welcomed death as the only escape from the constant rocking of the boat. It made her stomach roil in protest. Even the thoughts in her head seemed to rock and shift with the movement of the vessel. They floated from anger to fear to despair and back again as if a wave had pitched them around. The men on the boat didn't seemed to notice that constant moving and walked around as if on land. She'd glared at them at first, but soon her physical discomfort had turned her thoughts inwards so that she barely noticed them.

And they barely noticed her, a small favour for which she was eternally grateful, since she spent a good portion of the first couple of days retching over the side of the boat. But after she became too weak to move, it happened where she lay. By then her retching was dry heaves and the water forced on her; it mixed nicely with the seawater that constantly sloshed around the bottom of the boat, soaking her gown and freezing her to the bone. It felt as though she would never be dry again, and was caked in a layer of salt and grime that she feared would be fused to her skin for ever.

She didn't even know how long she'd been on the cursed boat, only that the light became dark in a nauseating cycle she couldn't keep up with. Every morning when the sun broke over the side of the boat to touch her face, the boy named Vidar, who'd been told to watch over her, offered her smoked fish. It tasted awful. The boy couldn't be but a few years younger than her, probably the same age as Godfrey, Alfred's eldest son. But he seemed much older, leaving her to wonder if these people only produced giants.

He was the one to supply her with water, but after she refused Eirik had been summoned. He appeared every time her thoughts turned to death and despair to stand over her with that ever-present look of disappointment. Apparently, she wasn't as well behaved as a good captive should be. Perhaps she wasn't supposed to be sickened by the constant motion. He never reprimanded her, though, only spoke to her in quick commands to eat or drink, but she could never get much of the smoked fish down. Not even after the nausea had subsided.

By the time land was sighted, Merewyn could barely rouse the interest to lift her head at the sound of the cheer that went up in the boat. But as the longship drew ever closer to the shoreline, her stomach crept further into her throat until she could barely swallow and the trembling in her limbs returned. What demands would be made of her in this new place? Was this their destination or simply another stop on the journey?

Before she realised that she had moved, she clutched the gunwale with a white-knuckled grip and searched the approaching shore for some clue as to her fate. She saw a long stretch of a sandy beach with slight green hills in the background; as they drew closer, she discerned the outline of what appeared to be a village. Numerous buildings were clustered together, most of them squatty and slight, but a few were a more substantial, rectangular shape. Farther past the village dark spots that she assumed were animals grazing littered a slight rise in the ground.

She hoped the perfectly tranquil setting didn't house something darker, such as a market that dealt in human flesh. She had always imagined those cities to be bigger, not villages with shepherds tending sheep and mothers tending hearths.

'This is home.' Eirik's deep voice was so near her ear, it made her jump.

She turned her head slightly to see him leaning close to her as he looked out at the shore. Her gaze traced the strong line of his jaw. The weight of his body was warm behind her, though he didn't touch her. His face wasn't cold and disapproving now as he watched the village get closer. Nay, his blue eyes had definitely taken on a glow of excitement, and for the first time she found herself wondering about his life. Who was he to this village and what did these people mean to him?

He looked down at her, his gaze raking her face before settling on her own. 'This is your new life. You'd do well to forget the old one.'

'You mean forget the life where I was free, to accept being your slave?' Her eyes flashed her anger, even as the words rang false to her ears. She'd gone to the beach in search of her elusive freedom, but had only managed to find a slavery that was more absolute than the drudgery she'd faced at home.

His strong jaw clenched, and the blue in his eyes burned with fire. 'Acceptance will make your life here better. Aye, accept that you are no longer the sister of a Saxon lord. You are mine to command now.' With those harsh words, he grabbed her shoulder and turned her to face him. Before she realised what he meant to do, he coiled a rope tight around her wrists and bound them together.

'You may command me, but I will never be yours.'

He glanced at her face and didn't reply. But the glance lingered and his thumb traced over the bruise she knew must be fading. There was no pain from the touch, just a strange trembling within her that made her jerk her face away. His hand dropped back to her wrists.

Merewyn looked at his fingers as he worked, noting that he made sure the bindings stayed on the outside of her sleeves. His nails were clean and trimmed, and she wondered how he had stayed so groomed while she was a mess. But then her thoughts moved to what was ahead. Despite the horror of being taken captive and the gruelling sea-sickness that had claimed her, there had been a strange reassurance to the routine of the boat. Eirik had stayed true to his word and hadn't harmed her. She was surprised to realise that she'd even come to rely on his strong presence as a sort of security to the unknown. Now that could change.

What demands would be placed on her in this new environment, his home? The look he'd given her when he'd held her against the stone was still a vivid memory. Then there was the way he'd just touched her. It meant things she didn't even want to think of, but an image from a morning she'd gone into the stable to visit a newborn baby lamb came to mind. She'd thought the place deserted. Everyone should have been in the fields. But there had been a sound.

At first she'd mistaken it for an animal, but as she'd approached the stall, she'd recognised it as human. It had been a moan followed by a series of groans that had heated her cheeks even when she'd been unsure of the source. Then she'd found them. A couple in a carnal embrace. White buttocks, luminous in the darkened space, worked between thighs equally as pale against the straw. Merewyn had watched for two heartbeats longer than was necessary to know what was happening. And she'd left with a strange feeling twisting deep in her belly and had promptly buried the memory.

But it had never really left her and came out to haunt her at odd times, such as nights when she couldn't sleep or when she'd catch one of Alfred's men looking at her with an odd expression. His men were universally disgusting creatures with bad manners and coarse habits. The idea of them having such thoughts about her had filled her with revulsion.

The memory of that day came out from hiding now as the Northman attended her. She knew his thoughts were similar to those of Alfred's men, but she wasn't filled with revulsion. But, fear? Aye, the fear was there.

'Why did you take me?' The white of those buttocks flashed in her mind. She couldn't banish them. Was that what he meant to do to her? His eyes had claimed her against that stone forge, even if his body hadn't had the opportunity. He'd wanted to. She'd felt the hard proof of his manhood as he'd pressed her hips against the stones.

Eirik's gaze touched hers briefly, giving nothing away, before he turned to see to their arrival. The fissure he'd opened widened and she slid ever closer to that abyss in her mind.

Eirik had been fighting for so long that he had almost forgotten what it was to stand on friendly shores, to not expect an arrow or the thrust of a sword to come his way. The air was heavy with salt and exhilaration as they pulled their boats ashore to be greeted by the villagers. They'd been spotted as soon as their boats had become visible on the horizon. By the time they reached shore, everyone in the village knew they had returned and stood on the beach to welcome them. It didn't matter that most of the men were from farther inland, from farms and villages farther along the river. A fleet of warriors returned home was cause for celebration. The high spirits always made the men willing to part with small tokens of their treasure to a pretty girl or an eager child.

The boats were unloaded amidst the curious villagers with the bulk of the treasure locked and guarded until it could be divided later. Then the boats were taken around to the river, where they would stay harboured for the winter.

Eirik approached his homeland with the excitement of a man who had been gone for too long. As much as he had anticipated his trip abroad, his first as leader of a fleet, he realised it had been nothing compared to his eagerness to return home. His flesh fairly tingled with it, something he hadn't experienced since he'd been a young boy awaiting his father's return.

He searched for Kadlin among the well-wishers, but wasn't surprised when he didn't see her. She'd likely be at her home, not staying with his father to await his return. An image of her as he'd last seen her passed through his mind. A goddess come to life with grace and beauty no mere mortal could hope to attain. She'd been a pretty child, but as a woman she was breathtaking. With hair that rivalled the silver moonlight in its radiance and eyes that shone the palest blue, he'd yet to see a woman more beautiful or good.

Why, then, did the face of another intrude on his thoughts? The slave's defiant eyes replaced those of Kadlin's to taunt him. His gaze followed the way of his thoughts until he found the girl standing near his younger brother, Vidar. The boy stood with his hand on her wrists.

There was a prettiness about her, in the curve of her cheekbones, the delicacy of her frame. But she was pale and slight while Kadlin was radiant, striking in her colouring and height. Still, there was something that called to him, that had drawn him to her from that moment on the beach. His gaze raked her, moving to where her gown clung to the curves of her breasts and waist, weighed down by the water that drenched the skirt. She stirred the darkness to life within him. He felt it deep in his gut, and it channelled the excitement already coursing through him to his groin.

He wanted to see her without the dress. To know what colour tipped her breasts. Would her nipples be light pink or coral like her lips? He wanted to lay her in his bed and stroke the pale flesh of her thighs before he pushed them apart to reveal her centre. He wanted to see every part of her. The awareness compelled him to look away, angry that she wielded that despised power over him.

He forced a few deep breaths before looking back at her. The colour had yet to return to her face, and she seemed more fragile than when they'd set out from Northumbria. Both were indications of the weight she'd lost on the crossing. He'd have to be more careful with her.

The girl didn't belong here. She wasn't as hale as the women here. It was plain to see that she was different from them. Eirik cursed the demon that had made him crave her as he stalked towards her.

'Come.' He walked past her with every intention that she follow, but the girl didn't move.

'Where are you taking me?' she asked when he looked back at her.

The fire that had intrigued him before was

flashing in the depths of her eyes. Eirik wanted to admire the courage the question had taken. He believed in facing whatever the gods meted out as the girl was doing and might have taken the time to appreciate her pluck under other circumstances. But he was too aggravated by the untenable lust she roused within him. Instead, he barely suppressed a growl of outrage as he nodded to Vidar and turned to lead the way home.

'I demand to know what will happen to me now. I have the right to know my fate.' Merewyn stood firm, refusing the boy's tug on her arm.

Eirik clenched his jaw and immediately turned back to her. He didn't stop until he stood just before her, causing her to take two steps back to look up at him. A flash of fear briefly tamped down the fire that burned in her eyes, but it flared back up again.

'You have no rights here. You're a slave.'

'I didn't mean—' She cut herself short and glanced away. 'I know my station here, I just don't know— Why won't you tell me what it means?'

Her eyes swung back to meet his, and he was struck by the same uncertainty and loneliness he had glimpsed on the boat. It tugged at something buried deep inside him that he didn't want to explore. Nor did he want to admit that he had no idea what her presence at his home meant or why he'd accepted her.

'You'll learn your place here soon enough.'

Before she could reply, he leaned down and picked her up, slipping her easily over his shoulder. She weighed almost nothing. The girl would be lucky to last the winter here. The thought didn't help his quickly declining mood. Eirik ignored the taunts and jests directed at them from some of the men, but was happy the girl noticed and ceased her struggling.

He kept her aloft until they reached the outside cooking fires and then wasted no time in dropping her to her feet. Hilla looked up from turning the newly spitted lamb and smiled when she saw them. His father's most trusted slave rarely smiled, and the fact that she did now was proof of her devotion. She'd spent his boyhood chasing him from every bit of mischief he'd managed to find in her domain.

'Welcome home, my lord.' Her gaze slipped to Merewyn, who was doing her best to look dignified after her unceremonious arrival.

Eirik had never brought a female captive home before, so he assumed he'd have to get used to the looks. 'Thank you, Hilla.'

'I see your trip was a success. It's good to see you well.'

He inclined his head in acknowledgement. 'Feed her and get her presentable for tonight. And make sure she gets meat with her gruel. She lost weight on the crossing.'

'Looks as though she fair near withered away.' Hilla tut-tutted.

'Watch for Gunnar. He feels he has a claim to her, but she's not to be touched.'

'Aye, that one will not be a problem.' She nodded to the long cane that was always present near her. It was almost as thick as a branch with a gnarled end.

Eirik smiled at the sight. He and Gunnar had felt the blow of that knot more than once. They'd had a lot of good times in their childhood. Standing toe to toe, they were of the same height and breadth. The only real physical difference between them was their colouring. Eirik was golden where Gunnar was blazing red. They had even been born mere months apart, with Eirik born to their father's wife while Gunnar had been born to the wife's sister.

It was almost as if they'd been destined to be rivals.

He turned his attention back to the girl and again noted her unnaturally pale skin. It was the fear.

While it was a good thing, it could sap the life right out of people if it went too far. He'd seen it happen and found himself hoping it didn't happen to her. It gentled his voice when he spoke. 'Stay with Hilla. She'll get you food and clothing.'

Chapter Five

Merewyn shook from a bone-deep chill that threatened to freeze her solid. She feared that if it did, she'd break into thousands of pieces with no one the wiser, to be swept up and discarded into the fire. That fire taunted her. She stood at the edge of the circle of light cast by the flames and watched them dancing, calling her. She wanted the warmth it offered; every fibre of her being craved it. But she stood immobile. The past days had seen her constantly damp and chilled—there was a comfort in the knowledge that she'd become accustomed to it. What would happen if she got warm only to have it taken away again? Could she become accustomed to the cold again?

'Merewyn?' The voice was Hilla's. 'Come to the fire and warm yourself, girl. I'll not have you catching your death.'

Merewyn nodded and pushed aside her reticence

to walk to the cooking fire. Hilla was bustling between the small shelter that adjoined the fire pit, where it seemed most of the cooking preparations were done, and the large longhouse. Men had been filing into it all day. The woman disappeared again towards the house before Merewyn even got to the fire.

Despite her activity, Hilla had managed to find time to see that Merewyn was bathed and dressed. Merewyn had been heartened to find that the woman spoke her language and seemed pleasant enough, even asking her name and how she'd faired on the voyage. It had been a surprise to have someone actually looking after her. But the woman had taken her into her fold as if a new captive being brought home was a regular occurrence. Maybe it was.

It almost made Merewyn laugh with a madness she was close to giving in to when she thought of how things had changed for her. It made her shiver anew to remember how Hilla and another girl had taken her behind the longhouse and poured buckets of frigid river water over her and scrubbed her hair while another had held up a blanket to shield her. Yet here she was thankful for even that much. The bath had been so cold she'd forgotten to be modest and hadn't even noticed if anyone else had been around to see her. It was worlds away from the warm water that a servant would bring to the chamber she shared with the children and the scented soap she adored. She brought her wrist to her nose, but only smelled the river on her skin.

Merewyn put her hands to the flame and welcomed the heat that thawed her frigid fingers. Even their grandest celebration back home had never called for a fire this large. It was a pit roughly two people in length and a person wide. Big enough for several spits and an area for roasting vegetables. Big enough to walk into and never come out of again.

As soon as the thought crossed her mind, she looked around in guilt, hoping no one had guessed what she was thinking. No one was paying attention to her, though, as they bustled around. She opened her palms wide and caught the tail end of an orange flame as it shot high, propelled by a crackle of grease. But it was too hot for her, and she gasped as she brought her hand back to cradle it against her breasts.

'Not too close,' Hilla admonished her as she came back to tend to a spit.

Not yet, Merewyn agreed silently, and checked

for damage to her hand. It was fine; no blisters would form. But eventually, if living there became so horrible that she had to, she would leave this place one way or another.

It wasn't that horrible yet. She latched on to the one bright spot in her new life. 'How is it you come to speak my language, Hilla?'

The woman grunted, but didn't seem inclined to answer as she pressed a wooden bowl filled with a watery gruel into Merewyn's hands.

'Were you taken like me?'

'It was long ago. I speak the Dane's tongue now. As will you, soon enough,' Hilla said.

'But what happened? How long have you been here?'

'I won't speak of that time.'

Merewyn frowned. 'Did you teach Eirik to speak our language?'

'Aye. Gunnar, too,' she clarified. 'It was required of me when they were younger.'

An involuntary shiver ran through her as she thought of the red-haired one. He'd grinned at her and told her she'd be going home with him in her language just before he'd taken her over his shoulder. Merewyn pushed the thought aside and found her gaze focused on the necklace at Hilla's neck.

Though she knew it wasn't a necklace before she even asked. It was a slave's collar.

'So you're a slave, then, too?'

Hilla's hand automatically came up to touch the wooden chip at her neck. Her thick fingertip traced the rune carved into it. 'Aye. I expect you'll be getting one of these soon.'

Merewyn looked to a few of the other women who scurried about the outdoor kitchen and noted they all had the collars, but couldn't see well enough in the firelight to determine if the same sign was inscribed on them all. Slavery wasn't a foreign concept to her. There were slaves at home, usually prisoners and captured enemies, who helped work the land, but only servants worked in their home. She'd never seen so many slaves working in such close proximity to free men. 'Do you all belong to Eirik?'

'None of us belong to him. We're household slaves of the jarl.'

'Does Eirik own any other slaves?' The thought had only just occurred to her that she might be the only one. What if she wasn't? Merewyn wasn't sure which she hoped for.

'You're the only one. He's had no need of a… personal slave. Before you.'

Before she could ask what that meant, Hilla

walked away towards the house again. Merewyn gently lifted the spoon in the bowl to examine its contents before taking a small taste. It was a grain porridge, but instead of milk and honey, it was flavoured with water and bits of fish and seaweed. It was horrible. But her stomach was growling, so she finished it all.

As she ate, she couldn't help but think of Hilla's words and the days ahead. Eirik had promised not to hurt her, but would he keep that promise now? What was a promise to a slave? Why had he been so intent to have her if he didn't intend to harm her? Would he force himself on her? Maybe he wouldn't think of that as harming her. The questions were endless and they wouldn't stop. But Hilla's next words did interrupt them.

'It's time to go inside now. My Lord Eirik calls for you.'

The now-familiar knot of terror returned to coil tight inside her. Merewyn stood looking at the closed door before her, knowing that Eirik, her master now, awaited her somewhere in the house. She shuddered to think of the night ahead. Would she still be chaste after this night? What new level of horror would she know? Images of what might happen poured through her mind, but she refused to give in to the panic that beckoned. It wasn't happening yet. Besides, he *had* vowed that no harm would come to her. Maybe he was an honourable heathen who followed his word. Maybe Mother Mary would see fit to intervene and grant her one miracle.

Merewyn clenched her fists at her sides and held her head high. Alfred had taught her the importance of bearing, so much so that she'd felt her eyes cross with boredom when he started one of those lectures. She'd hated those lectures. Hated how he would sit her down and drone on and on for hours about the importance of living up to her station in life. Now she hated that instead of listening, she had stared daggers at him until he'd sighed and dismissed her with a shake of his head. Then she'd go back to whatever she'd been doing. Usually dancing with Sempa in the forest as they collected herbs or swimming in the stream. Tears unexpectedly prickled her eyes, but she held them at bay. What she wouldn't give to hear him lecture her now about her morning walk on the beach, to hug him tight and beg his forgiveness for not listening.

For once, she vowed, his lectures would serve her well. With no other choice available to her, she squared her shoulders, determined to meet her fate in a manner that befitted her noble birth and would make her brother proud. She gathered her grace around her like a shield and followed Hilla inside.

Men, boisterous and loud, were packed shoulder to shoulder in the hall. They sat at benches lining the walls and tables that filled the middle of the floor near the hearth. She might have stared at them, wondering at their strange words and rowdy manner, if she hadn't caught sight of the raised dais on the right side of the room. An older man who she assumed to be the jarl sat at the middle of the table with Gunnar seated on his far side. She started in surprise when she saw him. She'd not realised he was so important, and the realisation of how potentially little stood between her and his mercy made her knees weak.

Neither of them noticed her. They sat watching a burly man who had taken a stand on one of the benches and seemed to be regaling the group in his immediate vicinity with a tale, judging from the dramatic sound of his voice and his arm gestures. But Eirik watched her from his place beside the jarl.

He was dressed in a midnight brocade tunic that stretched taut across the breadth of his shoulders, accented with gold piping and a small keyhole opening at the neckline. A dark gemstone button winked in the light, but she couldn't tell what it was. His trousers were tucked into calf boots, but she could see that even they were made of a finer material than most of the other men's clothing. He wore a gold band around each of his arms. His crimson cloak, trimmed in soft grey fur, was affixed to his tunic with two gold filigree brooches at the shoulders.

He was magnificent. For the first time since entering the house, her gaze dropped to the floor. Somehow it had been easier to maintain her dignity when she'd imagined him the barbarian she had painted in her mind; not the nobleman who sat across from her. The nobleman who held her life in his power. Merewyn resisted the urge to scratch at the coarse wool of the apron dress that had replaced her own fine clothing. The knot twisted tighter in her belly.

What did her own nobility matter here where she was a slave?

'Come.' Hilla grabbed her arm and led her around to the back of the dais. Some of the men noticed them now and made room for them to pass. Every one of them watched her with their speculative eyes, while some leered and openly appraised her.

She knew they were imagining her without clothing, imagining Eirik taking his pleasure and offering her up to them.

The thought was so unbearable, she might have stalled, but Hilla's strong hand helped her up the wooden steps and guided her to Eirik. He nodded to the woman, who motioned for Merewyn to sit. Merewyn did exactly as she was told and sank to her knees behind his seat, instinctively wanting to hide herself from the stares coming her way.

He waited until Hilla left before turning to look at her. She forced herself to meet his fierce gaze without wavering. The look of disappointment she'd noted earlier was still present. What did he expect from her?

'Eat.' He shoved a wooden bowl filled with pieces of roasted meat into her hands.

Merewyn knew she should have been hungry after the gruelling crossing and the single bowl of porridge Hilla had given her, but food was not appealing. It would have smelled delicious had her stomach not been in knots.

'I can't—'

'Do you intend to thwart my wishes at every step?' He raised an eyebrow.

'Nay, my lord, I'm just not feeling well. Perhaps if you tell me your plans for me.'

Eirik's gaze narrowed as he watched her, making her heart flutter wildly. 'Eat, girl. I won't ask again.'

She felt it in her best interest to refrain from pointing out that he had never *asked* her to begin with. But she had intended to argue about not being hungry when he rose, and her protest stilled on her lips. It was replaced with a gasp when his hand touched her shoulder.

'Courage.' His gaze met hers briefly, and then he turned to address the room.

He held up his arm in a gesture for quiet until the entire hall watched what was about to unfold. The bowl of food sat forgotten in her hands. Her attention settled on the breadth of Eirik's shoulders.

His voice carried around the room, and something about its deep, even cadence soothed her the slightest bit. It seemed as if he was telling a story because they all looked on with fascination and his speech continued uninterrupted. As she watched him, she realised that, here amongst his own kind, he was hardly a giant. Though one of the tallest, she had seen a few others that topped him. Even Alfred was only slightly shorter. It was Eirik's solid strength coupled with his height that had made him seem so big. The men she knew from home were not as broad in the chest and shoulders.

The jarl had turned in his seat to watch his son, but stood now as Eirik finished his speech. When the older man spoke she took the opportunity to observe him. His colouring was similar to Eirik's and he had the same strong jaw, but the face was subtly different. The nose was the same, except for the break, but the jarl's lips were thin and firm while his eyes were amber, like Gunnar's. It struck her then that the three of them were related, leading her to wonder if the jarl was Gunnar's father, as well. He must be, given that Hilla had taught him along with Eirik. She should have asked Hilla more about them.

The older man stopped speaking and turned his head to look towards the door from which she had just entered. Merewyn looked to see men bringing in three chests, which were set on the floor before the dais. Eirik gave the word and they were opened simultaneously. Her mouth dropped open at the riches they contained. One held coloured silks and brocades; the second glimmered with various metals in coins and chains; while the third held packages wrapped in leather and linen. She couldn't be sure what they held, but the aroma told her spices.

Though she couldn't understand the conversation, Merewyn knew these were all treasures Eirik had brought back from his trip. He'd probably stolen them all just as he'd stolen her. The jarl moved to leave the dais and walk amongst the riches. The man had yet to acknowledge her, but after he completed a pass of each of the chests, he stopped and looked directly at her. She instinctively held her hands clasped against her, pressing the bowl into her belly. His amber eyes were alive with merriment when he spoke and gestured to her. Eirik stiffened, but he didn't appear amused. Whatever the jarl had said made Gunnar laugh and drew his attention to her. They were talking about her.

She refused to look at him and instead held her gaze firmly on Eirik. His voice was low and solemn. His fingers were firm when he reached down to grab her arm and pull her to her feet. She dared not ask where they were going, but he took pity on her and answered the unspoken question.

'Time for bed.'

Chapter Six

Eirik led her towards the back of the longhouse. It was darker there because a loft area loomed overhead and blocked most of the light from the fire and candles. Chests and bundles covered in coarse cloths were stored in the loft, but she saw some movement there, too. Just before he led her beneath it she saw a pair of eyes staring down. She barely had time to meet them before she faced the darkness underneath.

It took a moment for her eyes to adjust enough to see that the area had been sectioned off into chambers on both sides, with wooden walls that rose up to meet the floor of the loft overhead. Four of the chambers had rough wooden doors, but the other two had scraps of cloth hanging down. The spaces along the walls between the doors were lined with bare wooden benches.

She had just begun to wonder, to hope, that one of those benches was meant for her, when he spoke.

'You'll sleep in my chamber.'

Merewyn swallowed as he pushed a door open and entered the chamber before her. She said a silent prayer for strength and followed him over the threshold. The darkness lingered for a moment, and then a lantern flickered to life, revealing the room to her. It was small in relation to the great hall, but much more lavishly decorated than she had expected. This was where he kept his personal treasures. Even Alfred didn't have this sort of comfort in his own chamber.

The floors were covered, wall to wall, with colourful carpets and thick furs. A large bed took up almost a third of the space. It was made of wood embellished with carvings of animals and piled with pillows. Heavy curtains hung from the corners for warmth, though they were tied back with braided cords. The outer wall was hung with tapestries while another held shields, armour and weapons. She recognised the chain mail he had worn hanging there. Chests lined the floor along one wall below shelves laden with assorted treasures in gold, silver and other materials she couldn't even name. It was the home of an exotic prince.

She stepped to the shelf nearest her to examine the figurines carved from a beautiful green rock she'd never seen.

'Jade,' he supplied. 'But don't touch them. Or take them.'

Merewyn dropped the hand she had raised to touch the one closest to her. The door closed and he slid the wooden latch into place. 'Stealing a jade figurine won't get me home.' Her glare would have melted him had he been a normal man.

'You are home.'

'This is not my home.'

'You live here now.' His voice was cool as he removed the brooches that affixed his cape to his tunic and then walked over to hang the luxurious fabric on a hook.

'By force.'

Eirik's brow arched as he loosened the ties of his tunic and then brought it over his head to hang it beside the cape. Her eyes followed him as he walked to deposit the brooches in a small wooden chest that sat on a shelf near her. He moved like an animal, sleek and smooth, with a confidence that irritated her. Her only solace was the sight of the wound she'd inflicted on his biceps. It wasn't deep, but the cut was still there.

When he was finished he came over to stand in front of her. She took an involuntary step backwards. 'If you obey me, you could have a good life here.'

'Are those my choices? Obey you, submit and I won't be harmed or fight you and…and live to regret it?' Merewyn couldn't stop herself from staring at his bare chest. She'd never seen a man without his clothing this close before. His skin was golden and looked like satin covering hard muscle. She took a deep breath to steady herself, but only managed to inhale his smell. That strange scent that was him—an exotic spice she'd never tasted mixed with leather—filled her and somehow made her feel more alone than she ever had before, even on the crossing. Everything about him was foreign. A strange longing flickered to life within her, and she realised that even she felt foreign around him.

'Submit to my commands, aye.' Eirik's hand came up to tip her chin upwards so she looked at him. His solemn blue gaze fixed on hers. 'But I've already vowed to not harm you. I'll never ask you to share my bed. It's not a demand I place on slaves.'

Merewyn's gaze flicked to the bed in a completely involuntary move, but then dropped to the floor when it only made her earlier fears return.

There was no need for him to lie to her. She was here in the chamber with him, completely at his mercy. He could do with her as he would and no one would come to her aid if she screamed. She could trust him—at least in this. Then something shifted in his gaze. She couldn't name it, but—just for a moment—the self-assurance was gone and she saw that he was unsettled. By her? The weight of fear that had held tight in her chest released the tiniest bit so that she could breathe freely.

'I believe you.'

'Do you?' The corner of his mouth tipped up. It wasn't a smile, but it was close.

'Aye.'

She did. But he traced over her bottom lip with his thumb, causing it to tingle. Then he was moving away from her, leaving only the ghost of his touch behind to linger on her skin. Merewyn pressed her own hand to her lips to smite it out.

'Eat.' He nodded to the bowl she still held and sat on the edge of the bed to remove his boots and woollen socks.

She chewed a piece of the meat, but only to keep the newfound peace between them. It was tender and flavourful, but she barely noticed. 'What happened in there with the jarl? He's your father?'

At his nod, she continued, 'Just before we left, he asked you something. About me.'

Eirik stood abruptly and his hands went to the fastenings on his trousers. She looked away when he began to push them down past his hips. Why didn't it bother him to strip bare before her? The man was a heathen. They were all heathens.

'Aye, it was about you. He asked why I was keeping you for myself instead of presenting you to him like a good son should.'

Merewyn closed her eyes against the unspeakable vision that raised in her mind. 'What did you say?'

She gave him a moment to answer, but when nothing was forthcoming she looked to him, making sure to keep her gaze from lowering. He watched her with an intensity she'd never known before.

'Obviously I denied his request.' His voice was laced with sarcasm, but his eyes were solemn.

'Why?' With that one word, his face closed. Merewyn knew she'd get nothing out of him that night and averted her eyes.

'You've already begun to address me as "my lord" and that should continue. The state of this chamber will be your responsibility, but we'll talk more of your duties and my expectations when we return.'

Merewyn studiously maintained her diverted gaze, despite the shock of that statement. 'When we return from where? When are we going?'

'I have to go on a short trip to visit a neighbouring jarl. No more than a week or so. I leave the day after tomorrow. You'll come with me unless you'd prefer to stay here alone.'

It wasn't really a choice. 'I'll go.'

He crossed in front of her again, completely unashamed in his nakedness, to reach into a chest at the end of the bed. She was forced to acknowledge him when he offered the woollen blanket to her.

'You can sleep on the fur.' Eirik indicated the dark brown bear pelt that was nearest the bed on the floor. It still had its claws.

She clutched the blanket to her chest as he walked away and couldn't help the glimpse she got of his backside. Solid muscle worked smoothly beneath his skin. That flare of foreign longing, exciting and unwelcome, ignited within her and shamed her into looking away. She waited for him to climb into bed before she sat her bowl down on a shelf and took her place upon the fur.

'Oh, girl?'

Her eyes shot open.

'If you think to attack me with one of those weapons, I'll stop you and you'll spend the rest of your nights tethered. Think hard if it's worth that risk.'

It wasn't worth the risk. Even if she hurt him, she had the others to contend with and an entire ocean to cross to make it home. There had to be another way, but she wouldn't tell him that. Let him wonder if he'd wake up to a dagger in his chest.

She thought she'd lie there contemplating the change in her living situation, but she fell asleep almost immediately. It was a deep sleep, the like of which she'd not experienced since she'd been taken.

Eirik did not fall asleep easily. Despite the fact that he was exhausted and in his own bed for the first time in nearly two years, the slave's face haunted him. Hilla had managed an extraordinary transformation. The chestnut silk of her hair shone with health and had reflected hints of red from the fire in the hall. Highlights he hadn't noticed in the grey light of the crossing. Her face wasn't as drawn as when they'd arrived, but her cheekbones were still too sharp under her skin. Nothing a few days of rest and proper meals couldn't fix. He'd even been pleased that she seemed to have regained some of her colour.

But none of that explained why she disturbed

him. It didn't begin to explain what happened to him when he looked at her. The way his body tightened with the unexpected need to possess her and protect her at the same time. The way he'd wanted to stand up in front of everyone in the hall and proclaim that she was his. Or the primal anger that had gripped him when his father had laughingly asked for her and the internal struggle he'd had to beat it down.

The girl was his. He wanted to possess her and liked the idea of her awaiting his pleasure entirely more than he should. But he couldn't possess her. Couldn't even let his mind take him down the path of imagining what it would be like to explore her body. It would be too easy to pluck her from her pallet and push her underneath him in bed if he let his mind wander there.

But even the mere thought caused his blood to thicken and settle low in his groin. He wanted her. There was no denying anymore that he wanted her in the primal way a man lusted for a woman. It was a visceral urge that gripped him in its tight fist and refused to let go. He knew then it was no demon that had possessed him to take her. It was his own dark needs—his desire for her.

Shame reared its ugly head, the usual complement

to his damnable lust. To want any woman was not something he permitted, but to want *her*—a slave who could neither fight him nor accept him—made him angry. He'd known what it was to have no control of his physical being before. He wouldn't, couldn't, force that on another. Had never even considered it before now. Before her. He never lost control, never let himself go so that he was at the mercy of his body's demands.

Eirik knew then that he should have left her behind. There had been no need to take her from her home. Aye, she'd been a gift, but gifts could be rejected. The girl had clearly wanted to stay, despite the bruises. Perhaps she would have been safer.

He rolled to his stomach to press the uncomfortable tightness of his erection against the blankets. He forced his mind to go black and his breathing to stay even. The lust would not overtake him. He would fight it.

Chapter Seven

The nightmares started near dawn. At first the blackness consumed him and all was quiet. But it wasn't a peaceful silence. It was heavy and expectant, like the stillness of the sky before the torrential downpour of a storm. The air sat heavy upon his chest and threatened to choke him with its liquid weight. Eirik struggled, but was only pulled down farther for all his effort.

When the screams began he jerked with surprise. He hadn't heard them in years, but he recognised them immediately. They tore from his own lips and filled him with shame even as they released some of the pain tearing through him. But this time, he was in control. Instead of allowing the vision to take hold of him, he fought it. Moments later, he opened his eyes to the darkness and breathed in the familiar air of the chamber.

The trembling of his limbs was nothing new. It

happened with every other nightmare he'd ever had, and he knew it would subside eventually. His throat wasn't raw, so he knew that the screams had been brief—this time. That was good. It was something.

He should have been grateful. There had been times when the nightmare trudged on for hours and he would awaken to Hilla or, when it was particularly bad, his friend Sweyn, dousing him with cold water. His throat would be inflamed and his voice rough from the screaming.

He wasn't grateful. The nightmares were gone, beaten. He'd closed his mind to the events of the day years ago that had caused them. He'd thought that they couldn't haunt him anymore. But they were back. Eirik breathed in and held the air in his lungs. He exhaled in a slow, steady breath of air that relaxed him and eased the trembling. Why were they back now?

Pushing up from the bed, he swung his feet over the side and hung his head until the pounding in his skull ceased. He sucked in a deep breath again and was assailed by her scent. The salt of her. Meagre light from the hall seeped around the cracks of his door to illuminate the girl. She was sleeping deeply on the rug, her hair streaming out behind her.

Eirik closed his eyes. The nightmares were back

because of her. Somehow they were her fault. His fists closed and gripped the blanket before releasing it as he forced the tension from his body once more and got up to dress. To try to sleep would be useless.

He wasn't surprised to find his father already in the hall, though he was disappointed. He'd hoped to sit in silence while the strength returned to his knees. At the moment, it was a struggle to keep his legs from trembling like a newborn foal. But there was no help for it, so he forced himself to join his father where he sat breaking his fast and drinking mead.

The man never slept. If it was because some demon haunted him and stole his sleep as well, Eirik didn't know. Sleeping men filled the benches, but the dais was clear, so Eirik took a place there across from the jarl. He waved away the offer of food, but filled a tankard from the pitcher that had been left on the table.

'Sleep well?' his father asked, and looked him over. Eirik hoped the despicable weakness didn't show on his face and breathed a sigh of relief when the man looked back down to his meal.

'Well enough. It's been a long time since I've had

a proper bed. I'm not used to it.' It was the truth. His back ached from the softness.

'Aye, I remember that. You'll get accustomed to it again.' The older man laughed before taking a mouthful of porridge. 'Go to the baths later. The hot water will help with the tightness. Take your pretty new slave. She can pound out the knots.' Hegard used his spoon to point in the direction of the bedchambers.

Eirik took a drink of the mead to fortify himself. The last subject he wanted to discuss was his pretty new slave. She was quickly causing more trouble than she was worth. He should have left her to her family.

Silence descended over them for a while as Hegard finished his meal, but soon he was pushing the bowl away and refilling his mead. 'Are you planning to visit Kadlin?'

'I'll leave tomorrow. I'd thought she would be here.'

'Nay, her mother's expecting again. Should be any day now.' Hegard took a drink, but his eyes never left his son's.

Eirik was aware of his father's scrutiny and was afraid he knew the way the questions would lead. Kadlin was also a subject he didn't want to discuss now. Not with his father. So he nodded and hoped the conversation would end there.

Of course it didn't.

'It's time you take her to wife. You're old enough, and with your take this last trip you can set up a household. Or even bring her here.'

His father's interest in his unmarried state wasn't new. Kadlin had been brought up as a likely candidate even before this last trip, but back then Eirik had hardly had the means to support a wife and family. That had changed, and there would be no putting it off now. Not that he would. Kadlin was everything a man could want and Eirik enjoyed her company.

'Aye, she'll make a good wife.'

Hegard smiled and continued as if Eirik hadn't spoken. 'Though I doubt she'll appreciate your slave as competition. Women are funny that way. Wouldn't you rather have a few weeks with the slave first and then pass her on to someone else before bringing a wife home?'

How could he explain to his father that he'd never intended the girl to be his bed slave? Hegard would never understand. The man had had his wife and her sister pregnant within a year of marriage and had never slept in an empty bed. Eirik could count on two hands the children the man acknowledged. There was no telling how many others existed.

But it wasn't only that that held back Eirik's explanation. If he hadn't taken the girl for a bed slave, why had he taken her? It had long been expected that he would marry Kadlin. She was the eldest and most beautiful daughter of Hegard's most trusted friend. They had spent their childhoods together. Eirik had known that marriage to her was imminent, and she wouldn't allow a pretty slave to share their household. No woman would.

Had he been too hasty in assuring the girl that he wouldn't harm her? He couldn't protect her if she wasn't his. He ran a hand through his dishevelled hair and glanced towards his bedchamber. Perhaps he'd wait until spring to wed, and that would give him the winter to figure out what to do with the girl.

It was as though Hegard had read his mind. 'Kadlin's been waiting long enough. The men go out of their way to stop at their farm and fjord just to catch a glimpse of her. Jarl Leif's already dissuaded numerous offers of marriage. He's waiting for you.'

Kadlin was lovely and kind. It was past time she became a mother. But the thought of babies made an unwelcome image flash behind his eyes of the act that created them. He'd never thought of her in that way. But then her image changed to that of the girl, and bedding her was something he could imagine all too well.

'It was kind of him to wait,' Eirik acknowledged.

'That bastard doesn't have a kind bone in his body. He wants you for his son.' Hegard's gaze narrowed. 'You want to be jarl after I'm gone, don't you?'

'Aye, it's what I've always wanted.' Eirik had imagined himself in his father's place since he was small enough to conceive of such a thing. But he clenched his teeth because he knew what was coming.

'Then you know you'll need the men to follow you after I go. There are those who would choose Gunnar when I'm gone.'

'I'm the better warrior. I led them all on every raid for the past three years. They're all wealthier because of me. The men will follow me when it's time.' His voice was hard and determined.

'Aye, that is true. You led them well, son. I don't mean to imply otherwise. But you must hold their trust.' The older man let the words linger in the air between them.

There was no need to elaborate. No one knew

what had happened on that day long ago. Even his father had only speculated, but he'd immediately installed a girl in Eirik's chamber. The men had assumed she'd slept in his bed, but she hadn't, and Eirik suspected his father knew that.

Eirik had never taken a bed slave, never once lain with any of the gypsy women who followed their camps, never taken a woman in a raid. He'd taken women into his tent, the ones who were reluctant to bed the others and grateful for his protection. But he never took pleasure with them and gently rebuffed the few who had tried to repay his protection with their favours.

'They have no reason to distrust me.'

'The slave was a nice touch,' Hegard agreed. 'I admit, even I wasn't expecting her. You've never taken a slave before.'

Eirik had to look away from his father's appreciative leer. It enraged him to have his father view her so casually, but there was no reason it should. She *was* only a slave.

'Bed your slave. But Kadlin won't wait. You need to wed her soon. Leave her with child when you return to fight in the spring. Then the men will have no reason to distrust you.'

'They have no reason to distrust me now.' Only

the few who followed Gunnar had dared to voice any dissent against him.

'They distrust what isn't like them. Marry a jarl's daughter and you'll prove to be even better than them.'

Eirik could read his father's eyes and knew that the seeds of distrust lived even in his own father. If it could live there, then how could he expect the men to trust him?

'It doesn't matter. I'll be married by spring and there will be no reason for it to linger.'

The jarl nodded, but kept a keen watch on his son's face. 'Good. Gunnar is learning, but he's not as temperate in his decisions as you are. The men need a level head to lead them.'

Gunnar was his main rival for his father's seat. It was his duty to make his claim as solid as possible to lessen the fight. Despite the rivalry, he had no desire to harm his brother. But Gunnar wouldn't sit by and allow what he deemed to equally belong to him to slip through his fingers. The fight was coming. It was the way of a jarl's sons.

'How was your bed slave last night?'

Eirik hadn't realised his brother had come out of his chamber when he joined them at the table, but the question shouldn't have come as a surprise.

Gunnar wasn't known for his subtlety or tact. He seemed to enjoy purposely riling both Eirik and their father.

'Gunnar.' Hegard shook his head in disapproval as he watched his son take a seat.

'A fair question, father. I only wish my brother happiness.' Gunnar grinned and raised his mug to them.

They were joined then at the table by Bram and Sweyn, who'd returned with Eirik and Gunnar, and the talk turned to the battles and raids over the past summer. The raids in Francia had been immensely successful. Much of their treasure had been paid in tribute, but the raids had been going on long enough and they were beginning to meet resistance. Which was why they had been patrolling the northern coasts. For years they had been raiding Wessex, East Anglia, Mercia and Northumbria to moderate gains. But now there was talk of more than raiding.

Hegard's brother, Einar, claimed the land was ripe for the taking. Hegard was doubtful that men could be such fools to suffer kings unable to protect them, which was why Eirik's trip had been so important. He'd confirmed Einar's claim. Every stop along the coast had proved the Saxons were unfortified and unable to counter a full attack against an organised fleet. Their leaders offered tribute too easily now. It had become second nature, as if they thought no other form of aggression was possible. Leaders like that didn't deserve to keep what they held. The only real resistance they had encountered was a skirmish just days south of where he'd taken the slave girl, and that had been pitifully organised. Judging from the lack of men at her home, Eirik suspected the group, or at least a part of it, had originated there.

Come spring, Eirik would return with even more men and join the group wintering just near Thetford. Then they would raid north to take Northumbria.

Eirik watched the excitement light up Hegard's eyes as he listened to their stories. There was no doubt in his mind that the jarl would be inclined to commit men to the battle. The exhilaration was almost contagious. It even pulled at him, making his hands restless and his heart pound. But he could be gone for years. What would he do with his pretty slave then?

Chapter Eight

Merewyn had awakened to the Northman's screams in the night. They had been so terrifying, she'd been convinced there was a demon attacking him until she'd risen to verify he was unharmed. Then she'd watched in fascination as he'd fought against something she couldn't see. It had occurred to her to try to calm him lest he hurt himself, so she'd reached out cautiously to touch his forehead. His screams had quieted, and the moment his struggles had ceased, she'd moved back to her pallet. It had seemed better to not let him know she had witnessed his nightmare, so she'd pretended to be asleep until he'd left.

But real sleep had proved elusive. She'd lain there as her mind had relived the previous days. Every time it was quiet, Merewyn would hear Blythe's words echo in the silence. She still didn't know what had possessed her actions. After a while, the door opened and Merewyn closed her eyes, unwilling to face the day. She opened them when it was quiet again to see that someone had placed a pitcher of water inside the door—Hilla, she imagined—so she made use of it to clean herself. She managed it as discreetly as possible, afraid that the door would open at any moment. But it didn't. She finally ventured out when her stomach began to grumble.

The first person she saw was Hilla, who directed her to an empty bench where she broke her fast surrounded by some of the men from the day before. She managed to remain unnoticed, so she slipped back to the bedchamber when she finished, where she was left alone until the evening meal.

Hilla was the one to retrieve her. This time the hall was considerably less full as she was led to the dais. Most of the men had probably left for their homes. Eirik sat eating, but didn't even glance her way as she took her place on the floor behind him, though once she was settled he handed her a bowl filled with bits of food from his. Famished again, Merewyn ate without reservation and finished it all.

She set the bowl aside and leaned back against the wall to watch the men as they ate and talked.

It had just occurred to her to wonder why there were no women—women who weren't servants or slaves—when Eirik got to his feet. Her heart leaped, as it had a disturbing habit of doing every time she thought he might address her, but he didn't look her way as he left the dais and headed outside.

Her mouth went dry as she looked around the room. She didn't like being left alone in the hall without him. Despite her earlier fears of him, he was all that stood between her and them, and he did make her feel safe. She was contemplating making her way back to the bedchamber when the jarl called Hilla over. It was clear they were talking about her from Hilla's glance her way.

That fear was confirmed when Hilla came over and knelt beside her. 'Merewyn, you must go attend to Lord Eirik. Jarl Hegard commands it.'

'Where is he?'

'The baths.'

Merewyn worried the inside of her bottom lip as she struggled to find the courage to open the door. The wind was cold, as Hilla had made her take off her woollen dress so now she wore only her linen undershift, and her feet were bare. Shoes were not allowed in the baths. But the cold did not spur her to enter, even though she could feel the heat from inside seeping through the door. She was too afraid of what she would find there.

'Go!'

She grimaced as she glanced to where Hilla stood tending the cook fire, which was a good thirty paces away from the bathhouse, but the woman watched. Taking a deep breath, she reminded herself of Eirik's vow to not harm her, then pushed the door open and stepped inside. It took a long moment before her eyes adjusted to the meagre lantern light that penetrated the steam. Her skin was immediately wet with it, but it was a pleasant warmth after the cold.

Empty benches lined two walls, and a third held a long hearth where flat stones had been laid upon a smouldering fire. Casks of what she assumed to be water sat near it, the source of the steam. She didn't see Eirik, but she heard someone just on the other side of a partition that quartered the room, so she stepped in that direction.

His deep voice filled the silence. He'd spoken a command, but it was in his own Norse language, so she was certain he hadn't realised that it was she who had joined him. Had the jarl really sent her without Eirik's knowledge? But the moment she rounded the corner, her ability to speak and alert him to her presence fled as quickly as any modesty she might have possessed. He had just stepped out of his trousers, his last garment, so he stood there gloriously naked before her, though facing away from her.

Hard muscles worked beneath the golden smoothness of his skin as he folded the garment and placed it on a bench. Merewyn couldn't help but notice how wide and powerful his shoulders were. His back was long and lean where it led to a tapered waist. It was marred by a patchwork of scars that she assumed were from battle. Perhaps from the nicks of the many blades he must have fought over the years. There wasn't a spare inch of flesh on him. Even his buttocks were chiselled with muscle. He exuded strength and confidence. It was then she admitted that under other circumstances she might have found him handsome. If Alfred had presented him to her as a potential husband, she would have encouraged his suit—had he been Saxon.

But Alfred would probably never present a suitor to her now, and it was all because of this Dane before her. The thought made her angry, so she was standing there with clenched fists when he turned around. She caught a glimpse of male flesh framed in dark blond curls before she pulled her gaze away, her face flaming.

'The jarl sent me, but if you don't require my… presence, I'll go.'

When he didn't immediately respond, she moved to leave, but his voice stopped her. 'Stay.'

Her startled gaze flew to his, but it was intense and unreadable and she found she couldn't hold it, but neither could she look at his unclothed body. His dark blond hair was damp with steam, causing it to curl and cling around his neck. It caressed him in a way that seemed too intimate for her to even look at his face. She shouldn't see him in this sort of dishevelment.

For lack of an alternative, she looked at the wall behind him, a safe enough place to settle her gaze as she tried to calm the strange fluttering in her stomach. He shouldn't affect her so. Why didn't she view him with disgust like she did Alfred's men? She *did* feel disgust. He was a filthy barbarian who was in no way handsome, she tried to reason.

But the anxiety of standing there awaiting his command was too great, so she looked to his eyes again. He was looking at her, but not at her face. His gaze was focused on her breasts, making her feel nude even in her undershift. The power he exuded touched her across the distance. An unfamiliar tingle began in her extremities and worked its way inward while her nipples tightened.

'What do you want me to do?' she asked in desperation to break the tension.

Her question seemed to break him from his study of her and his gaze returned to hers. 'Tend the fire.' It was the only explanation he offered before walking over to the tub of water she hadn't even noticed.

She watched him as he moved, deriding herself for doing so, but unable to tear her gaze away. The way his muscles moved and flexed under his skin fascinated her. She had the mad need to touch him, to see if his skin felt like satin and if those muscles would feel hard to the touch. Would he feel warm? Would his hair feel coarse or like silk? Would that male part of him that was growing rigid even as she watched feel hard?

The questions only stopped when he sat down in the steaming water, his head resting on the high rim, and closed his eyes. Her ability to function returned, causing her anger to return full force. In their brief time together, she'd yet to do anything in the way of serving him. She was a bit reluctant to cross that line. She'd never agreed to serve him and had only tried to bargain with him to save the pride Blythe had always said would be her downfall.

She didn't want to serve him. Particularly when he ordered it in so arrogant a manner. She was a noblewoman and he was the barbarian. If anything, he should be serving her.

'Nay.' She whispered the word and hated herself for her inability to say it louder.

His eyes flew open, but he held himself in control. 'Aye, you will.'

'You took me. I won't serve you willingly. You can't expect that of me.'

'But I do, slave.'

Her gaze went to his. 'Your taking me doesn't make me your slave.'

He almost smiled; she could see it in his eyes. 'That's exactly what makes you a slave. I took you.'

She shook her head and started to back up. Only her capitulating to serve him would truly make her a slave.

'Don't. Acceptance will make your life easier.'

Eirik knew she would run a moment before she did. The water sloshed over the edges of the tub as he pushed to his feet and ran after her. Whether or not he wanted her there, it was out of his hands.

She had to be made to understand that she couldn't defy a command.

He caught her just as she was rounding the partition and grabbed her arm. She swung back around and startled him by lashing out. He grabbed her arms and pulled her full against him, holding her wrists tight at the small of her back. She'd seemed so docile lately, he'd almost forgotten how she'd fought him that first day. His arm still carried a mark from her *seax*.

He held her silent until she stopped struggling and then lowered his head so he spoke nearer her ear. The words would be harsh. There was no need for his tone to be, as well. 'You belong here now. The sooner you accept that, the sooner you will adjust. You are not a noble here. Here you are a slave.'

The fight went out of her and she slumped against him, her head falling heavily against his chest. She might have sobbed, her body shuddering against him.

'There is no shame in accepting what fate has given you. The gods give us all challenges to overcome.'

'Do not speak to me of challenges. You are not a slave.' She spoke against his chest, but Eirik heard the hopelessness of her tone.

'You haven't been mistreated here.'

She did look at him then with heat and accusation in her eyes. 'Mistreated? Nay, I suppose I haven't been physically harmed, but my life is not my own. Everything is at your whim.'

'Is that any different than living with your brother? I've no doubt he would have seen you married soon, and then your brother would have been traded for your husband. At least I don't place the demands on you that a husband would.' It was the wrong thing to say, the wrong image to evoke with her in his arms. The vision of her compliant and naked stirred him. It didn't help that her body was pressed to him, and he found it softer than her slight frame had suggested it would be. Her breasts were full where they pressed against his chest, and her hips flared where he had expected them to be straight. He suddenly had the wish to reach down and feel how softly her buttocks would fill his hands. He suppressed the urge, but not before he'd imagined it.

'I hate you!' She struggled again, but he held her tight, and the friction only managed to stir his body to life even more. Her pebbled nipples moved enticingly against his chest, making him want to see them exposed to him. His shaft grew rigid against her soft belly, and he knew the moment she felt it because she stilled.

'You hate me because you have no one else to blame for your fate.'

'Isn't that enough?' But the hard edge had receded from her eyes. The dark orbs revealed the vulnerability and fear she'd tried so hard to keep at bay. He'd not seen that particular look in her deep gaze since she had tried to bargain her fate with him against the forge. It had a way of taking hold of him and making him want things that were unwise. It made him want to shield her, to take care of her, to make the fear go away. But even more, it brought light to the dark urge that wanted to own her, to possess her completely.

Before he even quite realised he'd done it, his thumb was stroking over that plump lower lip and he was watching it tremble beneath his touch. His breath came fast, matching the accelerated beat of his heart and the throbbing of his shaft. It would be so easy to lose himself. The lust firing his blood wanted to claim her. It was that part that took charge as he leaned down to her.

His hand moved from her chin so his fingers stroked her neck, revelling in her heat and the rapid beat of her pulse under them. Her scent overpowered him. It was delicate like a flower, with just enough of a hint of salt that he wanted to run his tongue over her flesh to lick it off. Just one taste of her, the demon within him urged. Just one taste and it would be enough. He breathed her in as his head lowered to her. His eyes fastened on her coral mouth. When his lips were just a breath from touching hers, she turned her head. He stopped just short of colliding with her cheek and paused, his breath harsh against her skin as he struggled for control. She just smelled too good.

Eirik closed his eyes and tried not to imagine pushing her against the wall and sheathing his length in her anyway, tried not to imagine how hot and tight her body would grip him, but the images played themselves over in his head with vivid clarity. He could even hear the sounds she would make with each demanding thrust. Tiny gasps of pleasure that would grow to helpless moans as she urged him to ride her harder.

To stop them he opened his eyes and watched her body tremble. He felt it shuddering against him and knew it for the fear it was. It was enough to make him win the battle for control. There would be no pleasure for her if he took her now.

Without warning, he released her wrists and went back to the tub, sinking beneath the water before she could see exactly how much he wanted her. He'd bet she'd never seen an aroused man before, and he knew the sight would frighten her. His head fell back and his eyes shut. Part of him was glad she had pushed him so far. Perhaps now she would see how compliance would keep her safer. If she hadn't run, he wouldn't have chased her and that moment between them never would have happened. But another part of him was angry that he had come so close to losing control with her. She had a way of accessing that darkness in him that shocked him.

From the relative safety of the tub, his hot gaze raked over her, and he saw that her shift was wet from being pressed against him. The turgid peaks of her breasts were on plain display against the fabric. Light coral. Her nipples matched her lips perfectly. Another surge of lust threatened to overwhelm him. For his own peace of mind, he decided he had to end this. Very little was stopping him from pushing her against that wall and acting out his fantasy.

'Get out. And, slave, next time obey me without question.'

Merewyn stood outside the bathhouse, letting the cool night air refresh her overheated body. It was the steam that had so unsettled her, or that was what she tried to believe. She'd never experienced its effect before and it had made her unusually warm and dizzy. But deep down, she knew the

Northman inside had something to do with how she was feeling now. The steam didn't explain her body's trembling or the pull that had made it so difficult to move away when he'd stared at her so deeply and almost put his lips to hers. It didn't explain why she'd suddenly become aware of that most secret part of herself that now throbbed between her thighs.

It was her body's reaction that shamed her the most. For just an instant, she'd wanted his lips to press against hers and had considered letting it happen before her better sense had prevailed. Nay, it wasn't even her better sense. She had wanted his mouth on hers, still wanted it. Damn him! The only thing that made her turn away was her sense of duty. He was her enemy, and his crimes against her and her family were atrocious. He'd made her a slave.

And yet here she stood, still trembling from his touch. Still wanting to know what would have happened if he had overpowered her token resistance and not stopped. She was weak, the worst sort of traitor.

A traitor to herself.

Chapter Nine

'Get up, girl.'

His gruff voice cut through her dreams, dragging her to consciousness. She blinked heavy lids and slowly looked around while allowing her gaze to adjust to the candlelight. It took a moment before she remembered where she was and whose voice called to her. He'd spoken in her language, but her sleep-muddled brain was slow to process the command.

'Up. We leave soon.'

That woke her fully. 'Where are we going?' She held the blanket tight to her chest as she sat up.

'I've already told you. We go to visit another jarl. Wash yourself and see Hilla to break your fast.'

She noticed then that he was dressed, his beard neatly trimmed, and wondered how long he'd been awake in the chamber while she slept. The thought bothered her for some reason. It suggested a level of intimacy that shouldn't exist, though it did. She didn't move as she watched his retreating back until he closed the door behind him. Then she scrambled to her feet, planning to ask Hilla what was happening.

But the steam rising from the basin of water on the table by the door drew her attention. She'd not washed in hot water since Eirik had taken her. The allure proved too much to resist. She made use of the cloth abandoned next to it, all the while pushing from her mind thoughts of Eirik using the same water.

When she was finished, she ran outside to find Hilla. Dawn was only just breaking when she approached her at the kitchen fire.

'Where is he taking me today? Do you know?'

A corner of Hilla's mouth tipped up in what Merewyn had come to understand was the woman's attempt at a smile as she pressed a bowl of that horrible porridge into her hands. 'Has he not told you?'

'Just that we visit a neighbouring jarl.'

'I only know he ordered for a cart and two of the men from the field. Some of the warriors who jour-

neyed with him did not come home. I think he goes
to deliver their share of the gains to the families.'

As she sipped the porridge, Merewyn mulled
over the revelation. It had never occurred to her that
the heathens would have a sense of honour, but it
gladdened her to know it. Perhaps if she could find
the right persuasion, he'd agree to take her home.
A layer of frost tipped the grass on the ground,
and as she moved closer to the fire she admitted it
would probably be a trip saved for spring. But that
she could accept, as long as she had hope that it
would happen.

She had just finished the last of the porridge when
Hilla brought a woollen cloak for her to wear on
the journey. It was as nondescript and scratchy as
her apron dress, but at least it was warm.

Eirik returned just then, mounted on a destrier
as black as his tunic, leading a horse-drawn cart
driven by two large men. He, she noted with bitterness, was cloaked in a lustrous fur that looked as
soft as it was warm. It made her think of her own
cloak at home. Though only lined with ermine, it
had been the most beautiful sea green with silver
embroidery along the edges. Merewyn had treasured it so much, she never wore it to the beach for
fear the salt from the spray would ruin it. It was

probably lucky that she hadn't worn it. If she had, Eirik would have taken that, too.

Alfred's wife would wear it now, she was sure. Blythe had always coveted it and had been peeved when Alfred had allowed her to keep it after their mother's death. She'd argued that Merewyn was a child and had no need for it, but Merewyn had refused to part with it. She'd even slept with it at night because it smelled like her mother. The thought that it was completely lost to her now filled her with such despair, she had to push it aside. In the spring, things could be different.

One of the men helped her into the back of the cart, where she sat down and snuggled into the warm folds of the coarse wool. Her gaze explored the chests, bags and leather pouches sharing the space with her. Some were loaded with foodstuffs, but others she suspected were filled with gold. They were divided out for half a dozen families, but put together would amount to a small fortune. The irony of the situation didn't escape her notice. Alfred would have given his best men for such wealth, but there she was surrounded by it and it couldn't save her.

If she hoped to convince the Northman to return

her, she'd have to think hard of something with which to tempt him. Gold wasn't enough.

They travelled south along the river with Merewyn walking much of the way because the jostling in the cart was too much for her. By evening they had reached the second farm where a family of six lived. She stood quietly by the cart as Eirik met the family who had come out to greet them. The older couple stood in front while their children hung back and watched with wide eyes. It was an almost exact re-enactment of the previous stop. As with that visit, she was left wondering if Hilla was right and he was relaying the death of their son. Their stoic expressions made it difficult to tell. This time, though, when he handed over the leather pouch filled with gold, he waved them forward.

Merewyn's heart leaped and she breathed a sigh of relief. They had been invited to stay. The prospect of spending the night out of doors held no appeal. Though the morning frost had long melted, she'd spent the past hour dreading its return when night settled.

Eirik followed the family inside their small home, leaving her with the two field men who had occupied themselves with settling the horses for the night. She was at a loss as to what to do and found herself perturbed by this unfamiliar state. Was she expected to stay the night outside like an animal after all? She clenched her teeth and decided Eirik could tell her that himself if that was what he intended. She was hungry and tired and longed for a fire.

So it was with squared shoulders that she approached the door. It wasn't latched, which prompted her to push it forward. Eirik was sitting at the table, but looked over and caught her eye when she stepped inside. It was the first bit of attention he'd given her all day, aside from that terse order to get up in the morning. His weighted gaze lingered on her face and moved down her front before he jerked it away to answer the farmer's wife, who was serving him food. The look prompted Merewyn to check her clothing, but it was fine, as fine as was possible for the hated slave dress.

She approached the hearth in the centre of the room with caution, drawn by the warmth, but half awaiting his direction. Nothing was forthcoming. The children huddled on the far side of the small living area and watched her warily, so she ignored them as she approached the fire. Her fingers were so cold, the first trace of heat to touch them actually burned. But it was a burn she savoured as the warmth seeped into her bones. Only when she'd begun to thaw did she realise how her stomach gnawed at her. Eirik was the only one eating, making her think it would be bad manners to serve herself. She, nevertheless, salivated as she eyed the pot bubbling on the hearth.

The woman of the house took notice of her stealing the heat from the fire and glared. Merewyn had no idea if the hostile look was because she was a foreigner, a slave or simply because she'd dared to seek out the fire's warmth. She was tempted to edge away, the good manners bred into her unable to allow her to presume her welcome within the home, but Eirik's voice broke the tension in a rough tone that was unmistakably an order.

Merewyn looked to him, and he motioned her over to sit beside him. The woman picked up a crude wooden bowl and began ladling soup into it, dismissing her. She walked to Eirik, intending to take the spot on the bench beside him, but his hand on her shoulder stopped her and he pushed her to kneel at his side. Her eyes widened at the insult—of course, she wouldn't be allowed a proper place at the table. Slaves were nothing but animals to them, unfit company for the table.

She jerked her shoulder from his grasp. 'If we were home, you'd be shackled like the criminal you are.'

'If we were home, you'd be attending me in the bath again.'

The warning in his words—a reminder of the previous evening—was undeniable, but it was the heat in his gaze and his smooth tone that unsettled her. A wooden bowl was pressed into her hands, and her grumbling stomach took over. She sank down and devoured the stew and the coarse bread that was served with it. The two men who had accompanied them on the trip came in soon after and took seats near the hearth, where they were promptly served with their meal. Merewyn couldn't help the tightening of her lips when she noted they were not subjected to the same hostility from their hostess.

Eirik spoke with the farmer who had taken a place across from him at the table, and the woman joined her husband after everyone had been served. They fidgeted as they sat, clearly unnerved by Eirik's company. Merewyn kept waiting for tears from the woman or some other telltale sign of mourning, but except for the anger she'd shown earlier, her face was stoic.

Her belly now satiated, Merewyn looked over to the children again. They ranged in age from about seven to a boy who looked old enough to be married with his own farm. He watched her with a carnal interest she recognised from the way men back home had looked at the serving girls. Her face flamed when the boy's gaze went from her to Eirik and back again, his thoughts plainly written on his face. He thought she served her master in that most physical way.

She looked away from him, but not before she saw the glint in his eye that told her he was envious. Her fingers moved with self-conscious grace to touch her hair, before she glanced up at Eirik. A jolt shot through her when she met his intense blue gaze. He'd seen it all, and that look burned as it touched her face and then moved down to the swell of her bosom. She squirmed beneath the weight of it and felt her body grow warm.

Did he want her to serve him with her body? She thought back to the previous day in the bath-house and how his male part had been stiff against her. She'd seen enough of animal mating to understand that was what would happen to a man in lust. Sempa had even gone through the entire explanation with her of how *it* happened. Aye, he did want to do that with her, but he'd said he wouldn't demand it of her. She believed him, and it kept her pulse steady and her breath even.

She was safe with him. Despite everything that had happened, he did make her feel protected. It was a strange knowledge that left her confused, especially as the look he gave her caused a peculiar ache to begin deep within her. His possessive gaze on her was meant to fill her with disgust, but the simple truth was that it did not—just as his touch had not last night.

Before he could recapture her gaze, she dropped it to look at his strong hand where it curled around his tankard. She easily recalled how those long fingers had curled around her wrists and pressed her close. The thought of them caressing the breasts he was so obviously admiring came to her unbidden, forcing her to close her eyes to shut it out. When she opened them, her attention settled on his broad thigh resting just inches from her face. A bizarre and inappropriate desire to touch him, to explore the thick, solid muscle with her hands, came over her. Why did she want to know how he would feel beneath her fingers?

She dragged her gaze along the length of the limb and stumbled upon the ridge of his maleness making itself known beneath the taut fabric of his trousers. For one breathless moment, she couldn't look away, could only stare at it as she became aware that, somehow, she had done that to him. Then she realised that if he was responding to her he must be aware of her scrutiny and raised wide eyes to meet his. The blue orbs were alive with a heady mix of desire and anger.

Caught spying, Merewyn blushed. Her lips even parted to inexplicably offer an apology, but nothing was forthcoming.

'Go take your rest.' He spoke in his own language, but repeated the command in her own. His voice was husky and warm.

The command broke the spell, and she looked to see if anyone else had noticed their inappropriate exchange. The couple at the table had continued with their hushed conversation and the children seemed equally oblivious, with the exception of the boy who still watched her with lust shining in his eyes. He might have seen. The men from the field talked in their own hushed voices as they ate their supper.

'Where?'

'There. Near the fire.' He nodded to the far end of the hearth, nearest the door and opposite where the children sat at the single partition that presumably separated the couple's chamber from the room.

Though she trembled with confusion and now anger at his curt dismissal—another reminder of the slave she was—she set her bowl on the table and made her way there. He could have spoken in her own language and saved her the embarrassment of being ordered about in front of these people. But he hadn't. Every time she began to think of him as a man, not simply her master, he found a way to remind her.

She held the cloak tight around her as she made her way. The boy still watched her; she could feel his gaze on her, so she gave him her back when she sat. Eirik stayed at the table, talking with the couple.

As she sat, she pondered what had just happened. Eirik desired her. That much was clear to her. But for some reason that desire made him angry. It was that anger that made him treat her so coldly, she was sure of it. She had no experience with men and their desire, so she didn't know if that was a normal reaction, though it seemed that it couldn't be. After all, her brother had got eight children on his wife and he didn't seem particularly angry with her about it. She'd heard some of Alfred's men carrying on with the female servants, and none of them seemed angry. On the contrary, often they would grin at each other across the great hall, thinking no one noticed their surreptitious glances. Could it be that, as a slave, he simply regarded her as too lowly to want to bed?

Merewyn didn't know what to make of this information, but she knew it was a key to him. Somehow it would be useful to figuring him out, and she needed to figure him out if she hoped to get home. The information was more than she'd had and it calmed her as she lay down and drifted off to sleep before the fire.

Chapter Ten

The house was dark when she awoke. Only the dampened light from the hearth lit the room. A movement from her side, too near for comfort, sent her heart fluttering in her chest. Merewyn's first thought was of the boy, so she sat up quickly to ward off whatever he had planned.

'It's me.' Eirik's voice, so near and rough in the dark, calmed her heart while at the same time setting off a disturbing fluttering in her belly.

'What are you doing?'

'Sleeping.'

'Are you not staying in the master's bed?' She was too groggy to stop the scathing reply before it escaped, as she looked around the small home. Everyone was asleep, littered like dolls across the living area. The master's bed might have been too generous a description. It looked to be a simple wooden bench tucked behind that partition in the far corner of the room.

'I wouldn't rob them of their beds on the same day I bring news of their son's death.' His voice was softer than normal, but still too loud for the sleeping room.

Arrogance, she thought as she watched him lay down on his fur and wrap it around himself. She still envied him the fur, and the reminder compelled her to scratch her belly where her rough dress irritated the tender skin. Then she recognised the darkness of sorrow lurking in his eyes just before they closed. The loss of those men bothered him.

He could've demanded a bed. He hadn't. Maybe arrogance had been too harsh.

She chewed her bottom lip as she struggled with her strange need to connect with him. It was rooted in the same twisted sense of security he gave her. It was inexplicable, but she reasoned she would need to know him to convince him to return her. 'It's kind of you to bring gold to their families. My brother wouldn't be so generous.'

He grunted, leaving her wondering why she'd even attempted to reach out to him. He so obviously saw her as someone less than relevant to him. The reminder made her earlier carnal thoughts of him seem even more shameful. She shouldn't entertain such depraved thoughts for a husband, much less a man who called her a slave and believed himself above her in every way. Something was obviously very wrong with her.

But that door, once opened, couldn't seem to be pushed closed again. She lay back down, remembering the sight of his muscled body and wondering anew what he would feel like beneath her hands.

'Your brother is a fool.'

Merewyn's eyes snapped open. From his spot on the floor just feet away, his gaze pinioned hers. 'You don't know Alfred.'

'It's a foolish leader who doesn't pay the family of a man who dies under his command. They have three younger sons. If I didn't pay, they wouldn't send them to fight with me.'

She licked her lips as she pondered her reply. He'd never engaged in conversation with her before, so the fact that he did so now made her wary. His words seemed to bait her, but his eyes were blazing, though not with anger. When his heated gaze moved down to watch her tongue where it moved over her lips, she understood it was some remainder of his earlier lust that emblazoned them. This information did nothing to tame her heart, which had begun to pound wildly again. 'Wouldn't your father order them to send their sons?'

'Every man here fights for his own gain, not because he follows orders. Is this how Alfred attains his warriors? Force?' He had turned on his side to face her and raised himself up on an elbow. The blue of his eyes seemed unnaturally bright and his lips curled in a sneer.

She opened her mouth to argue, but then realised he wasn't far off the mark. The families considered it an honour to have their sons fight under Alfred's command, or so she had thought. Was it possible that it was done under duress? 'Our lands are under attack. How else can Alfred and the king protect us without a reliable congregation of warriors?'

'If a warrior is worth his sword arm, he'll want to fight to protect his land. Without that desire, that free will, he's little more than a slave. A slave army has no chance of defeating one made up of warriors who are there by choice.'

'I'm sure most of them are there by choice.' What did it even matter to him? 'But either way, it's the way it's done. That doesn't make Alfred foolish.'

'It's only one of the reasons he's a fool.'

She wrenched her gaze from him to look at the wooden rafters of the ceiling. Anger was beginning to overpower the shameful desire, but it wasn't making it go away. The warring emotions merged into one confusing mass of something she couldn't name, but it was an energy she couldn't overcome. 'Why are you telling me this, Dane?'

'You should understand why your brother is a foolish man.'

'Why do you care what a slave understands?'

Eirik didn't answer. Aside from the occasional pop of wood as it burned in the hearth, the room was quiet until he was suddenly there, peering down at her. She pressed her back into the ground, away from the power he exuded. It caused her breath to stop altogether and then come faster. It didn't help that she noticed how the shadows cast by the glowing embers caressed his face, hiding his eyes now and leaving only his mouth visible. The effect could have been sinister, but her frail heart chose to humanise him. To notice the softness of his bottom lip. The intriguing lines that framed those lips.

The Viking god she had seen commanding the ship was gone. He was no longer a master. He was a man.

'There were no lookouts posted along the beach. Someone should have seen our boats or at the least expected an attack with the heavy fog. But they barely closed the gates against us.' His wintry breath caressed her cheek. How was that possible when they'd shared the same meal? He'd had ale. It should smell of ale.

'That's hardly Alfred's fault. He wasn't there. The king had called him away.' She couldn't tear her focus from those lips. The top one was a bit too thin, but the lusher bottom one made up for it.

'Is his home worth so little to him that he doesn't leave it protected when he goes?'

Merewyn had no answer to that. The Danes had never attacked them before, but she knew Alfred had had dealings with them in the past. Had he expected them not to attack? Had the men he'd left behind fallen lax in their duties? For the first time, she realised she had led a rather cossetted existence, insulated from the goings-on of war around her.

'And you, girl.' Her breath caught as his thumb blazed a trail across her cheekbone. 'You shouldn't have been allowed to go off on your own. Why didn't someone walk with you? Anyone could have taken you.'

She couldn't look away from his lips. 'H-he didn't allow my walks. I went anyway.'

Eirik went on as if she hadn't spoken. 'And his

wife should never have given you away. You are a treasure worth keeping.'

'I'm certain—' Was she? 'I'm certain he'll be angry with her for that.'

The thumb was still on her cheek and had moved up to caress the bruise. Or where the bruise had been. Merewyn had no way of knowing if it was still there. It didn't hurt anymore. His voice had gentled when he spoke. 'He allowed her to hit you. It wasn't the first time, was it?' When she didn't answer, he continued, 'Did he ever hurt you?'

She shook her head nay, but couldn't bring herself to voice a word to him as she fought the tears that stung the backs of her eyes. Alfred had never been physically violent with her, but he knew Blythe would occasionally raise her hand. He had never intervened.

'What does any of this matter?'

The corner of his mouth tilted up in a thought-ful smile. 'I said your brother is a foolish man and you asked for an explanation.'

'Well, you've more than explained yourself. It hardly matters. I'll never see him again anyway, will I?'

His gaze went to where his thumb touched her flesh. Merewyn didn't know how she knew, since she couldn't see his eyes clearly. The weight of it simply pressed there, heavy on her skin. 'Why are you so angry? I saved you.' He wasn't touching her belly, but she felt tingles there with every stroke of that damned finger on her. To add to the confusing mix of her emotions, she couldn't decide on his objective with this conversation. She almost thought he was teasing her, but the thought made no sense.

'You *took* me. You didn't have to. You could have left me.' Merewyn jerked her head away, refusing to be a pawn in whatever game he was playing, and moved to rise.

But he was on her, the weight of his body pushing her back down before she had barely moved. She shifted in a halfhearted attempt to dislodge him, but he was too heavy lying across her thighs, and her arms were like twigs pressed to the floor beneath the power of his hands.

'I took you because I couldn't leave you there.' The words tore from his throat in a hoarse whisper. It was almost as if he hadn't wanted them to come out, but they had anyway.

This close his eyes had become visible again and they burned into her own. All humour was gone from his face. 'Aye, you could have,' she challenged.

'Nay, she wanted you gone.'

'It wasn't your concern what happened to me. Why does a Viking raider concern himself with the well-being of a Saxon maiden anyway?'

'Because she would have given you to someone else and I couldn't bear the thought of another man having you.'

The air grew heavy and thick between them in the stunned aftermath of that admission. Those words should have repulsed her. Should have made her more determined than ever to put distance between them. But the simple truth was that they didn't. Nothing about him disgusted her as it should. Merewyn was helpless to stop the delicious tremor that his words had caused to work its way through her body.

Eirik felt it. His body pressed down to hers, as if to dissuade a fight. When he did, she felt the firm press of his manhood against her hip. She thought of the men and children sleeping so close in the small space, but even thoughts of them couldn't stop her body from responding to his desire. The blood thickened in her veins, causing her to feel strangely weighted, while a dull ache throbbed in that part of her that only he seemed to awaken. Her entire awareness became centred on that contact against her.

'I'll ask once more. Why are you so angry?'

Merewyn was so confused about her feelings, she couldn't have answered that question had she the slightest inclination to do so.

'I think it's because you don't feel nearly as angry as you believe you should.'

He was right to an extent. The fear was gone, but she didn't know what to call the emotion that had replaced it. She shifted her hips. It was an unconscious move to dislodge him, or so she tried to convince herself. As soon as she'd done it, she knew it had been a mistake. She could see the wave of hunger roll through him. But it had rolled through her, too, and taken her sanity to leave a very wicked, and barely glimpsed, part of herself in its place. The wickedness delighted in the fact that that look was meant for her alone. That she was the sole recipient of such intense attention. He'd cast a spell that pushed her dangerously close to forgetting that she was his slave, forgetting that she was anything but his woman. The thought shocked her to her core, giving her the wherewithal to buck her hips while jerking her wrists from his hold.

But he didn't let go, and his lower body pressed tighter to hold her immobile. Once she was subdued, his hips moved in a slow circle, grinding his length against her. He watched her face closely as she unwittingly arched into him and her lips parted on a gasp she managed to quell. Even through the layers of clothing, she could feel the heat of him, and that wicked, foreign part of her sought it out. He dropped his head so she heard his breath harsh near her ear. It was as erratic as her own.

Merewyn stifled a shudder when the touch of his nose stroked down along the column of her neck. He breathed in her scent, causing her to shiver when he exhaled, releasing the heat of his moist breath against her skin. Once, the coarse hair of his beard scraped along the sensitive flesh and made her insides twist with something close to antici-pation. It was followed by the supple contours of his lips dragging across the tender flesh. Her body came alive with the need to feel that abrasion again, particularly when it was followed with the touch of his impossibly soft, warm lips to soothe the pain.

Merewyn held her breath as he began the up-stroke and bit her lip to stifle another gasp when the tip of his tongue touched her. He stopped when he reached the shell of her ear, and she felt his la-boured breathing rasping against her.

'Don't tempt me, sweet girl,' Eirik whispered, his

lips moving against her, making her skin prickle with the touch.

Then he was off her, leaving her to watch his back as he left the cottage. Merewyn stayed immobile, trembling at the shock of her own arousal, before she could gather her wits enough to pull her cloak back tight around her. He'd hardly done anything, really. Why, then, did she feel as if he'd practically taken her there in the middle of everyone?

Eirik stood outside in the cold for a long time, letting the chill seep into his bones to war with the heat he felt for the slave girl. It unnerved him how close he'd come to taking her. The desire had roared through his body, almost uncontrollable in its vehemence. Giving fire to it was the knowledge that the farmer's boy was across the room. Eirik had seen the way he had watched the girl with lust on his face; even the two men from his own fields had looked at her throughout the trip with that flicker in their eyes. He had known an urge to make them know that she belonged to him. To take her before them with an animal's lust to prove that he was her master.

It was madness. He had nothing to prove to them. They all knew she belonged to him. None would touch her because of it. Besides, she wasn't a bed slave to be used at will. He wouldn't, *couldn't* use her in that manner.

He sucked in a deep breath to calm himself and closed his eyes. Only, when he closed them he saw her own looking back at him, dark and wide in their longing. Aye, he recognised the longing within them. Though fear lurked in those obsidian depths, he saw his own need reflected back at him. She recognised the dark lust within him, and it called to her woman's core. He wasn't sure if it was born from a slave's need to please a master or a woman's need to service her man.

It didn't matter. Those needs were two sides of the same blade. Whether she admitted it or not, she wanted to satisfy the demon urges. As he released the breath he'd been holding and opened his eyes to watch the cloud of steam dissipate, he knew now that the night would soon come when he would ask her to submit to him.

The shame and anger that accompanied those needs had shadowed him for too long. No matter how he tried to shove them down, they were there to bind him and sap his strength. His warning to her had come too late. She'd reached that part of him, and it wouldn't leave until it had been appeased. Eirik needed to fight it, to face it down, but he feared the only way to do that was through the girl.

He only hoped that when the time came, she told him nay.

Chapter Eleven

Their moment on the floor of the cottage might have never happened. Merewyn wouldn't have been sure that it had been more than a dream except that her heart stopped briefly when she awoke and her eyes were immediately pulled to him. He didn't return her gaze, didn't even look her way. Her heart, at least, hadn't forgotten it happened, even though he seemed unwilling to acknowledge her.

She had no idea what to say to him. Probably nothing would be said about it and they would continue as they were. Even if she had lain with him, she knew their roles would simply continue as slave and master, and the thought filled her with a heaviness that threatened to crush her. So she got to her feet and tried to push the memory out of her mind as if it didn't matter. It didn't matter. Life would continue.

After breaking their fast, it was time to leave. The

two men from the fields had already gone out to ready the cart and Eirik's horse, so they stood at the ready. But instead of walking to his destrier, Eirik walked before her to the cart and gripped her arm to help lift her inside. It wasn't done as gallantly as one of her servants back home might have completed the task, but it was attention. She despised how she lapped it up like a thirsty mongrel.

They rode that way for most of the morning, until the soil became too rocky for her to continue onwards in the cart. Even then, Eirik didn't speak to her. He simply motioned her over to him after she had climbed out and pulled her up to ride behind him.

She tried to maintain her distance, even with the close proximity, but it was impossible. After almost falling for the third time, she resigned herself to having to put her arms around him. He'd draped his fur across his lap to accommodate her behind him, so there was actually very little to keep her from feeling the heat and strength of his body all along her front. He seemed unaffected, and the knowledge left her wondering just how shamefully far she could fall under his spell.

The close proximity did have one unexpected

benefit. It allowed her to feel just how tense he became every time one of the houses they were to stop at came into view. Each time, the muscles of his back would stiffen, and she heard his harsh inhalation of breath just as he dismounted. Only knowing that was she able to look for and recognise the agony on his face as he approached the family to let them know their son had perished.

Each time he was silent when he came back to mount up in front of her. Her fingers gripped the fur in front of him, but she could feel the tension slowly leave his body with each step of the horse. She felt an inexplicable need to soothe the hurt he felt, though she recognised it as unwelcomed and unwise even as she searched for something to say to him. In the end, she remembered their words of the previous night and decided to say nothing. Words from a slave would mean little to him.

Their last visit was late in the day and, as on the previous night, they were invited inside to sleep. Eirik accepted, and this time she was allowed to eat at the hearth with the two field men. When it was time to rest, Eirik was still talking with the family, and she fell asleep before he came to her. Merewyn had no idea why she thought he would come to lie beside her again or even why she imagined some sort of repeat of the night before. It was to her detriment to have such a re-enactment play out. Yet when she closed her eyes the phantom weight of his body haunted her, eliciting shameful frissons of excitement along hers.

The grey light of dawn was filtering down through the only window tucked just under the roof when she awoke. She shovelled down her food and made her way outside, surprised to see the cart with the men riding in it already quite some distance away from the home and retracing their path from the previous day.

'Where are they going?' she asked, walking to stand beside Eirik where he watched them riding away. The gruel churned in her stomach.

'Home.' It was the only reply he deigned to give her as he turned to his horse and mounted.

There was no doubt as to his intention for her, because his arm came out to lift her up. Merewyn hesitated only a moment before taking it, but instead of lifting her up behind him, he settled her across his lap in front.

'What are you doing?'

He clicked his tongue and the horse started walking, taking a path to the east. 'Saving your arse from another pounding today.'

She blushed to realise he'd guessed correctly that she ached from the riding yesterday. 'I've never ridden.'

When she shivered from the cold wind, he pulled the much-envied fur around her and tucked her against him so her head nestled just under his chin. His arms cradled her on either side and his scent enveloped her, that exotic spice mixed with leather. It might have been a tender embrace had she allowed herself to believe he felt anything for her other than the care an attentive master felt for a slave.

'Aren't we going home, too?' The last satchel of gold and sack of grain had been delivered.

'Not today.'

Of course, the visit to the neighbouring jarl, but he wouldn't offer a further explanation to her. She clenched her fists in the fur, unable to accept her role as the biddable slave. 'Where are we going?'

'I have one more visit to make.' He gestured to the bolt of cloth wrapped in a length of oilskin strapped to the back of the horse.

She had to crane her neck to see it and felt a momentary pang of disappointment that it had usurped her place on the back—the real reason for the way his arms cradled her so tenderly. His biceps pressed warm and strong against her back, but she forced herself to sit up, away from the false comfort. Had she sank so low in her need for human companionship, her need for a simple scrap of affection, that she'd begun to see it where it didn't exist? Or long for it even if it was from him? Merewyn closed her eyes against the painful tide of truth that washed over her.

The reality was that her life had been lacking affection for a long time. Alfred cared for her, but Blythe didn't. The woman had given her away when the opportunity had presented itself. No one had touched her with tenderness since her mother had passed when she'd been six. There were times she barely remembered how it felt.

His truthful words of two nights ago came back to her again. He was right. She wasn't as angry at him taking her as she wanted to be, as she *should* be. Or, actually, she was angry for the wrong reason. She should be angry that he had taken her from her family, but she was angry that he had taken her from the promise of a family. She had been more than ready for Alfred to find a husband for her, to start her own family. It had been past time for her to leave Alfred's household. Merewyn was angry that she hadn't got that opportunity.

She'd never have a family now. Never know the love and tenderness that could be found there. That was the real source of her anger. Not the present he'd stolen her from, but the future he'd stolen from her.

I saved you. For the first time since he'd said those words, Merewyn believed him. Believed he thought that anyway. She wasn't sure if she agreed with him.

She shivered, and he responded by tucking the fur tighter around her. When he was done, his forearm settled on her lap. It wasn't an intimate gesture by any means, but it suggested a protectiveness that implied intimacy. Regardless, it warmed her far beyond the warmth offered by the fur. That was the danger. She couldn't allow whatever the Northman did to her to become something more than it was. He believed himself her master. There could never be tenderness or even real affection between them. As long as she could remember that, she would be fine.

And she needed to learn more about him. To figure out who he was so that she could convince him to return her. It would also help her to remember that he was a Dane—an enemy.

'What happened to the men who died? Did they fall in battle?'

To her surprise, he answered right away. 'Their boat sank when a storm blew in too fast for us to reach shelter. It was a few days before we reached your land.'

There was a hesitancy in his voice. One that she might not have noticed had he not consumed her so much since their meeting that she noticed everything about him. The loss bothered him. She felt compelled to say, 'I'm sorry.'

Yesterday he'd become tense before each visit to a family, and she was sure that she'd seen genuine sorrow in his eyes. Had she only imagined it? The need to know gnawed at her until she couldn't contain it anymore.

'Why did you deliver the payment to those families?'

He was quiet so long she might have thought he didn't hear her, except that he'd stiffened. 'We discussed this,' he answered, keeping his gaze steady on the horizon.

Merewyn observed his stony profile, but wasn't

fooled. 'I mean, you didn't have to do it yourself. You could have sent men for the task.'

'They were along the way. There was no need to send anyone else.'

He was being evasive. Although the sun had disappeared behind a low overhang of clouds, she'd seen enough of it to know they travelled northeast. The last stop, at least, had been out of the way. 'You wanted to do it yourself. Why?'

'Enough.' The word was spoken softly, but firmly enough that she knew he wouldn't elaborate.

He reached down to retrieve a small leather pouch tied to a larger one off the side of the saddle. After he opened it, she caught the scent of winter that she associated with him. Intrigued, she watched as he stuck his forefinger and thumb inside and came out with a bit of something that looked like dried leaves pinched between them. He chewed it and seemed amused as he noticed her interest.

'*Míntha.* Would you care for some?'

She nodded and moved to reach inside the pouch, but he beat her to it and offered her a bit pinched between his fingers. She hesitated only a moment before opening her mouth to accept his offering. Her tongue swept across his fingertips as she took the leaves. His sharp intake of breath was the only indication he gave in acknowledgement of the intimacy. The leaves were sweet and only slightly bitter as she chewed, coating her mouth with a coolness she'd never experienced. In a strange way, she felt closer to her captor, sharing in this small part of his life.

Merewyn grimaced and lowered her chin, unsure how to proceed with her warring emotions regarding him. She still needed information, still needed to convince him to take her home. As she chewed, she waited, watching the clouds roll overhead. She needed to have him share more of himself; perhaps then she could find something useful.

The temperature had dropped noticeably in the past hour, making her wonder if it might snow. A shiver shook her, and he responded by putting his arm around her and tucking her against his warmth. When she inhaled, her senses were flooded with his scent, manly and wintry all mixed together. She began to warm, but it had nothing to do with the fur wrapped around her.

'What do you Danes believe happened to those men who died when the boat sank?'

The blue of his eyes burned as his gaze raked her face from brow to mouth. Despite their close proximity, it was a shock how close his mouth was to her own. Almost as close as it had been that night on the floor of the cottage.

'Aside from drowning, you mean?' His breath whispered across her lips. She might have smiled at the dry humour had she been able to distract herself from its caress.

She nodded. 'What of their souls?'

'Why would you ask that? You despise Vikings as nothing but thieves and murderers. I know about your White Christ. Don't you think they go to hell like all sinners?'

His tone was almost teasing, so she didn't allow his words to bait her as he wanted. Besides, she wasn't interested in a theological debate. She simply wanted to learn more about the barbarian and his beliefs. So she kept her tone pleasant when she replied, 'I know what *I* think. I'm simply curious to know what *you* think.'

His discerning gaze assessed her for a long moment, but he must have decided her question was harmless because he finally turned his attention back to the rocky terrain they navigated and answered, 'They go with Rán to live under the sea.'

'Rán is a god?'

'Goddess. When at sea we all travel with a piece of gold in the event she decides to take us. It helps with the welcome. They'll feast at her table and, if they're lucky, maybe even share the beds of her daughters.'

'Lucky daughters.' Her voice dripped with sarcasm.

Eirik surprised her by laughing. 'I suppose you would see it that way. Though some would say the daughters are lucky to have the attention of virile warriors if the alternative is an eternity alone.'

'You Danes believe every woman is eager to lay down for you.'

His gaze drew back to her face and raked it so she felt its touch deep within. His eyes were smoky now and laced with amusement. A heady combination she hadn't been treated to before. 'Are you not?'

Did he know? Did he have any idea how her body had responded to him? Nay, it was impossible that he would know. Merewyn jerked her gaze from the hold he had on her and looked out over the hills around them. It didn't stop the unwelcome fluttering in her belly. 'It would not please me to be used for Viking amusement.' Except maybe for this particular Viking's amusement. She had begun to have serious doubts about her body's treacherous resistance to him. There was no denying that he awakened wickedness within her.

A shadow passed over them. Her words had altered the mood, extinguishing the brief flash of amusement and leaving a void in its wake. Merewyn knew it without even looking at him. The change happened in the subtle tensing of his body and the icy quiet that stretched between them.

'I won't allow anyone to violate you.' The words were pushed out between clenched teeth.

There was an unspoken depth in his voice that drew her attention back to him and made her wonder what he really meant to say. Merewyn studied his face, trying to determine what lurked behind his words. He refused to look down at her again, though, and kept his eyes on the horizon. Finally, she looked away, but couldn't shake the feeling. The silence stretched between them until it became all she could think about.

Merewyn's thoughts drifted to the night before last on the cottage floor. He'd wanted to take her then, of that she had no doubt. But he hadn't. Would he have pushed further if they had been back at the longhouse in his chamber? He'd wanted to.

Before she could stop herself, she said the very words that repeated over and over again in her head. 'But you wanted to.'

His hot gaze captured hers and the muscles of his

arm clenched tight against her. Reflected in the blue depths, she saw her own memories of that night and the fire that ignited so easily between them. Could he see her own shameful secret in her eyes? Did he realise the pleasure she'd discovered in his touch?

'Aye.' The word grabbed at something deep, primitive, within her and tugged a reluctant chord of sensual response. 'But you wanted it, too.'

Chapter Twelve

Eirik wasn't expecting the crowd that had gathered at Jarl Leif's. They rode in at twilight, having taken the path that followed the river and ended at the fjord. So many boats were moored there that more than half of them were anchored and bobbing in the deeper waters, with boys in smaller boats rowing visitors to shore. Ten years earlier, he might have been one of those boys charging for the convenience. It would have been a lucrative night, because it looked as though most of them had brought their women with them. Unless he missed his guess, the jarl's child had been born.

He'd hoped to speak the words he needed to speak to the jarl in private. Despite his father's urging, Eirik had decided that now wasn't the time to marry Kadlin. The declaration would make Leif unhappy, maybe even angry. The man had made no secret of his intentions that Kadlin and Eirik would marry. But Eirik hoped to make him understand that the fighting that would come with the spring invasion would need his complete attention. Besides that, it wouldn't be fair to leave Kadlin behind as a new wife to face her future without him. It was unlikely, but the campaign could take years. He absolutely refused to leave her pregnant.

The fact that his pretty slave was taking up so much of his thoughts didn't figure into things. Or so he tried to believe. The presence of the Saxon wench in his life had no bearing on his future. She was simply a minor complication in his present.

Someone called out a greeting to him, drawing his attention from her. He raised his hand, but the greeting alerted others to his presence and he was soon waylaid by others welcoming him back from his travels. The girl drew stares from the wellwishers that caused her to shift against him nervously. His hand automatically settled on her thigh to soothe her. It wasn't even a conscious thought on his part, just a natural action that was becoming all too common. His hands believed she was his to touch and stroke at will.

Her leg clenched beneath his touch. It was soft enough to be pleasing, with just the right amount of firm muscle. He imagined them clenching around his hips as he buried himself in her and immediately hardened. Even on horseback surrounded by people, he wanted her. It should have come as no surprise given how he'd wanted to claim her in the middle of the crowded cottage. Soon he needed to rid himself of her so his life could progress normally again.

'What's happening?' she asked as they made their way past the crowd that had gathered around them.

'The jarl and his wife have welcomed a baby.'

'Is that why you've brought a gift?' She glanced at the bolt of cloth tied behind him.

'Nay, I wasn't aware the child had been born when we left. The gift is for—' He stopped short, pondering how best to explain Kadlin to her. But then he wondered why he felt the need to explain Kadlin to his slave. It was madness, so he stifled the impulse. 'The gift is for a friend.'

She frowned, and he caught a glimpse of the hurt in her eyes before she looked away. Ever since she'd joined him on his horse, she'd been trying to penetrate the wall between them. Every question and comment had been an attempt to bring it down. He couldn't figure out her motive, but he knew she didn't realise the danger in her plan. The wall kept her carefully in her place as his slave. Without it, she became something else, someone he had no place for. Someone with no protection from the things he wanted to do to her.

Eirik walked the horse through the milling crowd until they came to the old man who tended a fire near the back of the large longhouse. Cnut smiled a nearly toothless grin as he rose slowly to his feet and raised a hand in greeting.

'Welcome home, my lord. I had wondered if you'd returned.'

'Aye, just a few days past. It seems your jarl has been busy.' Eirik dismounted and clasped the man's arm in greeting, before reaching up to grab the shapely hips of his slave and help her down.

Cnut laughed. 'He has at that, the randy bastard. Have you brought a gift or your own entertainment?' His question was unmistakably about the girl.

It was well known that Jarl Leif was too enamoured of his wife to partake of the entertainment a bed slave could provide. The question was simply a means of figuring out why the slave was there, but Eirik didn't feel inclined to elaborate on an issue he was still trying to figure out for himself. 'Neither' was the only explanation he offered as he untied the bolt of cloth from the back of the destrier.

'I see the black is still in his prime.' Cnut walked over and rubbed the horse's flank. 'Most folks came by boat or foot, so there's plenty of space for him.'

'Thank you. It's good to see you, my friend. I'll be out to check him in the morning.' Eirik turned his attention to the slave, who was busy watching the spectacle around them. Numerous fires hosted spits of roasting meat and gatherings of men who were laughing loudly and taking advantage of the occasion to drink copious amounts of ale. The girl looked as if she feared she'd end up on one of those spits. 'Come.' He gently took her arm and led her to the longhouse.

'Eirik!' The moment he stepped inside, Kadlin's voice came to him through the din of commotion. His eyes adjusted to the lighting inside just in time to catch her as she flung herself into his arms. 'I'm so happy you're here. When did you get home?'

'Just a few days ago. I'd thought to see you there, but Father said your mother was close to her time. The baby is well?'

'Aye, a strong boy, to my father's everlasting joy. After four girls in a row, I think he was beginning to doubt his prowess.' She laughed.

'He has other sons. I'm told daughters are trouble and, judging from all the trouble you've caused,

I can understand his distress,' he teased. 'Is your mother well?'

'Aye, she's wonderful and healthy. And I haven't caused a bit of trouble.' She feigned a frown, and Eirik had to admit that it only somehow made her more beautiful. Because of her height, she only had to look up slightly to him. He couldn't help but compare her to the slave's own delicate beauty and how she fit nicely tucked up against him. It was a disturbing thought, because he'd never once imagined how Kadlin felt against him. The unwarranted comparison made him release Kadlin and step back.

Her lips parted as if to remark on his abrupt movement, but then she noticed the figure beside him and smiled a greeting. But the smile faded as she noted the coarse wool apron dress and the plain braid. 'You've brought a slave?'

'She was a gift.' Eirik clenched his teeth.

'Do you think our welcome so lacking you had to bring your own slave?' Kadlin was still looking the girl over. She stared right back at her.

'I couldn't trust her safety to Gunnar and my father, so I brought her.' It sounded like a defensive statement and he despised it.

Kadlin's smile had returned when she looked

back at him. He'd feared that she'd heard far too much in his explanation. That she had noted his defensiveness and knew it for what it was. Guilt that he wanted the slave girl to belong to him in every way her position in his life implied. Eirik cleared his throat and changed the subject. 'I've been travelling for days. A dutiful woman would offer me mead and food.'

'Well, as you've realised, I'm a disappointment to my family and can be forgiven for forgetting my duties. But do come in and take a seat by the fire. Does your…?' She glanced at the girl, as if unwilling to accept the explanation he'd given. 'Does your slave need food, as well?'

'Aye, many thanks, Kadlin. I'd have her stay in the women's quarters if it can be arranged.'

She nodded her fair head and motioned over a stout woman who seemed to be hovering in the background awaiting her command.

'Go with the woman. She'll see you fed and show you to a bed for the night.' Eirik spoke softly in her own tongue while steadfastly refusing to allow the girl's wide-eyed hesitancy to affect him.

'My lord…' The girl lightly placed her fingers on his arm.

'You'll be safe in the women's quarters.' He

nodded to the loft near the back and unconsciously pressed his hand to her fingers for reassurance. 'I'll be down here all night.'

Two hours later, Eirik stared into the fire as Kadlin spoke of all that had happened in his absence. The flames made him remember how the slave's hair reflected the firelight, and he cast a glance in the direction of the loft.

'Then he tried to proclaim his innocence, all the while attempting to hide his muddy feet *and* the piglet in his trousers. When questioned about the squealing, he explained in all sincerity that it was a malady he had developed lately!'

Eirik couldn't help but chuckle and look to her younger brothers across the room. 'It appears they are even more troublesome than their older sister. Have you told them yet about the time you flattened Gunnar when he said you were more boy than girl?'

Kadlin blushed and sat back in her seat. 'Of course, but only so they know I'm perfectly capable of keeping them in line.'

Eirik smiled again at the memory. Being in her company had always been easy. As children she'd been determined to keep up with whatever machinations he and Gunnar were into and had always held her own. She'd eventually earned their respect by keeping up with them. Maybe he was a fool to pass up the opportunity to marry her now. She was perfect in all the ways he knew that a wife should be. But he had never once thought about what it would be like to lie between her thighs. Not like with the slave. He looked back at the loft before he could stop the inclination.

'She admires you, you know.'

'Who?' His startled gaze swung back to Kadlin.

'The girl.' She smiled. 'She seems very aware of you…as a man.'

'You've gone mad. She's a slave.'

'Slave or not, she's still a woman. A woman who looks at you like a woman looks at a man she notices.'

He despised that her words pleased him. 'What would you know of such things?'

'Women notice these things. I *am* a woman.' Kadlin sat up straighter in mock affront.

'I didn't mean to question your femininity.' He held up a hand in surrender. 'I only meant you barely saw her, surely not long enough to tell that. It doesn't matter.'

She kept up the knowing smile, and he forced

himself to look away from it, unwilling to discuss his thoughts of the slave.

'It wouldn't matter, I suppose, except you look at her that way too. It makes one wonder...' Her voice trailed off and her smile faded. 'That girl isn't like the other slaves working with Hilla.'

He knew what she meant, knew where she was headed and clenched his teeth.

'Her skin is too smooth and fair to have worked a farm. You have to know she won't be a good worker.'

'She's never worked a farm.' His voice was low and measured. Despite the noise around them, in their small alcove, the words carried to her. 'She's a noblewoman and was given to me. I didn't take her to be a good worker.'

The corner of her mouth tilted upwards. 'Well, that's not surprising. She has the look of noble birth. But I am surprised that you accepted her. Interesting.' Her fingers tapped rhythmically on the arm of her chair as she surveyed him. 'I know you weren't *forced* to accept her. No one could force a gift on you.'

His patience at an end, his voice was harsher than he intended. 'What's with this inquisition, Kadlin? Gunnar found her in a cellar, the lady of the manor gave her to me and she was clearly abused there. I couldn't leave her.'

'Oh.' For the first time, Kadlin looked uncertain. 'Gunnar is well, then?'

He nodded, but couldn't let the subject go until she understood. 'I had no choice but to take her.'

She was silent for a moment as she processed his words. 'It seems you didn't, but she's very pretty. There's only one position available to a slave like that.'

'Aye, I'm aware of the usual station offered to a pretty slave.' Eirik was more than aware. He'd been battling his own urges from the start. 'I haven't bedded her, if that's your concern. Have you always talked this much?'

'Always,' she countered. 'And that's not my concern, Eirik. I know you, but I do wonder what will become of her.'

'What do you mean?'

'You brought her here because you couldn't leave her with your father and brother. I agree that those two aren't the most trustworthy when it comes to pretty girls. But soon you'll have to leave to go off again or perhaps you'll marry. Do you suppose a wife would like your pretty slave to join your household? What will happen to her then?'

'You think I'd let a wife rule my decision regarding her? I don't know of a man who doesn't make use of bed slaves, married or not. It's a common enough practice and you know it. Your father is the only exception.' It was a stupid thing to say. Though it was true, it wasn't something he should be discussing with Kadlin, and it was his meagre attempt at assuaging his own guilt for those feelings.

'Oh, Eirik.' Her hand, tender and unexpected on his arm, drew his gaze back to her. 'You know that's not true, and even if it were, it doesn't excuse it. I know you desire her, but surely *you* of anyone knows what it would mean.'

Eirik took a deep breath and touched her fingers where they rested on his arm. 'Aye. I would not take away her free will in that. How can you speak of this so plainly?' He'd noticed there seemed to be no jealousy in her words.

'I care for you. I don't want to see you do something against yourself.'

Though he knew her words were true, there was more. 'You're not jealous of the girl yourself?'

She smiled, but it didn't reach her eyes before she averted them to the table. 'Why would I be jealous?'

'Because any woman in your position would have the right to be jealous.'

'My position?'

He watched her until she couldn't look away anymore and had to meet his scrutiny. It was clear to him then why she didn't feel threatened by the slave. 'You don't want to marry me, do you?'

Kadlin laughed and looked down again, clearly uneasy now that the inquisition had turned to her. 'My father has been talking to yours, I see.'

He nodded. 'But you've known they assumed we would wed all along. You don't want to be my wife.' The answer was plainly written on her face, a revelation he hadn't expected.

'Aye, they have. My father has failed to speak to *me* about the matter, however. He thinks he knows what's best for me.'

'You don't think marrying me would be best for you?'

'Look at my parents.'

Eirik found them at the large table across the room. The jarl held a small bundle tightly wrapped in blankets while his wife sat to his side watching the dancing girls who had made an opening in the crowd to twirl. They reminded him a little of the girl as she'd twirled on her beach. The jarl watched, too, but he kept turning to watch his wife, as if he'd rather experience it through her reaction.

'They love each other. My father doesn't even know other women exist. It's what I want, too.' She touched his arm again to soften her words. 'I know you care for me and that you'd provide well for me, but you don't feel that way for me.'

The weight he'd carried slowly began to dissipate, leaving him feeling free. He should have felt regret. But he didn't. She was right and, while he'd certainly never considered love—whatever that elusive emotion meant—necessary for marriage, it was clear that she did. His father would be furious. Eirik knew that he should be furious as well, but he couldn't rouse the emotion. He had never felt the match necessary to substantiate his claim, though he understood it would strengthen it. He'd have to figure out some way to placate his father.

His gaze automatically went to the dark loft again. He couldn't see anything, but he knew the slave was there. Free of attachment, the need for her roared through him. She could be his for as long as he wanted her.

'And you don't look at me like you do your slave,' Kadlin added. Her teasing smile was back.

'You *have* gone mad.'

'I've never seen you look at anyone the way you look at her. It's as though you want to possess her.'

'Cease this.' His voice was a low growl, provoked by how easily she saw his desire for the girl.

Undeterred by his gruffness, Kadlin laughed. 'I know how a man looks at a woman he wants. I'm not so sheltered I don't understand the happenings between a man and a woman. Like that dancing girl there...' She nodded to one with large breasts. 'Those men watching her want to bed her. But you, you look to the slave.'

Kadlin moved to stand behind him, her arms encircling his shoulders from behind and her lips near his ear. 'You're a fine man, Eirik. She knows it, too. I saw it in her eyes. I'm not sure why, but I think she could be someone special to you. She's a noble and she'd be a fine match for you if only she wasn't Saxon.'

'But she is,' he whispered.

'Aye, a Saxon slave. What a pity.'

Chapter Thirteen

Merewyn watched the embrace from her pallet on the floor of the loft. There was clearly something between them. The knowledge stung with a pain that brought tears to her eyes. She flopped onto her back and closed her eyes. The image of the beautiful woman putting her arms around Eirik—for the second time that day—was imprinted in her mind.

He laughed with her. When they had arrived, his arms had gone around her as if they'd done that many times before. The woman was clearly important to him, and she definitely wasn't his sister. It didn't matter. It shouldn't matter because he was nothing to Merewyn but her master. But it did matter.

She tried to tell herself that it only mattered because he was her security in this world. The woman could become jealous if she suspected their relationship was something…different than it was. Or what it threatened to become. Merewyn could still feel the phantom weight of his body on top of her, and she prayed for forgiveness when it wasn't at all a repugnant memory. If the woman became jealous, Eirik could give her away. Then what would happen to her? Some other man would use her as roughly as she'd been afraid Eirik would.

The thought might explain the reason her breath came heavy and almost panicked. It might even explain why her heart was beating so fast. It did not explain the tears that leaked from her eyes to fall into the hair at her temple. It did not explain the heavy tightness that had settled around her heart or the ache in her throat. Those could only be explained by the treacherous thought tumbling around in her head: her Northman was in the arms of another woman.

On some level the idea shocked her. But she accepted it, because it had been there for a long while hovering just outside her consciousness. It had crept in somewhere along the way and waited for just the right moment to reveal itself, that idea that he was somehow hers. She had no claim to him, but she wanted one.

* * *

The next morning Eirik came to see her as she was breaking her fast with the other women. She felt his presence as a prickling along her spine just before he touched her shoulder. Merewyn turned to him, uncertain what she would see in his gaze—guilt? Regret? Pity because he was giving her away? The woman would surely never allow him to keep her. But none of those was there. His blue eyes seemed pleasant and clear as they boldly met hers.

She nodded and walked the short distance away from the group so they could talk.

'Were you able to rest last night?' he asked.

'Aye, my lord.' It was a lie. She'd lain awake for hours thinking about him and that goddess, but that wasn't what he meant. He was only concerned with her safety. He'd probably gone to check on his horse that morning, as well.

Eirik surprised her by smiling and touching her cheek with the back of a finger. 'Your eyes give away your lie.'

Merewyn sucked in a breath and dropped her gaze. Not because he'd seen her so clearly, but because his touch was torture. It was tender when it should be cold. It promised things that were a lie. That ridiculous thought from the night before came back to taunt her. The light of day revealed it for the foolishness it had been. He would never be hers. He was her master and she was a slave. She had no hope of ever claiming any part of him. The knowledge left her bereft, and she hated the hollow ache in her chest. She'd been just fine in her life until he'd come along. He'd made things complicated, things that should be simple.

Even so, she felt the loss when his hand dropped back to his side.

'There will be a feast again tonight. Make sure you eat well and, once night falls, stay in the loft.'

She could hear him ordering the same commands to the boy who tended his horse. *Feed him well and, once night falls, keep him inside with plenty of hay.* It made her unreasonably bitter, as she realised that even Alfred might have spoken the same words to her. No one had ever cared if she needed more than food or shelter. She especially didn't expect the Dane to care, but she lashed out anyway to fight against his tender touches that lied. 'Aye, master, I know my place.'

His brow furrowed and his eyes clouded. The pleasant manner was gone. 'Do you?' The words were clipped, drawing her gaze back to his. 'We'll leave in the morning.' He turned and walked away.

The day did not get any better for Merewyn. She found herself hoping to catch glimpses of him among the guests who continued to arrive. Her task had been to take things back and forth between the fire in the house and the outside kitchen. It gave her ample time to look for him and the blonde woman. Twice she saw him talking with the jarl, but then he disappeared and she didn't see him or the woman again. She imagined them secreted away somewhere and it only made her mood decline even more.

By dusk, she'd worked herself into an angry frenzy. There was nothing left to do except serve the food, and that was more than she could take. She couldn't serve these people who thought they were so much above her.

Merewyn waited until the broad woman who seemed to be in charge disappeared into the house, then followed the smell of the salt air. She needed some time to herself to sort through her feelings. The beach called to her here just as it did at home, so she followed the smell until she could hear the water lapping at the shore and feel the land under her feet give way to sand. There were so many people around, it shouldn't have surprised her to find them on the beach, as well. She headed farther down the shore, away from everyone.

Only when the last fires had faded to flickering lights in the distance and the voices were barely distinguishable above the breaking waves did she stop. She unbraided her hair to set it free and closed her eyes so the gentle breeze could wash across her face. With each deep breath, the tension that was coiled around her chest loosened until she felt as if she was breathing freely for the first time since Eirik had found her. In her mind, she was transported back to the beach near her home with no thoughts of Northmen and slavery. She was Merewyn and she simply existed.

But that only lasted for a few brief moments. All too soon she remembered that when she opened her eyes, she would go back to the manor and everything would be the same. The same tasks, the same drudgery, the same Blythe. The home she wanted wasn't the home that she remembered. The home she wanted only existed in her head as a possibility. Alfred had promised to see her married and she'd always taken it for granted, perhaps naively, that she would be happy with his choice. Was that a realistic expectation? She was strongly beginning to suspect that no one would live up to her Northman in her mind.

Under any other circumstances, she would want him. He was strong, protective and good. He'd never made her feel real fear of him. Her fears had always either been self-nurtured or given to her by some other external force. Never by Eirik. She would be safe with him. A small part of her wondered if there could be more with him, too.

When he looked at her, there was desire, but she could see the beginnings of something else, too. Real interest, as though he was trying to figure her out. Though she was grossly inexperienced in those things, she hoped the depth of his glances meant more. He could have his choice of pretty girls at his home, but she realised now that he hadn't seemed to pay attention to any of them. And she loved that. A lot. She loved that his interest was with her.

She opened her eyes and she was firmly back on the foreign shore. A slave. But here there was more. There was Eirik and he wanted her. There could be a lot more if she was brave enough to embrace it.

And you wanted it, too. The memory of his observation made her shiver. Aye, she did want him. She wanted to know this thing that existed between them.

She took a deep breath and realised that the tension hadn't returned to squeeze the air from her. She was still free. Eirik had given her that. Though he hadn't said as much, he had promised not to violate her, but she knew that if she pressed he would take her. So the choice was hers to make. Eirik had given her choice, and wasn't choice part of freedom?

She looked down the shore in the direction that was dark and deserted. She could follow that direction if she chose and never return to him. Death might await, but it was also a sort of freedom. But she realised it wasn't what she wanted. She wanted him.

She wanted Eirik.

A smile tugged at her lips as she turned to make her way back to him in the village. There was a strange liberation in deciding not to fight. It had been a choice all along, though she hadn't seen it. She took a deep breath again and realised the tightness had not followed her from the beach. Freedom was following her. She almost laughed as she realised it had been within her power all along.

Kadlin—she had learned the Viking goddess's

name—might still be a problem. If the woman wanted Eirik, too, and it appeared that she might, then that could prove to be a setback. If Eirik really planned to marry the woman, then all would be lost. But she didn't know for sure if that was the case, and she was finished with being miserable over things she had no control over.

Maybe if she hadn't been so preoccupied, so hopeful, she would have seen the man before he grabbed her. But his hand had captured her arm before she could lurch away. He'd been a shadow among many leaning against the wall of a house. The big longhouse was just across the clearing, so close she could've called for help if the crowd hadn't created a drone so loud no one would notice.

'Let me go!' She jerked her arm, but he didn't give.

In the dim light she could see he was older, but his chest was still broad and his eyes were dimmed with drink. He said something to her in the Norse language. Even though she didn't know his words, she knew what he wanted. He was drunk and looking for sport. Faster than she would have thought possible, the man grabbed the front of her woollen dress and tugged. The pull was so quick and forceful, the brooches that held it in place were jerked right out of her shift.

Merewyn had just found her equilibrium to lash out at him, but he pushed her against a wall so hard that her next breath was knocked out of her chest. He stood before her, one hand wadded in the cloth of her shift at her chest while the other dragged it up over her legs. She looked wildly for someone to help her, but no one noticed her. In an area that had just been too crowded with Danes, not one of them paid any attention. It was probably a common occurrence, a slave being taken against a wall.

When she could finally draw in a breath, she shrieked and kicked out at him, but her foot contacted with hard muscle, and a shard of pain wrapped itself around her ankle. She barely noticed as she tried again. This time she was rewarded with his grunt of pain, but the unmovable pressure of his fist on her chest didn't let up at all. She screamed. He dropped the skirt, and her eyes stayed glued to that hand as it raised to strike her. She knew that if his meaty fist hit her, she wouldn't wake up until it was too late.

But then he was gone. The tug where his fingers had been wrapped in the front of her underdress happened first. The weight was there one second and then it was gone and he was falling. She almost thought he had passed out from too much drink, but she could feel the heavy presence of another there and knew that someone had intervened.

Eirik.

Merewyn might have fallen to the ground in relief if her body wasn't frozen in place against the wall. All she could do was watch as he pummelled the offender. A few men walked by, but none took much interest in what was happening. Merewyn couldn't look away. Her eyes were wide as Eirik pulled back his fist and struck blow after blow. If the other man struck even one, she hadn't seen it. He wasn't even moving.

'Lord Eirik.' It was all she could manage, but when the man didn't even get up and Eirik kicked him hard in the gut, she got worried. 'Eirik! Stop!'

That got his attention. He stopped and turned the intensity of his gaze on her. He was all tousled hair, bloody knuckles and blazing eyes. Violence incarnate. And she had his full attention. The old Merewyn might have trembled from fear, but the Merewyn she was afraid to become—the one he had created—trembled from something else.

Something darker than fear.

Chapter Fourteen

He approached her slowly, as if wary of the power held barely leashed within him. If she was honest, that power held her in thrall. Merewyn had never seen him lose control like that before. He was always so *in* control, so self-possessed. It was one of the reasons she had begun to feel so protected with him. It was such a part of who he was that to see him without it now was like looking at a completely different person. Eirik, but untamed and fierce.

His eyes were vivid blue in their intensity as they stared at her through the night. His golden hair wild about his face. Her heart pounded a wild beat in her chest as he came closer. Her hands pressed hard against the wall behind her hips. In the periphery of her vision, she was aware that the beaten man struggled to his feet and limped away, but then he was forgotten.

The air between them was charged with a tension

she didn't recognise, but it excited her. Her breasts tightened and somehow became fuller, while lower, that utterly feminine part of her began to throb and ache. Somewhere deep down, Merewyn knew it shouldn't excite her, that her body's reaction was wrong, but there was no room for right or wrong just then. There was only Eirik.

Inches remained between them when he stopped. His gaze locked hers in its trance and the ferocity gripped tight something equally as tumultuous within her and pulled it out into the open. He broke the stare when he looked down to her breast. The weight of his gaze settled there, scorching her bare skin with its touch. Merewyn realised then that her shift had been torn away, leaving one breast completely exposed. She had been too focused on Eirik and the fight to even notice the cold that prickled her flesh. Even now, she couldn't move.

The sound of his breathing filled the air, but then she caught the movement of his hand coming towards her breast and she held her breath. That was when she realised the sound had been her own erratic breathing. His was shallow and quiet, like a predator stalking prey. Her eyes widened as his hand moved towards her. She knew he was going to touch her and she wanted it, had to stop her back from arching to reach him.

Her eyes widened when his flesh touched hers. The back of his finger brushed across her taut nipple and, though the touch was slight, a shard of pleasure shot through her. And just like that, the fissure she thought was mending widened irreparably. The back of each finger brushed across her nipple, and she bemoaned the loss when he drew back. But he wasn't finished.

Eirik pinched the pink flesh lightly between his thumb and forefinger and rolled the tender nub before letting go with a tug. Merewyn was unprepared for the dart of pleasure that shot to her core and gasped aloud, drawing his attention to her face. He repeated the movement, watching her response, knowing that it gave her pleasure. Her face flamed, but she couldn't tell him to stop or even stop herself from arching into his touch.

Her eyelids fell closed, and she was suspended there against the wall as he played her. The throbbing between her thighs beating in time with his touch. Her breathing was erratic, filling the air between them. At that moment, she was his, would have done anything he commanded. When his arm came around her hips to lift her up against him, she was surprised, but didn't open her eyes and didn't struggle against him. She simply savoured the feel of her breast crushed against the warmth of his rough palm as he gently squeezed the plump flesh.

Her arms went of their own accord around his broad shoulders to hold him close when he buried his face in her neck. She jumped and cried out in surprise when his teeth scraped the tender flesh. He didn't bite hard enough to break the skin, but even if he had she didn't know if she would care. It sent a surge of excitement throughout her, so she held him tight, her entire body throbbing with her need to get closer to him.

'You are mine.' The words were spoken roughly against her ear so she felt every one against the tender shell.

Just hours ago, she would have fought against those words, would have hated them and everything they implied. But not now. Maybe it was that she wanted to belong to him, wanted those words to be true. But even more than that, she wanted to say those words back to him. She finally understood that she wanted him to be hers in a way she had never imagined, never planned on in all the days of wanting to get away from him.

'Do you hear?' Eirik pulled back just enough to

look into her eyes. He held her up high enough so that they were level with his own.

She met his eyes, but then let her gaze travel down to his mouth. That full bottom lip held her attention for far longer than it should have as she imagined his mouth on her again and wondered if his teeth had left a mark. 'Aye,' she whispered.

'Say it.'

'I'm yours.' With those words, her defences crumbled. The abuse by Blythe, the fight to get away, her surrender, the assault by the unknown Northman—it was all too much. It began as a lump in her throat, becoming first one tear and then another. Her body shook with the effort to keep the emotion inside, but it kept coming, and when both of his arms went around her to pull her close against his chest, she lost control. The tide of emotion rolled over her until she was gripping him tightly and sobbing into his neck. Somehow his familiar scent soothed her and made the tears come all the harder.

She was hardly aware when he gathered her into his arms and began walking back to the longhouse. He took her through the back door, away from the festivities, and disappeared through a doorway she hadn't seen earlier. He walked right to the bed. Merewyn sat up when he placed her upon it and realised *bed* might not be the right description. It was a wide bench covered with furs and opened only on one side. A wood encasement closed both ends, separating it from the line of connected benches, while the far side was against the wall. It must have been where he'd slept the previous night.

Before she could say anything, he pulled the torn apron dress from her legs and threw it behind him. Then he was climbing in with her, blocking her senses from the rest of the chamber. There was only him and no time to consider what he meant because he gathered her into his arms and she stopped thinking. Nothing mattered except his large body solid against hers and the warm feeling that spread throughout her body.

She was safe. Nothing could harm her with him holding her so close. The tears still came, but she fell asleep listening to the steady beat of his heart under her ear.

The next morning Merewyn awoke to the horrible realisation of what had transpired the night before. She had said the words she never thought to say to him. She had acknowledged, nay, she had agreed that she was his and wanted it to be true. But even worse than that, she had cried in front of him. Both were things she had never thought to do and she wondered if she had betrayed herself—again—by giving into those weaknesses.

It was so unlike her to cry at all. Even when Blythe had been particularly harsh with her, Merewyn had learned to hold the feelings inside. By not acknowledging them, it somehow made everything better, or at least seem better. How had she broken down so completely with him? It shamed her to remember how she had clung to him and taken strength from his embrace.

Then she remembered what had preceded the embrace. He'd touched her. A vision of his tanned fingers plucking her nipple taut made her groan and sit up. She looked down to see that the fabric of her shift was tucked neatly between her breasts, but her hand came up to cover the tear anyway. Her heart pounded fiercely under her palm.

Where was he? Merewyn started to get out of bed, but her gaze collided with his and she froze. He was sitting across the small chamber, staring at her as though he'd been there for a while waiting for her to wake up. His legs were braced wide with elbows on his knees while his hands were folded beneath his chin. He'd changed into a dark blue tunic, similar to the one he'd worn on her first night in this new world. The fabric was rich, but the decorative gemstone was absent. His clothes proclaimed him a prince of this world; his manner proclaimed him king.

Gone was his gentleness that had ended the evening. In its place was the ferocity she had seen earlier, but it was tempered with the return of his customary control. She couldn't help but notice the dark scabs that graced a few of his knuckles. Merewyn trembled on the inside, but her embarrassment at succumbing to tears before him gave her the courage to raise her chin, determined that he wouldn't see her weak again.

'I told you to stay above in the loft once night fell. You disobeyed me.'

Merewyn bit the inside of her lip to keep it from trembling. There was nothing she could say to that that wouldn't sound petty and childish. She had disobeyed him, but she'd never promised to obey. Never considered herself his. Until last night.

I'm yours. What had possessed her to say those words? Even in the light of a new day, there was an undeniable flawlessness to the simplicity of those words. They rang with truth. She had chosen him on the beach.

'I can't protect you if I don't know where you are,' he continued when she didn't offer a defence.

Her gaze shifted to the fur in her lap. Of course, he was right. The rustle of clothing indicated he had risen, but her body was aware of his movement in other ways. She knew that he came closer because every part of her came alive with a tingle. She despised it, but at the same time she revelled in it. There were two people inside her with no hope of coexistence.

He sat down on the bed, drawing her attention to his broad thigh resting so near her own. 'I've spoken to Kadlin.'

At the woman's name, Merewyn's gaze jerked back to his. Kadlin had accepted his suit. She had lost before she'd ever really tried to win. Her immediate thought was that he would give her away now. Her lips parted to beg him not to, but as soon as she realised that was what she would say, she shut them tight again.

'She's agreed to take you in.'

Those were not the words she expected. She'd expected that he would marry Kadlin and give her to another master, not to give her to *Kadlin*. 'Why?'

The word hung in the heavy silence between them as she searched his gaze, but he wasn't giving anything away. Did the way he had touched her the night before mean nothing? She'd forgotten about the bite, but now her hand went to her neck. There was nothing there. Of course there was nothing there. It hadn't really been a bite and he wouldn't really feel anything for her. It had been nothing to him.

'Because I can't keep you safe anymore.'

Had her actions done this? 'But that man— I don't understand. Even if you leave me here, someone like that could—'

'That's not what I meant.' His jaw tightened. 'From me. I can't keep you safe from me. You should stay here with Kadlin because if you leave with me, I won't be able to keep my vow to keep you safe.'

'I don't understand.' But deep down she knew.

His eyes flicked down to her breast and back again. 'Don't you?'

Before she even realised that he'd moved, he had one hand tangled in the hair at the nape of her neck and she was on her back with his body on top of her. There was no denying the hard press of him against her thigh. There was no denying the little flip her stomach gave. It wasn't from fear. It wasn't from fear at all.

All she could look at was his mouth and wonder where it might go next. But nay, he was still in control. The faint lines that framed his lips told her that. 'I want to be inside you more than I want my next breath.' His fingers tightened in her hair, pulling her head back so she met his gaze. It might have hurt had she not already lost her mind. 'You can't fight me off, and I can't promise not to take you.'

The words hit her low in the belly and crawled lower. He wasn't as in control as he seemed after all. She flushed as the full impact of that statement washed over her and made that strange throbbing begin between her legs. 'Are you offering me a choice?' *Freedom?*

'Aye, the choice is yours. If you stay with Kadlin, you'll be her personal slave. She's agreed to honour my vow that you not be harmed. No other man will have you.'

'But last night—' her voice lowered to a whisper '—you said that I'm yours.'

Possessiveness flared hot and fierce in his eyes. 'And you will be…if you agree to come with me. This is my last offer. Stay or we leave in an hour.' Eirik rose from the bed and strode from the chamber, leaving his words to linger behind him.

Chapter Fifteen

She was going to go with him. As she stood in the shadow of the doorway and watched him readying his horse for travel, Merewyn couldn't help but imagine what that would mean. What it would mean to truly be his. He was magnificent. His back was broad and strong. The muscles moved under his tunic as he swung a bag across the back of the horse and tied it to the saddle. Those muscles had been hard under her hands. Even his stomach had been hard when it had pressed tight against her own as he'd lain on top of her. The memory had the power to warm her from the inside.

His austere, chiselled profile made her envision anew the Viking god who had landed on her shore. Powerful, focused, so in control. But the man he had been last night had not been in control. She closed her eyes to see the sheer violence Eirik had unleashed on the man who'd attempted to assault her. Last night he had lost the control that he tried so hard to maintain.

For her.

But when he'd approached her afterwards, his touch had been so tender and caring that it had brought her to tears. No matter what he said, she knew that a man who could be such a tender lover would not hurt her. Not intentionally, at least.

The tense set of his shoulders as he worked let her know that he was still just as bothered by their morning talk as she was. He kept glancing to the house, but she stayed in the shadows so he wouldn't see her observing him. A part of her entertained the notion that maybe he was wondering about her choice. Perhaps he was anxious that she wouldn't choose to go with him. But the reasonable part of her couldn't give credit to the notion. Why would he care about a slave?

That thought had haunted her from the beginning and refused to be banished. But again, thoughts of the previous night soothed her. A man like him was too measured, too calculated, to allow himself to lose control because he thought of her as a mere possession. He did care. He cared enough to gentle his touch when he reached for her just moments after unleashing that violence. She blushed anew at the reminder of his tender touch on her bare breast. He cared enough to cradle her in his arms when she'd cried despite the undeniable evidence that his body wanted her. Merewyn didn't know how long he'd held her, but she'd fallen asleep with a sense of peace that had everything to do with him.

Some part of him cared for her. It was that knowledge that gave her the courage to accept his challenge. Even if it meant he would touch her again. Especially if it meant he would touch her again and awake those strangely wonderful feelings he invoked within her. Her gaze went to his fingers where they were tying the knot of another bag. They were strong, graceful and rough from years of work. And so gentle.

She bit her lip and clenched her fists against the longing that washed through her. This was freedom. This was a choice. He was her choice, and now that she realised it, she was anticipating what was to come at the same time her stomach churned with anxiety of the unknown.

She forced herself to relax and smoothed the skirt of her dress. It was the hideous slave dress, but it was all that she had. At least she looked presentable thanks to Kadlin. She had surprised Merewyn by coming to retrieve her from Eirik's bed and taking her to her own chamber to wash and dress in private. In her efforts to communicate and her gifts of new clothing, Kadlin had been nothing but kind. Merewyn might have been a dear friend instead of the slave that she really was. The encounter had left her hopeful that she had misunderstood Eirik's relationship with the woman.

'Merewyn.' The softly uttered word drew her attention to Kadlin, who had come up to stand beside her.

Merewyn blushed, uncomfortable to have been caught with her thoughts by the woman who might have a rightful claim to him. If anyone should be having those thoughts, shouldn't it be her, not his slave? He'd not even told the woman her name. She'd had to ask Merewyn in a series of gestures when she'd come to collect her from his bed.

When Kadlin had returned to her chamber, she'd had to use further gestures to ask Merewyn if she wanted to stay. Merewyn wondered if Eirik had explained to her why he wanted his slave to stay with her. If he had, Kadlin didn't let on. She had only smiled brightly when Merewyn had refused the offer.

Now Kadlin spoke a few words in the Norse language and pressed a bundle into her arms. Merewyn looked down to see a second pair of fur-lined leggings—she'd already donned the pair given to her when she'd washed—and a small burlap sack tied together with twine. At Kadlin's urging, she opened it to find small, crudely made cakes of a wonderfully fragrant soap.

'Thank you.' It was an unexpected gesture of friendship that Merewyn was unprepared for. The woman had every right to feel threatened by her, to want her removed from Eirik's life, but that didn't seem to be the case. Merewyn thought again that perhaps she'd misunderstood their relationship.

Kadlin spoke, but the only word Merewyn understood was Eirik's name. Then she smiled and nodded towards him. Merewyn turned to see him standing, openly watching the doorway now. Waiting.

She took a deep breath, then took a step in the direction of the fate she had chosen. This would be her last day as a chaste woman. The thought in itself was jarring, but not any more so than the delicious expectation it brought to life within her.

The moment she appeared, Eirik tightened his grip on the reins. He'd had no inkling as to whether she would stay or not, but even more, had not known whether he wanted her to stay. She should stay. For her own safety, she should stay as far away from him as she could get. And yet she continued to walk closer. His nostrils flared when her unique scent reached him. After sleeping so closely to her the night before, it was imprinted on his senses for ever. It carried the power to immediately make him hard from the memory of her body pressed to his, her body curving to meet the shape of his and her buttocks pressed against him. His body was eager to consummate the alliance she was agreeing to with her presence. He was glad his tunic was long enough to cover the evidence of how she affected him so easily. She heated his blood like no other, and he forced himself to recall the violence she had pulled from him the night before.

Eirik fought so hard for control, it angered him that she could so easily make him lose it. He so rarely unleashed that sort of violence on anyone, even in the heat of battle, but the threat against her had been too much. The simple notion that anyone would dare to touch her made him crazed. Something had to be done so he could get back that control. He either needed her out of his life or he needed to slake his need for her, break the spell that she held over him, before it destroyed him. Afterwards, he could go back to how he had been. As he watched her walk to him, he was strong enough to admit that he was glad she had chosen to come with him. Even if it meant his body would ache all day anticipating the evening ahead, even if it meant he would finally have to face down the demons that haunted him, because there was no doubt in his mind that he would have her before the day ended.

When she stopped before him, she looked down as if bashful and unable to meet his eyes, before finally gaining the courage to look up at him. He took a deep breath as he studied her. She was beautiful. He wondered how he had ever thought her anything less. The way her ivory skin curved gracefully over her cheekbones, tinted pink now either from the wind or her own thoughts of the previous night. Her fine nose, turned up slightly at the end that always seemed to hint at defiance. Her lush mouth with those pink lips he had yet to taste.

But he would. Soon.

The excitement coiled in his gut and he clenched his fists to beat it down. The need to have her under him, to be inside her, controlled him.

'Why are you here?' The question was a growl brought on by his own perverse need to hear the words from those lips he planned to claim.

It took a while for her to answer, so long in fact that he almost ordered her back inside. He was too far gone now to accept anything less than her total capitulation. But when she spoke, she surprised him. 'Because the alternative is unbearable.'

Eirik closed his eyes against all the possibilities that answer implied. That she wanted to explore the pleasure he was sure his touch had given her. That by coming with him she meant to align her fate with his in ways that went far beyond the mere protection he could give her. When he opened them again, she was watching him with an odd expression. A knowing that hadn't been there in the days before. An acceptance. It made his breath hitch.

Eirik couldn't say anything as he took her bundle from her and stuffed it into the sack already tied to the saddle. When his hands went to her hips to lift her up onto the horse, she surprised him by putting her hands on his to stop him. He raised a questioning brow at her, but didn't trust himself to speak without revealing the raw need coursing through him. It was too late for her to change her mind. If she refused to go now, he feared he'd throw her over his horse and take off with her anyway.

'Wait. I need to know…' She looked away again,

unable to meet his gaze as she continued. 'What of that woman? Kadlin. Is she your betrothed?'

His heart leaped in his chest. The question was further proof of her understanding of how things had changed between them. 'I have no betrothed. We are childhood friends.'

'Then you...I saw you with her... It looked... intimate.' She fumbled over her words before falling silent.

Eirik would have smiled at her reticence if he wasn't fighting his need for her so valiantly. 'The only woman in my bed last night was you.' His thumb caressed her cheek in a gesture that was developing into a dangerous habit for him. The need to touch her was becoming overpowering. He liked how his words made her skin pink and felt the need to drive home the point. 'I will never have Kadlin the way I intend to have you.'

Before she could respond, he sat her on the horse and mounted behind her. His arm pulled her to him and her body settled against him as if she belonged there. He had to fight to keep his hand from closing over the breast he had fondled the night before. He wanted to remind her that it was his. To tear the fabric away to reveal the pretty nipple he had discovered and make it pebble beneath his touch.

It belonged to him now. He wanted to discover the rest of her, claim the rest of her, just as he had that perfect mound of flesh. His arm tightened in a grip that was unmistakably proprietary. Before this day was out he would make her his.

Chapter Sixteen

'What is this place?' Merewyn asked.

Eirik walked before the horse, holding its lead while she rode. He'd set a slower pace today, often walking while she rode or letting her walk if she chose. There had been almost no conversation between them. After the night that had passed and the intimacy of his touch, she didn't know what to say to him that wouldn't sound insincere or forced.

The truth was that she had spent far too much time reimagining it. Every time she would look at him, her gaze would drift to his gracefully long fingers and she would feel them on her all over again. And then there were the times he *would* touch her. His hand would grip her hip and squeeze gently as he helped her dismount, or his arm would tighten and pull her indecently close to him, despite the awkwardness of the pommel. If the lingering touches were intentional or simply imagined by her hypersensitivity, Merewyn didn't know.

When they stopped at midday to eat cheese and bread and allow the horse to rest, the air hung thick between them. It was awkward, but not entirely unpleasant. Especially not when she caught him watching her. No one had ever looked at her like that before. A few of Alfred's men had looked at her with lust in their eyes. She knew that look. This one made the intensity of those pale in comparison. Eirik did more than look past the clothes she wore to see what was underneath. He seemed to look deeper, into her very soul, so that nothing was hidden from him. The more it happened, the more she wanted to open herself to him.

By the time they approached the sod house in the distance, she was distinctly unsettled and aware of him. Every nuance of his breathing and cadence of his step was noticed. He'd been tense for the past hour and becoming even more.

'This is my farm.' When he answered he didn't even bother to glance back at her. His body had become tighter, his steps less fluid.

Merewyn glanced again at the sod house that blended in so well with the landscape. It appeared to be a part of the hill that was behind it. She hadn't even seen it until they were almost upon it and the wooden door became clearly visible. She didn't see any animals or people around to indicate it was a working farm. There were fields in the distance, but they were dormant now that winter was settling in. She couldn't tell if there was a fire inside the house.

'I thought you lived with your father.'

'I do. This farm belonged to an uncle. My mother's brother. He died a few years back without issue, so it's mine now.' They had drawn even with the door, so he dropped the lead and walked to reach for her.

A flicker of anticipation came to life in her belly the second before he touched her. His strong hands tightened on her hips as he pulled her swiftly from the saddle to stand before him. But he didn't let go and instead held her there. She was entirely too close to him for sanity's sake and held her breath as she looked up to meet his deep blue gaze. The fire in them threatened to scorch her as it warmed the air between them.

'Are you hungry?' he asked.

Food was more than her churning stomach could handle at the moment. Merewyn shook her head, afraid that to give voice to a reply would reveal her feelings. Feelings she wasn't certain she was ready to verbalise. She just wanted him like he'd been last night. The anticipation was almost unbearable.

'Me either.' He surprised her by grinning. A sight rarely seen from him and made all the more wolf-ish for its scarcity. Eirik's hand on her hip urged her towards the house.

The door opened into what appeared to be the main room, where there was already a small fire blazing in the hearth and a bit of meat roasting on a spit. A row of low benches sat against the wall with a hallway just past them that led into the interior of the home. There appeared to be other rooms but they were all dark.

'Is someone else here?'

'A man and his sons worked the farm while I was away, but they live on the other side of the fields. Jarl Leif loaned me a messenger that I sent ahead to give notice of my arrival.' Eirik gestured to the low benches that lined one wall near the fire. 'Sit and rest. I'll see to the horse and return soon.'

Eirik barely glanced her way as he left. Merewyn drew her arms about herself, uncertain how to proceed. Eating was the last thing on her mind, so she walked to the benches and unrolled the pile of furs and blankets she assumed the caretaker had left there. She spread them out along two of the benches, but the task was completed all too quickly and she was left to her restless thoughts. Filled with nervous energy, she found wood piled in a corner and added a few sticks to the fire, prodding it until it was blazing and filling the small space with its warmth.

Task accomplished, she rubbed her hands together as she perched on the edge of a bench and closed her eyes to see him as he had been the night in the bath. His body bare to her gaze. Even then, even with her fears and uncertainties, his masculinity had attracted her. From the beginning she'd been aware of his strength, but that night she had seen it. His chest, arms and legs were all muscle. His stomach was roped in muscle. That night she had wanted to touch him, to feel that firmness beneath her fingers, to know how his skin would feel. Tonight she could know if she allowed him his way.

Could she do it? Could she actually give herself over to him? She wanted to, even knowing that it was a traitorous thought. He wasn't a Saxon. He was an enemy to her family, to herself. But he wasn't. Not really. He'd kept her from harm when she was sure no other Dane would have. He could have pressed his advantage last night when she spent the night in his bed. But he hadn't even touched her except to hold her against him. Did it make her weak to turn to him now? Nay, she reminded herself that she was making a choice. She took a deep breath and the tension slowly abated.

When she opened her eyes, he stood there, watching her from just inside the doorway. That she hadn't even felt the cold blast of air he was sure to have let in was a testament to her emotional upheaval. From across the distance, Merewyn could feel the power of his gaze. It was the slightly wild look of the previous night. The look that said he wanted her.

He walked towards her, and she swore she felt each step as a tingle up her spine. Even without his touch, fingers of pleasure spread from her belly down her thighs. He came to a stop just before her and raised his hand to brush a stray lock of hair from her face. The heat of his gaze warmed her lips, the flush spreading across her face and chest as his gaze moved to her own. The unspoken command in his eyes pulled her to her feet.

Eirik leaned down, making her remember the bath when he'd almost kissed her. This time she didn't turn away, but he stopped when his lips were a breath from her own. Whether it was to give her time to revolt or to give himself time to abstain, she didn't know. She only knew that suddenly the most important thing in her world was for his lips to finally claim hers. Every beat of her heart throbbed through her in anticipation of it.

'My lord—' The words died with the subtle brush of his lips across hers. The caress was light and surprisingly gentle, though it carried the power to ignite a frisson of pleasure in her belly. Her hands went to his arms to steady herself, and she marvelled again at the strength of him and how hard he felt beneath her touch.

As if her movement had given him permission, his hands captured her hips and pulled her flush against him. But then they moved downwards to fill themselves with the flesh of her bottom. He squeezed and pulled her forward so the firm length of his arousal was clearly outlined against her belly.

A thrill of excitement shot through her, and she couldn't contain her gasp of surprise. When her lips parted, he pressed the advantage and gently sucked her bottom lip into his mouth. The unexpected sensation of his tongue stroking her so intimately made the newly awakened muscles between her thighs clench in anticipation.

She was just warming to the seductive kiss when

his mouth abruptly left hers. While her lip was still wet from his tongue, she drew it into her mouth to taste him. Should it excite her so much to have the taste of him in her mouth? She wasn't sure anymore about should or shouldn't. He was her Northman. He *shouldn't* affect her in any way. But they had moved far past that.

A strong hand came up to twist in her braid and tilt her head back. Their eyes met briefly in a scorching look of control and surrender before his lips crushed hers in a more powerful kiss. This one was a bit more savage as his tongue forced entry to stroke her own. Merewyn was shocked by the strength of her own responsive arousal, and gripped his shoulders tightly to steady herself.

Eirik growled at her acquiescence and tightened his grip on her bottom. His hips moved against her, grinding his hardness into her soft belly. Its obvious size and potential for pain frightened her, but stronger than the fear was the desire it called forth within her. Excitement welled and created a delicious throbbing between her legs. She'd felt an inkling of desire for him that night in the baths and, especially, that night on the cottage floor. But not like now. Now her body swelled and softened in anticipation of opening for him.

He pulled back just far enough to look down at her, though with one hand twisted in her hair and the other on her buttocks, he kept her body imprisoned against his. The intensity in his eyes was almost her undoing. The way he looked at her as if he already knew her intimately. 'If you intend to deny me, tell me now.' His voice was hoarse and rough in a way she had never heard it before. Feral. It rasped across her sensitised body so she felt it deep in her core.

'I want this,' she whispered.

Triumph flashed in his eyes briefly before they softened and moved down to her lips in a caress she swore she felt. 'Have you ever had a man before?'

Merewyn flushed anew and attempted to look away, though his fingers tightened in her braid to hold her still. 'Nay.'

'I don't want to hurt you, but it's unavoidable. I'll be as gentle as I can.'

She wasn't completely ignorant of the sexual act. She knew to expect pain the first time, but Sempa had explained that there could be so much more than pain. Merewyn had always been sceptical of that, but now Eirik's touches promised that, as well. So it wasn't in ignorance that she moved her hands up his shoulders to tangle her fingers in the silky length of the golden hair at his neck. It wasn't in ignorance that she pulled herself tight against him to press against the hard, aroused length of him. She did that with the desire of a woman who wanted to know his touch.

'I know, but I trust you.'

Chapter Seventeen

She shouldn't trust him. His hands had begun to tremble with the effort of holding himself back from her. If she had any idea of the man he really was, the man who wanted to push her down on to the bench, spread her legs and ravish her until his lust was sated, she wouldn't trust him at all.

Eirik released her completely from his grip to deny himself the temptation. It would be so easy to overpower her, but he refused to give in to that desire and become what he most feared. He wouldn't hurt her any more than was necessary. If she'd already had a man, it might have been possible to have her experience no pain at all, but that thought brought with it a possessiveness he still wasn't used to feeling in regards to her. Just the thought of her with another man was enough to enrage him.

He could go slowly for her and give her some

pleasure. She'd responded so unexpectedly to his touch the night before that he wanted to see her do it again. 'I want to touch you again.' He slowly brought his hand up so that his thumb stroked the tip of her breast through her clothing. 'Here. Will you undress?'

The blush already staining her cheeks darkened. 'But it's not dark.'

'I want to see you. With the light.'

He expected her to shy away again and decline, but she surprised him when the corner of her mouth tipped up and she challenged him, 'Will you undress?' He didn't miss the way her appraising gaze dipped to his chest.

He hadn't expected to like the fact that she was interested in his body, but her request pleased him. He took a step back, and with slow, deliberate movements, unfastened his belt and pulled the tunic off over his head. The undershirt followed, and when her eyes widened in obvious appreciation, he couldn't deny the swell of pride he felt at her assessment. Her breathing quickened and he realised that she drew just as much pleasure from looking at him as he did from the sight of her own body. Eirik knew that he was attractive to women. It wasn't unusual for women to watch while the men sparred, often shirtless. But he particularly liked that *she* enjoyed the look of him. He liked that he pleased her.

'Now you,' he prompted.

'What about the rest?'

He laughed then, a hoarse rumble of sound he barely recognised, when her wide-eyed gaze dropped to the length of him surging within the confines of his trousers. She was curious, and the knowledge hardened him even more, if that was possible. 'Not yet.'

Her lips parted in what he was sure would be an argument, so he closed the distance between them and stopped her protest with a quick brush of his lips against hers. 'Later. I want to see you.'

She nodded and gave him a shy smile as she turned her back to fumble with the brooches. He almost smiled at the unnecessary modesty. After all, she was disrobing so that he could see her. But he allowed her the indulgence and fisted his hands at his sides to keep from helping, though the urge to take over was nearly overpowering.

When the apron dress fell to the floor, his breathing became shallow, but it stopped altogether for a moment when she pulled her underdress off over her head and held it to her chest. She stepped out of the puddle of the dress at her feet and looked over her shoulder at him, clearly uncertain of herself. But there was no reason for her reticence. She was beautiful. The creamy skin and delicate curvature of her back was more alluring than he'd anticipated. It wasn't supposed to be so attractive.

But hers was. She shivered when his fingertips travelled the length of the indentation of her spine to its end at the waist of her leggings. The elegant curve of her lower back fascinated him, so he spent extra time there, letting his fingertips stroke over her. Her skin was like satin. Both of his hands flattened against her and moved in massaging strokes up and down the length of her back.

'You enjoy my touch,' he mused when she closed her eyes and her head fell forward. She muttered an affirmation, so he kept stroking until the need to see more of her took over and he pulled her into his arms. Her back fit nicely against his chest.

She didn't fight or tense when his hands came around her waist and slipped under the cover of the wadded-up linen to cup her breasts. When he squeezed gently and tugged the hardened peaks between his thumbs and forefingers, her head fell back to his shoulder. He couldn't see her nipples, but her parted lips were pink and inviting, so he took them instead and dipped his tongue inside to sample her sweetness.

One of her hands moved to his nape to hold him close for the kiss. Eirik took advantage and tugged the underdress away from her. The moment it pulled away, he broke the kiss to look down at her. He was struck anew by her beauty. The creamy mounds of her breasts filled his palms nicely, and the taut peaks seemed to strain towards his fingers, begging to be plucked again. He obliged them and watched as her eyes closed in bliss from his ministrations and her breasts seemed to grow fuller in his palms. She arched against him, pressing her luscious bottom against him. By the gods, he wanted her. He didn't know if he could hold out as long as he'd intended.

Never in all of her life had Merewyn known that this feeling was possible. She'd never expected to feel like this: drunk on his touch, her body heavy and languid with the pleasure of it. The entire universe had centred to the surges of energy that rippled through her when he tugged her nipples. Except it widened slightly when he moved and his hot mouth touched her neck. He was tasting her, savouring her if the sounds coming from his throat were any indication, and then he bit the tender lobe of her ear, making her shudder with a pleasure she felt deep within her molten core.

'More, I need more of you,' he whispered.

She had no intention of denying him more of anything that felt so good. Her fingers threaded in his hair and her eyes closed in anticipation as his hand moved down her stomach to disappear inside her leggings. His fingers parted her and slid down to find her centre—she jolted in surprise when one dipped inside. But then she forgot to be self-conscious, forgot everything but the way he made her ache as his finger moved in soft circles as he explored her. She bit her lip to stifle a groan when his thick finger pushed inside her as far as it could go.

'I want to hear the sounds you make. Don't quell them.'

His finger retreated just to push farther inside and she did as he asked, letting a soft cry pass her lips. When he coupled the repeated movement with a tug on her nipple, she cried out louder, her voice filling the house.

'These have to go.' His voice was harsh against her ear as he withdrew abruptly, leaving her mourning the absence of his touch. His hands had gone to the waist of her leggings and he was pushing them down her hips and then her thighs, before she could collect herself. 'Lie on the bed,' he ordered after he'd helped her step out of them.

She paused as the enormity of what was happening washed over her. It was one thing to think about it, to imagine it, to want it, but quite another to expose herself to him with nothing between them.

'You're perfect in every way.' His fingertips brushed her cheekbone, an action she was coming to love, and he leaned close to kiss her lips and murmur against them, 'It pleases me to look at you. Let me look at you.'

She kissed him, reminding herself that he wanted to please her, too. Breaking the kiss, she turned and sat on the bed, her heart pounding in her chest as she pushed herself to lie down as he'd asked. When she gathered the courage to look at him, he was studying her with the heavy-lidded gaze of a man in the deep stages of arousal, as though he wanted to devour her. She had no idea how she knew that, except that instinct had taken over and her body answered that look with an intense response that left her shifting restlessly for fulfilment.

She took a deep breath of anticipation when he moved to join her on the bed. He settled so close to her that she could feel the heat of his body and moved towards it. His gaze was still almost reverently exploring her, but she wanted his touch again and reached for his hand to bring it back to her. It was all the prompting he needed to begin exploring her again. This time his mouth followed his fingers. Her breasts, her ribs, her stomach all received the same lingering attention. But when he began to move farther down, she tensed and would have sat up had he not put a hand on her shoulder.

'I want to see you here.' His free hand had moved down to rest between her hips, resting just over the mound between her thighs.

Automatically, she shook her head. 'No one ever has.'

He smiled, a knowing smile tinged with amusement, but somehow filled with tenderness. 'And no one else ever will. Open for me.'

She didn't resist when he moved partially over her and urged her knees apart with his thigh. But when he pushed them farther apart to make room to kneel between them, she closed her eyes; in part because she couldn't believe he would look upon her in that way, in part because she couldn't believe how much it pleased her that he wanted to.

It wasn't a surprise when he touched her there but she jumped anyway, before giving into the languid pleasure of his caress.

When he suddenly pulled away from her, she felt bereft, greedy for more of him. But his hands had gone to his trousers, and he pushed them down his hips and then kicked them away as he climbed back over her. His arousal stood thick and firm against his belly, but she only got a glimpse before he was resting over her and nudging at her entrance.

'I don't want to hurt you.' The tension in his arms as he held his weight off her made him tremble slightly.

'I know.' She wrapped her hands around his shoulders to pull him close. 'I know, but I want this. I want you, Eirik.'

He groaned in surrender and dropped his forehead to rest against hers as he pushed into her. She had anticipated the incredible fullness and the tight, burning pain, but the reality was so much more than she could have imagined. There was just too much of him. She bucked to shift him away, but he kept coming, the press of him hard and insistent.

'You're so tight,' he groaned. 'I never thought—

Nay, don't move.' His hand went to her hip to hold her still. 'It feels too good.'

How could it feel so good to him while she simply felt...*impaled* for lack of a better word? Her nails bit into his shoulders and she cried out as he pressed forward the last few inches, until he was finally seated completely within her. The touches, the kisses, the throbbing were lies. She felt betrayed by the lot of them. They had led her to allow this, then fled the moment she had. How had she wanted this? Even her thighs ached where they were awkwardly stretched around his own.

'My lord?'

'Hmm...' He wasn't listening. He was kissing her neck, the abrasive rasp of his beard prickling the tender skin and giving her goose bumps. Then he pulled back his hips and pressed forward again in a shallow thrust that brought with it a strange pleasurable sensation.

She must have made some sound, a gasp of some kind, because he did it again. His breath came harsh against her ear, exciting her. Coupled with the gentle movement of his hips, that part of her began to throb again, and she could feel herself softening around his invasion. She couldn't help but move. When he withdrew again, she inadvertently arched into him, seeking more of that tender pleasure. He growled, a purely masculine sound of conquest, and drove his full length into her. It was more than she'd expected, and while the movement brought back some of the initial discomfort, it brought with it so much more.

He barely gave her time to question the amazing sensation before it was there again. His manhood dragging across some hidden place within her as his hips pumped relentlessly against her. Unrecognisable sounds of pleasure were coming from her throat as she arched, unable to do anything other than accept him as he drove them higher towards something she couldn't identify. She simply held on as he took them there, her body quickening in time to his rhythm, and then he cried out harshly near her ear and she was filled with a liquid warmth before he lay replete above her.

She held him tight against her, unwilling to relinquish him after the amazing wonder their bodies had created together. Aye, the pain had been there as Sempa had promised, but a magic had been created. Something she had never thought was possible and was already imagining exploring again. How much better could it be without the pain of her maidenhead to mar the pleasure?

* * *

Eirik closed his eyes and buried his face into that soft place between her neck and shoulder, breathing in her scent. She smelled incredible, delicate like flowers, but with the undertone of a woman's salt that made him half-rigid with wanting her again. Her cry of pain still echoed in his head, reminding him of just how harshly he had used her. It had happened exactly as he'd feared. He'd lost control and taken her too roughly. He recoiled from the darkness within him that had demanded he take her and was urging him to do it again.

He wanted to stroke the smooth creaminess of her skin. To kiss her the way he knew brought her pleasure and thank her for the gift of her body. It had happened too fast. Her small body lay trembling beneath him, reminding him of how he had become the monster he'd feared lurked within him and abused her delicate beauty.

He was unfit for her presence, much less the pleasure of her body. Eirik pushed away, and without looking at her, drew a blanket up to cover her. When he noticed his hands shook, he let it go and clenched them into fists to stop their trembling. He should have left her with Kadlin, despite her protest. He'd known there was no way to stifle his desire, yet he'd taken her anyway. He'd avoided women all these years because he'd instinctively known how it would end. Or maybe it was only she that made him lose control. He should have slaked his lust on a whore used to servicing men like him, men who were wild and uncontrolled in their desires.

Determined to save her from his presence if he could do nothing else, he rose and put his trousers on. She sat up as if to speak, but he couldn't bear to hear her recriminations. On his way out the door he retrieved the rest of his clothes and, furious at himself, made his way to the river that ran some distance away across the field. Once there, he discarded his trousers and paused when he caught sight of her virgin's blood where it smeared on him. It brought back images of another day. A day he had long thought buried.

Eirik realised then that he was just like *them*. Drawing pleasure from the pain he had caused. He'd known the size of him within her had been painful, but he'd spilled his seed anyway. For that brief instance he had given in to his own pleasure without concern for her. He closed his eyes against the sight and dived into the icy depths of the water. The shock of it was almost painful, but he welcomed it as no less than what was due to him.

* * *

Later that night, after he'd taken the horse across the field to Harold's stable, he bedded down on a lonely, furless bench as far away from her as he could get in the house. It was cold. He deserved cold. Let her have the warmth of the fire and the furs. His still-wet hair had turned icy, but it didn't matter. He'd known cold before. Besides, the pain of cold kept other thoughts away.

But somehow sleep claimed him. In between thoughts of her and his conscious attempt to not shiver, the dreams got him. It started with that familiar liquid weight holding him down, only this time the force manifested into a hand so large that it covered the entire bottom half of his face, cutting off his air and making black spots dance before him. Eirik fought until he was able to bite, and the warm coppery taste of blood filled his mouth. After that there was only pain, exploding in his head and almost crippling him. But he fought them anyway. He would always fight them.

Until they took away his fight because his hands wouldn't work and his legs wouldn't obey his commands. It was the part of the dream he despised. Usually the part where he started screaming, but he was too cold to sleep too deeply and was able to shake himself out of it. Eirik came to with a start that landed him on the wooden floor. The trembling was back, so he just laid there until it eased off and thought of Merewyn, of how good it felt to hold her. Her scent had stayed with him despite his dip in the river, so he let it soothe him now.

Chapter Eighteen

An awful silence filled the room after he left. Awful because it was bereft of the tender ministrations she had been expecting. He had left her. Merewyn lay back down and tried to recall what exactly she had imagined would happen after such a mating. She'd always expected it to happen with her husband in her marriage bed. Not with her captor. Perhaps he would hold her or kiss her brow and tell her how important she was to him. Perhaps he would tell her that she was treasured.

The Northman had simply left. Was it because she was a slave or because she'd displeased him? He hadn't even looked at her.

The sudden chill in the room prompted her to rise and pull on her underdress. The apron dress she left alone, unwilling to bear its itchy discomfort, and moved back to the bench to huddle under the blanket, preferring to be cold rather than wear the coarse woollen garment to sleep. She intended to wait up for him, hoping that he'd gone for more wood or something else to explain his absence. But when it became clear she would spend the night alone, she removed the meat from the fire and laid down on the bench.

Eirik was a Dane. Theirs wasn't a love match or even a marriage. It had been a simple mating. Nothing more than his desire to slake his body's need. Perhaps she should content herself with the fact that it hadn't been entirely unpleasant. When she thought of how he'd felt moving above her, within her, her breasts began to respond. How did the memory of his touch ignite her even now that she knew there was no pleasure ultimately to be had from it? How had she let it convince her that mating with her Dane captor was a good idea?

She rolled onto her side and pleaded for sleep to come, too confused to figure out how she should feel.

The next morning she awoke to an empty house. There had been no stable or outbuilding, so if he'd brought the horse inside during the night, she hadn't been aware of it. If he'd come back at all during the night, she didn't know. A hollow of disappointment formed in her belly, but she refused to let it bother her. There were too many other ailments bothering her.

Her breasts were aching—more specifically her nipples felt as if they had been well attended to. When she sat up and swung her feet down to the floor, she noticed a distinct soreness between her thighs and became aware of an ache present in the muscles in that general area of her anatomy. Out of curiosity, she stood and raised the skirt of her dress to find faint markings left where his fingers had grasped her hips. She should feel shame and outrage, but the truth was that her blush was from the remembered pleasure. Her thoughts treacherously lingered on that languid heaviness his touch had built within her. The delicious tingle that had somehow touched her entire body and made it come alive.

Why did the Dane have to be the one to make her feel those things? Why couldn't any one of the men back home have caused half the chaos within her that he did? He'd hurt her, but here she sat thinking favourably of the encounter. Even believing that it was her own untried body instead of his hard shaft that had caused the majority of the pain.

'Stop thinking of it!' she whispered, afraid to

let her voice carry far, but needing to hear the admonishment aloud. 'Forget it happened like he has forgotten!'

Despite the warning, she could do nothing but remember. She was bewitched. That was the only reason she could accept. He was a sorcerer who had cast a spell she was too weak to resist.

Her suspicion was confirmed when he appeared in the doorway only moments later. His mere presence stole her breath and made her heart race. Every fibre of her body was awakened by him, a state that seemed to be a permanent affliction in his presence, but she refused to give in to the desire to look away from his piercing stare. He studied her with that same intensity she always found so exciting. When her nipples began to respond, she crossed her arms over them.

Eirik swallowed and looked away as he walked towards the fire. Only then did she notice that he was carrying a pitcher of water in one hand and a small stack of wood under the arm of the other. He set them both down and shrugged out of the sack of moss he'd slung over his shoulder. The fire there was still smouldering, and she realised that he must have come in at some point to add more wood.

Merewyn didn't know what to say to him. What

did one say to the man she had known so intimately, but in many ways didn't know at all? So she watched him work as he added the moss to the fire so it flared higher and then added wood. When he was finished he notched an iron rod with two pots and positioned them over the fire before splitting the water between them. From a sack he retrieved from a shelf, he put two handfuls of grain in one and finally looked at her again.

'Breakfast. The other you can use to wash yourself.'

Her face flamed as she realised he must know her need for washing. Though she had barely looked, she remembered seeing the streaks of red on her thighs the night before. Even as she stood before him at this very moment, his seed leaked down the insides of her thighs. Did he carry any reminders of their time together? Something about the way he stood there, tall and intense, made her think he didn't. It had been nothing to him. The hollow in her belly grew larger so that it threatened to swallow her whole, but she refused to give in to it. If he didn't want her, then her choice had been the wrong one and she had to but persevere and get through her life here until she could get home. Nothing mattered until then.

'Are you injured?'

She swung her head to look at him. He was watching the fire, but his jaw tightened. She despised the flare of hope the question ignited within her and reminded herself that he had left her. The act had been a common mating to him, nothing more. He'd probably had a hundred women that way. What did she matter?

When she didn't answer right away, he walked over and came to a stop just before her. He lifted his hand as if to touch her, but then dropped it again. 'Did I hurt you, Merewyn?'

He'd said her name! She hadn't even been sure he'd known it since she'd refused to tell him on the boat. The genuine concern reflected in his eyes was unmistakable. But if it meant something more, she couldn't tell.

'I'm fine, my lord.' It was best to keep formality between them. If there was nothing between them, then it behoved her to not foster illusions. 'Thank you. If you have things to do this morning, I can see to breakfast.'

His raised brow was the only indication that she had surprised him. If he was expecting her to dissolve into a puddle of tears and screaming hysterics, he would be disappointed. Thanks to

Blythe, she'd been trained well in the art of pretending. She could pretend that she had felt nothing and that last night had never happened. She could pretend that she hadn't wanted him to stay and sleep with her. She could pretend that she didn't want tenderness from him, because it was the only way to insulate herself from the inexplicable pain his rejection had caused. She could be the slave. She could be mindless and not expect anything from him beyond protection, food and shelter. That way, everything would make sense and she could stop being so confused by him. He was a Dane, an enemy.

Eirik paused a moment as if he would speak, but then thought better of it. With a final nod, he left and she was alone. When the door closed, her eyes unexpectedly filled with tears and her lip began to tremble. Merewyn refused to give in to the weakness to cry and moved towards the fire. She was fine. She would recover from her momentary lapse in judgement and be the same person she was before. Nothing had changed.

But everything had changed for Eirik. He had succumbed to his physical urges and become the man he had sworn to never be. The man who couldn't control his urges; the man who took advantage of those weaker than himself. That was bad enough. But even worse than either of those was the fact that he couldn't stop thinking of her. She filled his senses so that her soft, sweet scent was the only thing he smelled and he still tasted her on his lips. When he closed his eyes, he imagined that she was sprawled gloriously naked beneath him. In those imaginings, she was asking for his touch, her body warm and responsive in his hands.

By the gods, he wanted her again. Even with his need for her so recently slaked, he could think of nothing but laying her beneath him and pushing into her hot, tight sheath. It was as if he lost control of his very thoughts when she was around. He cursed to himself and raised the turf knife above his head to drop it so it embedded in the ground at his feet. He repeated the motion again and again until he had a large square outlined. Then he angled the flat blade to cut the roots of the grass. His earlier inspection had revealed a corner of the roof that was failing. The house would be mostly unattended over winter, so he hoped to get it fixed before the failure caused a bigger issue.

If he'd returned home sooner, he might have had the time to ready it with supplies and more repairs for the coming winter. But he hadn't intended to stay there. It was only after the night with the girl that he imagined endless days and nights alone with her.

Eirik shook the thought from his head and called for Harold, the caretaker, to pick up the square of turf and add it to the others in the wagon. He dug into the next one with a ferocity he hoped would banish the girl from his head.

He managed to avoid her for the rest of the day and was relieved when Harold and one of his sons agreed to stay and sup in repayment for their help that afternoon. The conversation turned to what was happening across the sea and Eirik welcomed Harold's interest, anything to keep from thinking of her. The man had been partially lamed by a fall in his younger years and now walked with a pronounced limp that had cut his seafaring years short. Harold now lived his fantasies of adventure through the stories of others.

But later, when the ale had run its course, the older man's speech had turned slurred and the boy lay snoring by the fire, Eirik looked to her where she reclined on the bench. As if she felt his attention, she cast him a quick glance and blushed. She'd done that all day and then her gaze would move downwards over his body as if she were remembering the way he looked without his clothes. She did that again now, those beautiful eyes touching his chest and shoulders, before turning her attention back to the clothing on her lap that she was mending. He watched those long, graceful fingers as they tugged at a stubborn length of thread and then smoothed over the stitches.

In his mind, he heard the soft mews of pleasure that had spilled from her lips when he'd touched her. He might have hurt her last night, but she'd found enjoyment in his touch before he'd taken her. The longer he sat there, the more he wanted to relive that pleasure again. As he watched her hands, he took a long, deep breath as he imagined those fingertips gliding along his cheek, the line of his shoulder. It came as a surprise that he enjoyed her touch, as well.

If Harold and his son were gone, Eirik knew he would go to her again, whether it was the right thing to do or not. He couldn't control himself with her. But it looked as though they were staying the night, so Eirik pulled a fur over and covered himself. There was no reason to alarm her with his body's ready reaction to her.

There would be time. It seemed one taste of her was not nearly enough.

Chapter Nineteen

Eirik slanted a glance at the girl where she sat perched on a rock overlooking the stream. He wrapped the rope around his forearm as he pulled the net free of the water. It was no surprise to find it empty. His poor concentration was making his throw off, so the net had closed in on itself. A despicable mistake he was grateful no one else was there to see. His concentration was on her rather than fishing. She consumed him.

He took a deep breath and returned his gaze to the water, where it should be if they were to eat that night. It took three more drags of the net to snag a handful of minnows to use for bait. Even then, he almost lost them when he looked to her again. The cloak she wore was spread out on the rock around her while she sat with her knees to her chest. It was her face that arrested him. The simple beauty of her features had caught his attention before, but now it struck him anew.

'You're not a very good fisherman, are you?' Her face was serious, but there was a teasing note in her voice that he didn't think he was imagining.

His lips twitched in a smile. 'Not with a pretty distraction so near to me.'

The blush returned to stain her cheeks. He'd found himself catching her gaze all day just to watch it bloom across her skin. It was proof of her innocence and proof that he shouldn't touch her again. But more than that, it made him know that he affected her. That knowledge attracted him like a moth to flame. He wanted to drink in her innocence, to let it seep through his body until it became a part of him—until she became a part of him. Why this need for her had begun, he didn't know. When it had become something far more than physical, he couldn't even begin to guess. He craved the very essence of her, and monster or not, he needed it.

As day was turning to night, he wanted to know if he could give her pleasure without pain. And if it was possible to redeem himself.

Her face finally cracked a smile, a very small one, but it made his heart beat faster.

'Perhaps you should stay with raiding.'

'Aye, look what it got me.' He tipped his head to indicate her. 'I do seem better at it.'

She smiled, though she bit her lip and turned her face away to hide it.

Eirik looked back to the icy waters and resolved to ignore her until he'd caught their supper. Taking her to his bed with any regularity was never a decision he'd thought to make, but now it seemed the only option. It seemed only natural that she belong to him in every way. Excitement gripped him and he had to force himself to keep his calm composure. He was resolved to go slowly with her. There was no need to repeat the pain of the first time. Her body was made for his; she would accept him. He could give her pleasure.

He thought perhaps she sensed the change in him when he approached her, fish in hand, to go back to the sod house. He had tied the fish to string and carried them at his side, but instead of continuing on in front of her, he walked with her. She gave him a puzzled glance, but didn't speak as she gathered up the bundle of wood she'd collected. However, he sensed a nervousness about her that hadn't been there before.

After they'd eaten the fish he'd prepared on the fire, he disappeared to the back of the house to dig into the stone cellar to retrieve a cask of wine. The need to please her was new to him, but it seemed only fair given the pleasure he would ask of her body. Though there would be no pain for her this time, he hoped, he felt he owed her something.

'Wine.' He opened it and brought it to his nose.

'I didn't know Vikings drank wine.' She smiled. It was good to see her smile.

'Vikings enjoy many things from all over the world.' He smiled back and knew he had surprised her. She wasn't used to this smiling man in front of her. He wasn't used to him either. She made him do many things he wasn't accustomed to doing. 'It's Lotharingian. Brought it back a few years ago. I'm not sure if it's still good though.' He poured some into a cup and took a drink. 'Ah, still good.' Then he passed it to her.

She took a tentative sip and then a larger one. 'It's better than the wine I've tried at home,' she proclaimed.

Eirik's smile lingered as she handed the cup back to him and he took another swallow. The rich liquid washed over his tongue and left a faintly sweet aftertaste. It felt good to please her. He thought again of spending more time with her at the farm and decided that when he returned from the spring raid he would bring her here. It would be years yet before he assumed his place as jarl. He could have her to himself here until that time came.

Though Merewyn resisted her place with him now, she would come to accept it and even enjoy it. He was as endowed with riches as her brother, if not more so. He could bring girls to help her care for the house and keep her in furs and finery. Here, away from the longhouse, she could even wear dresses that were more comfortable, not the undyed wool reserved for slaves. It could be a good life. It *would* be, and she'd see that leaving the Saxons had been a good thing. He would provide for her better than a Saxon could. *He* would never beat her.

'Tell me of your home.' Eirik surprised himself by voicing the command aloud. Now that he had imagined her life with a Saxon man, he found himself wondering if she'd actually been partial to one.

Her brow furrowed as she watched him. 'What do you mean? You already know of my home.'

The smile vanished as he looked down and swirled the wine around the bottle. It wouldn't do to let her know that he was jealous of a man who would never have her now. Eirik didn't even know if the man actually existed or not. 'I know what I saw,' he agreed. 'But tell me what I didn't see. Who was important to you there?'

She hesitated, but after a moment she began to speak about her family. The younger nieces and nephews she had spent her life attending to. It wasn't what he wanted to know, but he found himself listening anyway. Some part of him was eager to know any morsel she was willing to divulge about herself. He told himself it was because it would make her feel more comfortable with him, but on some level he knew that was only the partial reason. The need was his own.

'And your parents?' he prodded.

'My parents died when I was young,' she began. 'My father I don't even remember, but my mother died during my sixth year. I'm not even sure what happened to her. She fell sick that winter and one day didn't wake up. But I have nice memories of her. She used to take me swimming in the summer. Though Alfred never approved, we did it anyway.' She smiled and her voice trailed off as she became lost in the memory. 'And then there's Sempa, my nursemaid as a child. After my mother's death, she took her place—at least with getting me in trouble with my brother. Not that I needed much help with that.'

He smiled at her obvious fondness for the woman. 'Was she there in the cellar that day?' The question was out before he could think better of it. It probably wasn't the best idea to remind her of the circumstances of their meeting. Not if he wanted her willing again. But he couldn't take it back so he sat waiting for her answer.

Merewyn shook her head. 'She goes out every morning to gather herbs. I'm sure she hid until everything was over.'

An uneasy quiet settled over them. They were in unchartered territory. Intimate, yet not. Lovers, yet she was still the captive and he her master. To be fair, he liked that she was his and had no interest in changing the arrangement. But he also realised that he wanted her to give herself to him, to submit to being his. It could happen. He was sure of it now, after the way she had responded to him. She could accept his touch.

Finally, she spoke through the silence. 'What of your mother, my lord?'

Eirik ran his fingertips across his bearded chin. His mother had been so overpowered by his father that it seemed as though she had been gone years before her actual death. He tried not to think of her, but wanted Merewyn to feel comfortable in opening up to him, so he answered. 'Vidar's birth was a difficult one. He was strong, but she never seemed to recover her strength.'

'And do you have sisters or is your father only capable of siring boys?'

He smiled at her humour. 'I have two. Two from my mother anyway. They were born between myself and Vidar, but they've both been married off. My father betrothed them young and, just after my mother died, sent them to their new families.' He allowed the silence to stretch between them just long enough that the next question seemed natural. 'Were you betrothed?' It was his reason for starting this conversation, but he despised that the answer meant so much to him. His breath lodged in his chest as he waited.

'Nay, not betrothed,' she answered easily, completely unaware of his interest, as she stretched. Their shared wine was making her lethargic. 'Alfred had planned to see me wed in the coming summer, but I wasn't promised to anyone.'

His relief was palpable. He wanted her exclusively to himself without the shadow of another in her heart. Startled by the depth of his feeling on the matter, he took another long drink of the wine. It was dangerous to want her the way he did, but he didn't care. He was past that point. Already he was half aroused, thinking of having her again, and his acknowledgement of the thought pushed him over the edge.

Merewyn barely managed to hold her smile in check when he asked about her betrothal. She'd toyed with the notion of lying to him just to see his reaction, but she hadn't because he seemed so eager to know. His behaviour towards her over the past two days had convinced her that she had been wrong to judge him so harshly. He had left her after having his way with her, but there was a tenderness now that he couldn't hide as well as he had before.

He went out of his way to spend time with her, to tease her and make her smile. Sitting there with him in the easy silence that had fallen, she could almost imagine that they lived there as husband and wife. Obvious newlyweds who barely knew each other, but wanted to know more. The rational part of her realised those were dangerous thoughts, because the truth was that she was as far from a wife as one could get. But the part that wasn't entirely rational, the part that had convinced her that choosing him was a sort of freedom, recognised that he liked her and that…maybe they could have a good life together.

His eyes had that intense and hungry look she'd come to recognise. It wasn't an unpleasant thing at all to be on the receiving end of that look. Even knowing the pain of the first time and the pain of his rejection in leaving her, her body warmed in response, and it made her wonder if it could be different this time.

He didn't watch her as she went to the far corner to remove the apron dress and leggings, but his attention jerked to her when she approached him wearing just her underdress. The heat of his gaze made her stop and press her thighs together to combat the power of her desire for him. Her lips parted, but then she realised she didn't know how to tell him that she wanted him again.

But it seemed she didn't need to say anything at all. Setting the wine aside, he rose and stepped up to her, making the air heavy and hard to breathe.

'I foolishly thought that once would be enough.' His mouth quirked in an attractive smile. 'But I want you again.'

She nodded and watched his eyes become heavy. Her heart pounded furiously against her chest when his hands moved to her waist. She took shallow breaths, afraid to move for fear that he wouldn't continue. He didn't move either. Even without his touch, her body was ripening to the pull of his. Her nipples were taut peaks beneath the linen of her underdress and he hadn't even touched her.

Finally one hand curved itself around her hip while the other came to hover just above the neckline of her dress. His thumb ran lightly along the string of the tie there.

'I know that I hurt you before, but I believe that's because you were untried. I think it's possible to have you without pain.' He'd watched his thumb caress the string as he spoke, but then turned the full force of his sapphire gaze on her.

'You don't know, my lord? Have you never had a virgin?' she whispered.

Eirik shook his head once. 'Never.'

For some reason, knowing that he was as lost as she was settled her. They were equal, in this at least. 'I'm told that if...' She blushed and looked away. Just because they were both ignorant didn't change her embarrassment in discussing it. 'I'm told that, if properly prepared, there should be little pain. Perhaps none if I'm lucky.'

'Who told you that?'

'My nursemaid.'

Eirik was silent for a moment, but then seemed to come to a determination. His eyes flicked to her mouth, and when it came back to her eyes a promise lurked in their depths. 'You don't have to rely on luck, Merewyn. I want you to crave my touch, and I'll do whatever it takes to make sure that you do.'

Chapter Twenty

Merewyn didn't speak as she watched him unlace the strings holding her bodice together and force it down to reveal her breasts. He looked at them with a reverence that made her breath hitch, until he leaned forward and took the pink tip of one into the scorching heat of his mouth. Then she let her breath out in a harsh rush of air that ended on a moan when he sucked gently. He drew away with a tug that made a wet popping sound when he let go, leaving the pink flesh glistening. Slowly, he moved to the other to lavish it with the same attention. And she felt vividly exactly what it had been like before the pain of his entry and knew why she would capitulate to his touch again and again. He touched her as though she was precious.

Her arms came up to tangle in his hair and hold him captive against her. The coarse hair of his beard was abrasive against her tender skin, but even that felt wickedly delicious. But he pushed against the restraint of her arms and raised to look down at her, his eyes dark with wanting.

Her hands fell away to clutch at the fabric of her dress as she gathered it and pulled it off over her head. It had barely touched the ground before he grabbed her and pulled her to him, his mouth devouring hers. Merewyn threaded her fingers in his hair, relishing the groan that came from deep in his throat. The rough silk of his tongue stroked hers, and it ignited that all-too-familiar throb within her. When he picked her up in his arms, excitement fluttered wildly in her belly.

He sat her gently on their bed and moved back to pull his shirt off over his head. It was quickly followed by his boots, socks and trousers until he stood gloriously bare before her. He was so perfect, she might have been intimidated by him if he had given her the time. But he was pushing her back and climbing in beside her, his lips on hers again as his hand moved between her legs.

Though she'd felt the pleasure of his fingers the other night, she was still jolted by the shock of sensation they sent through her. His thumb parted her and massaged, making her groan against his kiss.

When she did, he pulled back to watch her face as he repeated the movement. 'You like this.'

'Aye,' she whispered, and grabbed his shoulders as her hips moved involuntarily against his touch.

'Tell me what you want. Don't be afraid.'

Merewyn wasn't sure how to tell him what she wanted when she wasn't even sure herself what it was that her body was moving towards. So she told him what she had liked. What she wanted him to do again. 'I like your mouth on me.' She was incapable of speaking above a whisper. To say the words aloud was almost more than she was able to do.

Eirik immediately complied with her request and kissed a trail down the sensitive skin of her neck to her breast. Except instead of taking her nipple as he had earlier, he lapped at it with his tongue. And then when she was straining upwards to him, her back bowed from the bed, he scraped his teeth over the sensitive peak. She cried out from the pleasure, the sensation moving like a bolt of lightning from her breast to the place between her legs that his thumb caressed. Only then did he take the entire nipple into his mouth and suckle. The ache between her legs had intensified so much, she knew that she needed something more.

'There.' She moved her hips. 'I want you there.' Without even thinking, she reached for him, that hard, wholly male part of him that she knew her body craved. She instinctively knew that only his shaft could ease the swollen ache within her.

The back of her hand brushed the hard, flat planes of his stomach, intent on touching him, exploring him on its way to her goal, when he suddenly jerked away from her and held her hands pinned against the blanket beneath them. For a split second, she registered the look of fear and alarm in his eyes, before he blinked and the facade of control had returned.

'Don't touch me.' His voice was back to the authoritarian master, not the tender lover who she was learning existed just beneath the surface.

'But...' She thought back to the times she had touched him and then realised there hadn't been many. On the horse, her body had rested against his back and then his front, but she'd never actually *touched* him intentionally. His hair, his shoulders, his hands, but not really his body. 'But I want to feel you.' The hurt in her voice was impossible to hide.

Eirik shook his head and the husky timbre returned to his voice when he spoke. 'You're perfect, Merewyn. Just lie there while I have you.'

He moved slowly, as if unsure of his welcome now that the mood had shifted, and gently brushed her lips with his. She parted for him and he dipped inside, a soft, tender atonement for what she couldn't have. Her eyes closed and she gave herself up to him as his mouth moved down her neck and onto her body, reigniting her with his touch. When his tongue dipped into her navel, he pushed her knees apart and she tensed, but didn't stop him from settling his wide shoulders between them.

'Eirik!' she cried out when his mouth replaced his fingers on her sex, her back arching off the bed. His hot tongue stroked her deliberately as his thumb pushed into her. Her own fingers tangled in his hair, determined to pull him away, but only managing to hold him close as ripples of pleasure pulsed from where he kissed her.

Finally, when the ache within her became unbearable, she whispered, 'Please. I need more. I need you.'

'Say that again,' he commanded, his voice harsh against her pulsing flesh.

'I need you.'

He immediately let her go and moved up her body

until his hips rested between her thighs, his weight on his forearms. His gaze raked her face, coming to rest on her eyes as he aligned himself to her and ever so gently pushed the tip of himself inside. 'Are you in pain?' he asked when she gasped.

She bit her lip and shook her head, but to speak was beyond her as his exquisite length filled her. Everything narrowed to that place where he coalesced with her so completely it felt as if he'd been made just for her. Her hips angled instinctively, greedy for more of him, and he answered by rocking into her in a gentle but steady rhythm. His gaze never left her face, as if he could gauge her pleasure by her expression. But she wanted him with her and pulled him down to kiss him.

When her tongue stroked his, he made a soft groan of capitulation and ground himself into her. He wasn't gentle anymore, but with each stroke something tightened inside her. Then suddenly her entire body clenched, especially that part gripping him so tightly, and everything came apart. Nothing mattered, nothing was real, but the solid weight of him above her and inside her.

He pulled back to watch as she cried out her pleasure and shuddered beneath him. But then, a strong arm went around her waist to hold her steady and he rode her harder until his own cry filled the room and he fell atop her, heavy and sated.

It took several minutes for the euphoria to fade and Merewyn to realise what had happened. Though she still wasn't sure what to call it, only that it had come over her body and swept her away. When she found the strength to open her eyes, Eirik was there looking down at her.

'What happened to you?' His voice was tender and soft and just a little bit awestruck.

'I'm not sure.' Despite everything, she blushed. 'Don't you know?'

'Merewyn, I—' But he seemed to think better of whatever he planned to say and simply shook his head. 'Are you certain you're not hurt?'

'I'm not hurt.' In fact, she wanted to explore what he had awakened within her. 'That was incredible.'

She shifted, but he must have assumed it was a subtle reminder that his weight was smothering her smaller frame, because he moved to leave her. It wasn't a reminder. He could crush her for all she cared as long as they could go to that place he had taken her. The intimacy had been so vibrant, so real between them, she was afraid that he would leave like he had the first time and it would be gone. She didn't want to be used and discarded like she was a slave. When he touched her, it became more than that between them.

'Don't go.' Forgetting his earlier admonishment, she grabbed at his waist to pull him back to her, but he flinched as if she'd struck him. She touched the back of his hand instead.

He surprised her by dropping to his side beside her instead of leaving. His eyes were closed as he struggled to slow his breathing back to normal. She smiled because she knew that she had done that to him, because he had done it to her. Her gaze caressed him all over, settling on his face. He was a beautiful man. But she realised now that he was also a broken man. There had been real fear in his eyes when she'd reached out to touch him. He'd hid it well, but she'd caught a glimpse of it before he'd managed to hide it.

She didn't know what could create that sort of fear in a warrior like him—it seemed ridiculous to even think that was what she saw. The intimacy they created swirled around them, drawing them close in its cocoon, but the gulf between them still existed. She knew that gulf was rooted in his fear. They laid there together, her touch on his hand the only thing between them, but there could be so much more. She was sure of it. If only she could breach the fear that he held like a shield between them.

* * *

Eirik laid there in the semi-darkness, savouring her touch but unwilling to do what he knew she wanted. He'd spent his entire adult life avoiding every woman except Kadlin, avoiding any entanglement that would make him relive things better left forgotten. But now, with her small hand on his and her warmth so close, he wanted to pull her close. To bury his nose in her hair and drink in her scent as she slept, to know the comfort she offered him.

The urge to touch her, to stroke her back and whisper how she'd pleased him, was there within him just as it had been the first time. But he stayed the impulse. She would have to be happy with what he could offer her. He liked her happy, eager to please him and be pleased by him. There could be nothing more than that simple pleasure between them. If she became too comfortable with him, she'd want things from him that he was in no way prepared to offer.

The way she wanted to touch him was a good example of that. A barrier had to exist between them. She had to know her place, and that place didn't include intimacy. They found pleasure in their couplings and that was all it could ever be. Physical pleasure. Anything more would cross a wall he wasn't ready to breach and make him vulnerable to her, to the dark things that hid within him.

He wasn't ready to face them.

Chapter Twenty-One

The next few days were more blissful than Merewyn had thought possible when Eirik had carried her onto his ship, away from her home. Actually, they were more blissful than any of her imaginings on her morning walks to the beach. He made love to her every night and usually in the mornings, as well. Every time he moved slowly and thoroughly until she experienced that soul-shattering climax they had discovered together.

But it was more than the care he took in taking her body that made the days so idyllic. When he went fishing, he took her with him, and she would gather wood while he caught their food. If he was doing something more laborious, then she tended the house, but he'd come to chat with her frequently. They prepared the evening meal together and he told her stories from his childhood. It occurred to her on an evening almost a week after their arrival that their lives were exactly that of a husband and wife.

Except it was even better than any match she'd dared to hope that Alfred would provide for her. There was not a grand manor or any servants to see to their every need, but she didn't need those things. Not when her prize was her Northman. Sometimes she would feel pangs of guilt because she knew that he wasn't really hers and she should want to return home. But she couldn't summon those longings anymore. She wanted Eirik with every fibre of her being. She wanted him and everything he could offer her. He accepted her as she was, he made her feel wanted, but more than either of those…he valued her. She felt that in every tender glance he threw her way and in the time he took to teach her things, such as how to properly tie on a hook or to keep the fire burning consistently to cook their supper. Things she'd never had to know before because someone else had always taken care of them.

She could happily stay there with him for ever. But some nagging voice deep inside would always remind her that it wouldn't be for ever and he wasn't her husband. He was her captor. No matter how happy she ever felt, that cold thought found a way to intrude.

She'd purposely not broached the subject of going back to his home, back to his family, because she hadn't wanted to face what that would mean. Though she hadn't fully realised it until that moment, a part of her had come to hope that their stay at the farm would be indefinite, or at least through the winter. It was so cosy with just the two of them and the occasional presence of the caretaker and his sons. Going back to the longhouse would be a break, perhaps an irreparable one, from this idyllic world they had created.

Here, he made her feel cherished. He made her feel everything she had always assumed, always hoped, that a husband would make her feel. But he wasn't her husband. Even though he treated her better than her family ever had, even though she found herself imagining a fantasy life with him, that was all it was. Fantasy. Because she was his slave and that wouldn't change.

Eirik's hand on her cheek brought her back to the present. He stood above her where she sat on the bench that had become their bed, but sat down beside her once he had her attention. 'What are you thinking?'

'How happy I am here…with you,' she whispered.

He pressed a kiss to the crease that had formed between her eyes. 'You don't look happy.'

'Are you happy here?' It was foolishness to broach the subject, she knew that, but couldn't still her tongue.

When he pulled back, the corner of his mouth was tipped up in a smile. 'Aye, sweet girl.' He pushed her back at the same time he trailed kisses down her neck. She closed her eyes and gave herself over to the desire that he could so easily rouse within her.

Once she was on her back, Eirik raised up to look at the prize he'd taken from the Saxon shore. Only, she'd become so much more than a prize to him. She opened her eyes and smiled, and he felt that smile deep in his chest. It was as though she'd somehow reached inside and taken out some of the heaviness that weighed on him. 'You make me happy.' And as he spoke the words, he realised how true they were.

He was supposed to keep himself removed from her, to keep a wall between them. But, somehow, she was breaking it down without even giving him a chance to defend it. When she reached up and cupped his cheek in her hand, he turned to place a kiss to the tender pulse on her slender wrist. He wasn't sure how it had happened, but all he wanted to do was show her pleasure. To make her eyes light up with it and make sure every part of her body felt it. She deserved so much more than he could offer her; he felt that he needed to make up that lack to her in any way that he could.

So he slowly pulled up the skirt of her dress and nuzzled his face in her breasts. He knew how she liked to be touched, how she liked to be tasted, and spent the rest of the evening showing her all the things he could never say to her.

But afterwards, when she had turned to sleep on her side, he laid beside her and stared into the fire and wondered how much longer they had left. Their days at the farm were numbered. His father would send for him if he didn't return soon, Eirik was sure of it. There was too much to be done before the invasion in the spring. Besides that, his father would be angry about Kadlin and looking to vent his disapproval. For the first time in his life, thoughts of returning home were unsettling.

He rested his hand on top of hers and smiled to himself. The need to touch her was happening more and more lately. And it wasn't just for comfort that he sought her out. Somehow, this small woman gave him strength. He longed to take her in his arms and soak her in until he was as strong as she believed him to be. But this simple touch was all that he could allow, because he was afraid of breaking in front of her. If he did, she'd turn away from him.

He didn't know what he would do when that happened. In one week, she'd made this place more of a home than the one he'd lived in all his life. The one he should be anxious to return to because he hadn't spent more than two nights there in the past two years. But he didn't want to do anything but stay with her.

He closed his eyes and tried not to think of their return and what it would mean. She wouldn't like her life as a slave, but there was no alternative for her. When he took a deep breath, her scent washed over him, drawing him closer to her warmth as he fell asleep.

Eirik took a deep, gasping breath and sat straight up in bed. His lungs were deflated, deprived of air as though he'd been underwater for too long. Grey spots danced before his vision, but slowly they cleared and his breathing wasn't quite so desperate. It was only at that point that he became aware of the water running in rivulets down his bare chest. And then he noticed Merewyn. She stood watching him as though she was wondering if he was the same man who had touched her just hours earlier.

He realised then that he'd had a nightmare and it must have been bad enough to wake her. The dreams became worse, more vivid, during times of anxiety. Thoughts of leaving their sanctuary, of returning home, must have triggered it.

He raised his hand to reach out for her and realised only then that his body was trembling in the furious aftermath of the dream. The entire bed was shaking. He couldn't even remember the dream, only the horrible feeling of dread and despair that settled heavy in the pit of his stomach. And with it, that remembered feeling of helpless pain. He despised it.

A fur dropped around his shoulders, surprising him so that he jerked away from the comfort.

'I'm sorry. I just… You're shaking and I think maybe you're too cold.' Merewyn stood at his side, her voice gentle and hesitant, the way women sometimes talked to people who were injured or infirm.

He despised that, too. Not that she would try to help him, but that she would see him as infirm because that was exactly what he was. Damaged in a way that would haunt him for ever. If only she knew, she would be ashamed of giving herself to him, ashamed that he wasn't the man he pretended to be. He jerked his gaze away from where she stood beside him to her empty spot in the bed. He wanted to leave so she wouldn't see him this way, but he knew from experience his legs wouldn't be able to support him just yet. It occurred to him to order her away, and he opened his mouth to do that, but there was nowhere safe for her to go. The other chambers would be too cold for her.

'Here.' She moved slowly so she wouldn't frighten him and he hated that she would have that worry. He closed his eyes so he wouldn't have to see what she thought of him now and the fur slid back up around his shoulders. He gripped it tight so she wouldn't have to.

Sounds of her adding wood to the fire reached his ears, followed by the soft pad of her bare feet as she moved to stand beside him. She paused and he heard the sound of rustling as she put on her underdress.

But she didn't leave him as he expected, and the heat of her thigh warmed his as she sat beside him. After a moment, a dry cloth blotted the water away from his forehead. He jerked away, but she surprised him and followed, 'You'll catch your death if we don't get you dry. I'm sorry for the water, but I couldn't wake you any other way.'

He kept his eyes closed and suffered through her administrations as she wiped the water from his face and hairline. After a while, he realised his skin tingled under her repetitive touch and his shoulders weren't as tight. He didn't know when it happened, hadn't been aware of shifting his position so that he faced her, but when he opened his eyes, she was smiling at him.

She chewed the inside of her bottom lip, the way he noticed that she sometimes did when she was uncertain, and gently touched his hand. When he didn't pull it back, she brought it very slowly, but very deliberately to her own face so that his palm cupped her cheek. 'Just feel me and know that I'm here. You're not alone.'

His hands still shook, but as he focused on them, the trembling subsided slightly. He felt like a babe as she attended to him. But she was helping. She felt warm, solid, *alive* beneath his hand.

'I'm going to dry your chest.' She held up a length of linen and moved slowly to bring it to his chest. He watched it the entire way and sucked in a deep breath when she touched him through the cloth, but he refused to follow the impulse to stop her and watched as she dried him. When he was as dry as he was going to get—his hair would be damp for a while—she gently pushed him down to lie on his back and threw the linen to the floor. Then she climbed back to her side of the bed and pulled a blanket over them both.

She smiled at him again, a timid smile of understanding, as she snuggled against him. 'I'm going to put my arm across your chest, but I'll only rest it on your shoulder.' Then she did just as she described, and he put his arm around her as she stretched out to lay full length against him, her arm across his chest.

Tears stung his eyes, and he blinked them back furiously, determined to not further unman himself before her. The fingers of one hand bit into the soft flesh of her hip as he pulled her closer. He'd never had this. After the nightmares had started, he'd sometimes awaken to Hilla or Sweyn bringing him out of it, but never to this. Even before the nightmares, when his mother had been alive, he'd never known the comfort of touch. His father had taken over the care of him and his brothers, while his sisters had been under the care of their mother.

No one had ever held him.

He closed his eyes against the memory, but it wasn't enough. As much as her touch comforted him, it threatened to tear him apart. There was pain in her arms, because they demanded too much. They demanded to know, demanded that he face what he refused to remember and threatened to bring the knot of pain that he'd tamped down to the surface. A tear slipped out, and he flipped their positions so that his face was buried against her chest and his arms held her tight against him. He couldn't let her see how dangerously close to breaking he really was. He couldn't let her know the blackness that existed deep within him, so he took deep gasping breaths to keep from telling her.

Her hands stroked his back in long, slow caresses, and he closed his eyes to savour the sensation. They stayed that way for a long while, until his trembling stopped completely. It was amazing how she soothed him. Her warmth became his, and there was an indescribable comfort of having her in his arms.

'What do you dream about?' The question wasn't a surprise, but he'd thought—hoped—that she'd gone to sleep.

He didn't want to lie to her, but there was no way he was telling her about the nightmares, about what had caused them. Perhaps he was selfish, but he wanted her and had no intention of giving her up. Eventually she would find out. Someone would mention that day. He didn't know how he would face the day when she told him she didn't want to be with him anymore, but he knew that he wouldn't force her to stay with him. So he had no intention of hastening its arrival. She wouldn't want to stay after she knew, of that he had no doubt.

'I don't remember the dreams.' His voice was husky and almost unrecognisable against the steady beat of her heart. His throat was scratchy and dry, but he didn't want to leave her for water. He needed her right now more than he could admit.

'You never remember the nightmares? But they're so…so disturbing. Do you have no notion of them?'

He shook his head, but he knew exactly what they were, had very vivid recollections of the earlier ones when he was younger. He was sure now that they had come back; they were the same. 'Forget them, Merewyn, they don't mean anything.' But he knew from the way she lay so quietly that she wouldn't forget them. He couldn't say that he blamed her.

'But—'

'Forget it.' Stronger now, he pushed up on his

elbows to look down at her, but he immediately bemoaned the loss of her warm body against him. He knew that she must notice the redness in his eyes—his weakness would be on clear display for her to witness, and he hated it.

Her only reply was to beckon him back, and he crushed her to him again and closed his eyes until he wasn't aware of anything except the beat of her heart.

When she awoke the next morning, he was still wrapped around her. She smiled and rubbed her palms along the warm skin of his back. She didn't want to wake him, but she couldn't resist the impulse to touch him. But he must have already been awake, because he lifted his head to look down at her.

'Good morning.' Her smile widened as she noticed his expression. Things had changed between them. His eyes were as raw and exposed to her as they had been last night. Maybe the barrier wasn't gone yet, but there was a definite chink in the wall. Her heart almost flipped in her chest when he smiled back. It wasn't a large smile. In fact, it was more a barely perceptible quirk upwards.

'Good morning.' His voice was still raspy from his screams.

'How are you feeling?' His hair had dried pressed flat against her breast, so it was quite messy. It looked adorable, but she kept that thought to herself as she ran her fingers through it. Something told her he wouldn't take the description as a compliment.

The question was a subtle reminder of the night before, and it made his eyes immediately shutter. She wanted to smack herself for even asking. Instead, she brought her hands to his shoulders to hold him in place when she felt him tense to move. 'Don't go. I'll get breakfast started.'

He hesitated, but eventually moved to the side to let her up. But when she rose and turned towards the fire, she flinched when a sharp twinge of pain shot through that part of her he had so enthusiastically enjoyed over the past few days.

'What was that?'

She laughed and pulled on the woollen apron dress. 'We've been rather active lately. Or have you forgotten?'

'You've been letting me hurt you?' His voice was so solemn that it immediately drew her attention back to him.

'Of course not. I enjoy our...' What was she supposed to call it with him? Lovemaking? Surely he didn't think of it that way. 'I enjoy our coupling.' She blushed because that word made it sound like the hurried, clandestine activities of that couple in the barn. But it wasn't. Whether he admitted it or not, it was something special. She'd bet everything she had—which was nothing, but even if she'd had a boatful of treasure, she'd bet it—that he'd never felt the things with another woman that he felt with her.

He was so deathly quiet, she moved back to sit beside him. 'I don't want to hurt you, Merewyn. Ever.'

'You didn't hurt me.' She gently touched his hand.

'You're limping.'

'I'm only sore from all of the...activity, and it's morning. My body isn't used to the things we do. I'm sure it's normal.'

He pulled free of her to run his hands through his hair. 'I hurt you,' he whispered.

'Nay, Eirik, I like what you do to me.'

The look he gave her was so filled with disbelief she felt the need to prove it. So without thinking she grabbed his hand and brought it to her breast. 'I'm sore here, too, but only from an excess of attention, not because you hurt me. You know you haven't hurt me here. You've been nothing but gentle.' When he seemed dubious, she brought his fingers up to press them to her lips. 'Even here. I'm sore from your kisses and your beard, but nothing more, my lord. I'm your captive, remember? I hate you and have no reason to make you think I enjoyed something when I didn't.'

That made the corner of his mouth tip up in a half smile. But she knew he had capitulated when his thumb traced the slightly swollen curve of her lower lip. 'I like that you're my captive, sweet girl. That only makes it worse.'

The words made a shiver work through her core, and she had to agree with him. But she was only his captive when they weren't making love, if then. While she was beneath him, he catered to her every want and need before seeing to his own. 'I was there with you, Eirik. Don't forget that. I wanted you.' She pulled him down for a kiss.

His other arm snaked around her and held her close as he kissed her back. But he set her away quickly. 'No more until you heal.'

'I can agree to that—' she nodded '—if you can tell me what your nightmare was about.'

'Nay.' His face closed off to her. There was a

flicker of fear and then there was nothing. The warmth in his eyes turned to ice. And despite their intimacy and his caring, she was reminded that he was her master, and perhaps she'd never be trusted enough to get too close to him.

She didn't bring up the nightmare again, and after they ate breakfast, it was as though it had never happened. He was kind and considerate with her and their relationship settled back into the pattern of familiarity that had developed between them. But their respite from the world would be brief.

Chapter Twenty-Two

Merewyn smiled as she leaned back against Eirik's chest and followed the line of his finger as he pointed to the third hill in the distance. They were leaned back against the side of the house, with his thigh wedged between hers to offer some support to her bottom, while his other arm rested comfortably around her waist. She loved the easiness that existed between them. Even more she loved how, ever since the nightmare, he pulled her against him to sleep now.

He still didn't seem to want her to return his touches, but she could still tease him. As she nodded while he pointed out some rock structure he and Sweyn had made as children, she settled her bottom more firmly against him and was rewarded with the brushing of his lips against the top of her head. She'd almost convinced herself that it was possible to bring down that wall between them.

'You play with fire,' he growled, and nuzzled her neck.

'It's been days. I only want what you've promised me when you warned me away.'

He chuckled, and the sound filled her with warmth. He'd refused to join with her since the day of her limping.

'Please, Eirik.' She was smiling as she turned in his arms and put her arms around his neck. 'I know you want to.' The evidence of his arousal was firm against her thigh. 'I'm healed, I swear.'

His thumb brushed across her lip and the humour in his eyes changed as they darkened with intensity. There was an answering flutter in her belly to that look. His mouth covered hers and his hands slid down her body until they were cupping her buttocks, giving each globe a squeeze as he pulled her up his thigh, pressing her womanly softness into the hard muscle.

'Don't tease me unless you mean to follow through,' she whispered when he moved his mouth from hers to trail hot, open-mouthed kisses to her neck.

'I'll tease you, but then I'll take you.' His teeth nipped her tender skin, eliciting a serrated groan from her.

He might have taken her there had something in the distance not drawn his attention. It took a moment more for the fog of her arousal to clear enough that Merewyn heard the hoofbeats followed by a horse's whinny. By then, Eirik had grabbed her hand and was already on his way to the door of the sod house. 'Get inside and stay there until I tell you it's safe.'

The wait was horrible. Merewyn's heart was in her throat where she waited just inside the door with a kitchen knife in hand. It wasn't much, but it was the only thing she had found in her hasty search that could even be considered a weapon. She wasn't able to breathe again until she heard Eirik's voice and then another one. Neither seemed to be angry. She cast a glance at one of the smoke holes tucked under the roof and was considering how to boost herself up to it to see outside when Eirik called to her and opened the door.

'It's Vidar and Sweyn.' He looked grim as he walked inside with a cask of what she assumed to be mead under his arm.

A sick feeling festered in the pit of her stomach as she turned to the open door and watched as the boy unloaded a stack of furs from the back of his horse and gave her a nod as he passed her to come inside. She felt ridiculous holding the small knife, so she gave him a tentative smile and walked to put it away.

Vidar spoke to Eirik in their language, so she was surprised when Eirik answered him in hers. 'Looks like snow tonight. You'll stay the night.' Eirik nodded to the blazing fire and both Vidar and Sweyn, who had just come in and shut the door, walked over to it with their hands out, eager for the warmth.

She'd been unaware that Sweyn and the boy knew her language, so was surprised when the boy answered, 'We can head back. It's only midday.' Vidar's voice was halting with his lack of confidence, but he spoke as well as Eirik did. Hilla must have taught him, as well.

'Fool boy!' Sweyn smacked Vidar with a good-natured open-palmed swat on the shoulder. 'When you are offered fire and food, you accept.' He spoke with a heavy accent that she had to strain to understand, and gave her a wink. Her contact with him before this had been limited to observing him on Eirik's ship, but the fact that he spoke her language when it obviously wasn't easy for him to manage caused her to instantly like him. The wink made her think that he must know how she and Eirik had been spending their evenings…and mornings. The fact that Sweyn didn't treat it casually, as though she was no one but a slave, made her hope that others might come to see their relationship as something more. Though, even she wasn't sure exactly what it was.

'You won't make it home before dark. There's no need to freeze outside again tonight. We can all leave in the morning.' Eirik placed another piece of wood on the fire and stared at the flames, his back to the room.

Merewyn started at his words and knew that her worst fear had been confirmed. This wasn't a visit. The two had been sent to retrieve them. To retrieve Eirik—she was only excess baggage. 'We're leaving tomorrow? To return to your home?'

Eirik didn't speak for a moment, and neither of the others was brave enough to break the sudden tension in the room. Finally, Eirik turned and she could see the truth confirmed in the bleakness of his handsome features. Only then did she realise how he had been dreading their eventual return to reality as much as she had. 'Aye, my father has summoned me.' He met her gaze for only a moment before walking out the door.

It was ending. Her stomach lurched and she fought a wave of nausea. It was ending. The tenderness, the unexpected freedom, the late nights in his arms, the sound of her name on his lips when he called to her from across the room or whispered it against her neck when he found his release inside her. Their time together had only just begun, but already it was ending. It wasn't fair. Why couldn't they stay hidden away on his farm just a little longer? Why did the world have to intrude on the tiny bit of happiness they had been able to carve out?

Tears pricked her eyes, but she blinked them back and turned to the benches to hide them under the guise of folding the furs and blankets. Vidar and Sweyn spoke behind her at the fire, but they had reverted back to their own language. She probably wouldn't have understood their words even if they conversed in her own. The pain and fear were too great to allow room for anything else. She hated this. She hated the idea of going back there and being nothing but a slave again. Would Eirik treat her differently? Would they go back to the way things had been before? Nay, she couldn't believe that would happen. Perhaps it was possible to take this bit of happiness with them.

Still, she couldn't stop the thought that it was too

soon. If they'd only had a few weeks to explore their discovery, to savour it, then maybe it could survive in his brutal world, but their love—*their* love?—was like a newborn being tossed to the elements. They needed more time to figure out if love was even possible.

A strong hand on her shoulder made her turn to see Sweyn standing there. 'There are long winter months ahead.' He spoke gently. 'Don't fret.' He gave her a nod as he walked out the door.

Merewyn had no idea what to make of that. It was disturbing that her thoughts were so plainly seen by everyone, but she'd been surprised and unable to hide them. Maybe there was some truth to his words. Maybe there would be time.

The day wore on quickly, too quickly to suit her for their last day, but it hardly mattered. With Sweyn and Vidar around, there was very little in the way of privacy. The four of them spent the evening drinking mead. Sweyn regaled them with stories of past adventures, but Eirik wasn't listening beyond the cursory addition to clarify the random fact that had been exaggerated. Often she'd catch him watching her or gazing absently into the fire. Did he feel their time slipping away, as well? She longed to ask, but couldn't, so as soon as it was acceptable, she excused herself to go to bed. It was torture to be in his presence with all of the uncertainty.

She gave him a brief glance as she left the fire, remembering what had been happening before the sounds of their guests' arrival had broken their embrace. A thrill of remembered pleasure coursed through her belly. If the momentary flare of heat in his gaze was an indication, he also remembered. It made her wish for privacy more than she'd ever wished for anything.

Sleep proved elusive at first, but eventually the murmured voices lulled her to sleep, though she didn't sleep deeply and was awakened from her doze numerous times by laughter. At some point, Eirik slid into bed behind her. His arms came around her from behind and she melted into his warmth. This was the closeness she had craved from him all day. His face buried in her hair, and she felt his heavy sigh against her ear, his facial hair making her skin tingle.

'I missed you,' he whispered.

She smiled as the words warmed her. 'I missed you, too.'

One hand found her breast and teased the nipple

with insistent gentle pinches that awoke her body. 'Didn't I warn you about teasing me without following through?'

'What will you do?' he challenged, and his other hand began to work the skirt of her underdress, the only clothing she wore, up her thigh.

'Eirik! You can't.' She tried to turn in his arms, but he held her fast. So she turned her head to look at him, her eyes desperately trying to look beyond his broad chest to the room beyond.

His fingers found her damp and swollen. His eyes were solemn now, with no hint of the playfulness from just moments ago. She understood then that he felt the same desperation she did, as if something was slipping away from them before they'd even had the chance to know it was there.

'They're both asleep. Out cold with drink.' As if to emphasise his words, one of them let out a loud snore from where they slept on the other side of the hearth. 'But if you tell me nay, I'll leave you be.' To dissuade her, he began circling the spot they had discovered made her mad with desire.

In a purely reflexive move, she pushed back against him, so he rocked his hips into her in response. He was straining against his trousers. She couldn't deny him, couldn't say nay to their potential last night of happiness.

'Aye,' she whispered, and brought his head down for a kiss.

His mouth plundered hers while his fingers rubbed and tortured until she moved restlessly against him. Finally, he pulled away and brought the large blanket of furs over them before catching her beneath the knee to push it forward. She longed to reach back and caress him, but knew he wouldn't let her, so she kept her forearms braced on the bed. A moment more and he grabbed a handful of her hair and an arm went around her waist to hold her steady as he pushed slowly into her. She bit her lip to stifle the cry of pleasure that begged to escape. There was no pain, no soreness, only unimaginable pleasure.

'You're mine, Merewyn. Say it.' His voice was both rough and soft against her skin.

'I'm yours.' There was no hesitation. It was the truth. As surely as he drove her body higher towards release, he carried her heart right along with it. It was his.

'Everybody out!'
Eirik winced as the words boomed throughout

the great room. The four of them had just stepped inside his father's longhouse, where everyone had been enjoying the quiet after the evening meal, so there was no doubt that it was their arrival that had provoked the command from his father. It was confirmed when he happened to catch sight of the man standing on the dais, his hard gaze directed their way. A few of the men greeted him on their way out, but others avoided eye contact as they moved past. Even Vidar found it better to abandon him than to face their father's wrath. The little ingrate.

'Everyone! Go!' This bit was directed at a couple of older women who appeared intent on staying to work on their weaving.

They grabbed their shawls and made a show of putting them on as they left. A twinge of guilt prickled because it was steadily snowing and had been all day and the previous night, but he pushed it aside to face the bigger battle that was his father.

He grabbed Merewyn's arm and pulled her along as he approached the dais. 'Stay behind me,' he murmured. Her hand burrowed in the fur of his cloak. Sweyn moved to his side, helping to shield her.

'What do you mean by refusing to marry Kadlin?' A vein on the jarl's forehead bulged. His voice held the hard edge that foretold of fury.

'I'm not aware of refusing her. She decided we wouldn't suit.' Eirik played semantics in an effort to defuse the situation until he could get Merewyn to safety.

'By the gods and all the hounds in Helheim, do you expect me to believe that girl would have refused you? You who would become jarl?'

'There are many would-be jarls. Surely you realise that she could have her pick of them.'

His father slung down his tankard and Eirik clenched his teeth. 'But she wanted *you.* Leif has said she's done nothing but wait for you. But now there will be no marriage.'

'Perhaps her father was misinformed.'

The jarl cursed and knocked the tankard from the table so it flew halfway across the room. Merewyn jumped behind him. Eirik gave Sweyn a nod and half-turned to her. 'Go with Sweyn. He'll take you to my chamber.'

Her eyes were wide with fright, but she nodded and was stepping away from him when the jarl spotted her.

'Is it the slave? One taste of her and you're giving it all up for her.'

'Father.' Eirik's voice rose slightly in warning. 'Halt before you go too far.'

'I'm the jarl here. I can't go too far. It's you who goes too far. I knew I should have given her to someone else as soon as I saw her. Or maybe I'll even sample her myself.'

'Nay!' Eirik pushed her behind him and faced his father squarely. His other hand gripped around the sheathed blade of his sword. 'She is mine. You have no right to take her away.'

'Right? You challenge me about right? Whose ship were you on when you took her? Whose ship brought her here? Everything you brought back with you belongs to me by *right* if I want it. Everything! That includes your slave.'

There was no denying the absolute truth in those words. But it was almost unheard of for his father to so exert his authority that every man wasn't given his equal share. Almost. A blade of fear knifed through his chest as he realised just how precarious Merewyn's position could be here if his father chose to make it so. 'All right. You can have her, but you'll have to take her from me first.' His voice had gone deathly calm and his fists clenched tight around the sword.

The words broke through his father's red rage.

The older man collapsed back into his chair and took a deep breath before speaking again. When he did speak, his voice was lower and more measured. 'I don't want to take her from you. I don't want to do you harm. What I do want is for you to be jarl after I'm gone. I *want* you to establish that as your rightful place so there will be no question between you and Gunnar. I don't want some slave to ruin that.'

'I have established my right to be the next jarl. The raids were successful and the men already—'

'Enough! I'm speaking of a wife. You need a *wife*, not a slave.'

'Aye, I agree, but it won't be Kadlin.' He nodded again to Sweyn, who immediately ushered the girl back to his chamber.

'It should be Kadlin! Keep the slave for the winter. Bed her all you want. But don't cast Kadlin away while you do it. Be done with the girl and marry in spring before you leave.'

'It won't be Kadlin. She doesn't want our marriage. Whatever agreement you and Jarl Leif have made will have to be dissolved, or you can marry her to Gunnar.'

The jarl guffawed. 'Gunnar! Gunnar? He leads the men on his boat well, but he's a warrior. He's too reckless and wild to be a jarl. The men need a level head to lead them. And you are the rightful heir.'

'The men know that. They will follow me when the time comes.'

'You've made a mistake, Eirik. I only hope you realise it before it's too late.'

Eirik nodded to his father and turned towards his chamber. The jarl could be right, but it was a mistake he was willing to make.

Most of the men would follow him, but that didn't mean there wasn't a small contingent hoping to gain more for themselves by installing Gunnar as jarl. He agreed that with the power of Jarl Leif behind him his claim would have been virtually unbreakable. Maybe it was unwise not to pursue her, but marrying Kadlin had never held much appeal. His thoughts inadvertently went to Merewyn, and he was shocked at how easily he could imagine her as his wife with their sons and daughters playing at her skirts.

She could be with child now. His chest tightened so much at the idea that he had to force a deep breath. He'd have to leave her in the spring for the raids. There was no help for it, but perhaps by then his father would have come to terms with his decision and she would be safe. However, there would never be the question of marriage for them. She was a slave, and even if he set her free, her station in life would never be elevated high enough to become an acceptable wife for a jarl.

He'd have to make it up to her somehow. He wasn't fool enough to think that a noblewoman, even a noblewoman slave, wouldn't want marriage. He'd have to show her that they could have a good life together anyway. Make her realise how he valued her, so that she could be happy. Perhaps it was time to tell her how important she really was to him.

Chapter Twenty-Three

Merewyn jumped to her feet when Eirik walked into the chamber. She was exhausted from the long trip, but their dramatic welcome had unsettled her so much that sleep would be impossible for a while. Her stomach was in knots that churned against each other, twining tighter.

His gaze met hers briefly before he walked by her to the chest at the foot of the bed and dropped his burden of sword, furs and a leather satchel. His jaw was clenched and rigid shoulders told her he was angry.

'What happened? What did he say?' She wrung her hands as she waited for him to speak. She'd heard the jarl—even in Eirik's chamber, she'd heard him clearly. But her knowledge of the language was so poor that she'd only picked up a couple of words.

He shook his head and knelt to open the satchel and slowly, maddeningly, empty its contents one by one and put them away. His comb and straight blade wrapped in a leather sheath were placed on a small corner table. His spare woollen socks were thrown into the opposite corner with his extra trousers to be washed later, and finally his sheathed sword was carefully placed onto hooks affixed to the wall by the bed.

'Please, Eirik! Tell me.'

He was unfastening his cloak and flung it angrily onto the bed before he spoke. 'He's angry that I've decided not to marry Kadlin.'

'Oh.' She had expected the jarl's anger to be about her, not Kadlin. It seemed the woman and Eirik had been more than friends after all. 'So you *were* betrothed, then?'

'Nay, only in his foolish head. We played together as children and her father is a jarl.' His voice trailed off on a frustrated sigh, and he ran both hands through his hair. 'Our fathers think we should marry. But she doesn't want it. I don't want it. I've never wanted it.'

Merewyn looked at him. *Really* looked at him and tried to put herself in the place of any other woman. The breadth of his chest was impressively displayed by his pose. Her eyes followed the line of his lean hips down to his muscular thighs before roving back up to the ropes of muscle that banded his exposed forearms and finally settled on his face. Despite the fact that his nose had been broken once, his features were almost too perfect, his lips too sensual, his eyes too blue.

It was impossible. No woman in her right mind would refuse him. Even the thought of another woman laying claim to him made her heart lurch in jealousy.

'I don't believe you,' she accused. 'Did you lie to me about her? That night, I saw her with her arms around you—'

'Nay, Merewyn, I've not lied to you.' He'd not been oblivious to her thorough inspection, and lowered his arms to his sides. His eyelids had gone hooded and the corner of his mouth ticked upwards in that almost smile she had come to love. A coil of heat unfurled in her belly, unwinding the knots and making her short of breath. He moved the short distance between them, leaving only a small gap.

The fact that he could be so nonchalant in the face of her anger only added fuel to the quickly blazing fire. 'She touched you as if she *knew* you, as if she had the right to you.'

When she would have backed away in anger, his fingers went under her cloak to grab her wrists.

The way his thumbs rubbed circles over the sensitive skin was distracting, but not distracting enough that her heart didn't stop with his next words. 'We did discuss marriage, but decided against it.'

'Why wouldn't she want you?' She hated the envy she felt towards the woman who had been so kind to her. To have a claim to him and then to throw it away was beyond comprehension.

'She wanted a love match, and I don't love her. She doesn't love me. Besides, Kadlin knew that I only wanted you.'

'Now I really don't believe you.'

'Then there's something you should know.'

When he looked down at her small hands in his, she took a deep breath to try to slow her racing heart. He wasn't meeting her eyes; in fact he seemed to avoid doing so and she didn't know how to take that.

'What should I know?'

'You're the only woman I've ever known.'

He couldn't mean what her feeble heart tried to make those words mean. It was impossible. He was... Well, he was Eirik. Women noticed men like him. Women pursued men like him. 'What do you mean?'

His solemn gaze met hers and she knew he spoke

the truth. 'I've spent most of my life trying to control my urges—my tolerance for pain, my endurance in battle, my need for sustenance, my need for women—but you broke me. I avoided that need until you.' When he saw that he needed to elaborate, he dropped a wrist to run a hand through his hair and clarified. 'I've never been inside another woman—only you. I couldn't stop myself from taking you. Now it's all I think about.'

'How is that possible?' She was too stunned by the admission to say anything else.

'You're quite tempting.'

'But how, Eirik? Why?'

'It doesn't matter, Merewyn. Just know that I only want you.'

'But it does matter. It doesn't make any sense.'

He changed their positions so quickly, she was struck off balance as he swept her up into his arms and turned towards the door. 'Right now I want you to join me in the bath. I've wanted to have you there since the night you were there with me.'

She bit the inside of her lip to hide her urge to smile, too smitten to care that just moments ago she'd been anxious and angry. He carried her out the back way to the bathhouse that already had a steaming tub of water waiting. He must have arranged it before meeting her in his chamber. When he set her down, he let her knees go so she slid along his length, and then he pulled her close so she felt the hard bulge of his manhood against her belly.

'Tell me why, Eirik. I want to understand you.'

'Not now,' he whispered, and pushed her back firmly to undress her.

When he had finished and she stood nude before him, he bid her to go to the tub, where she sank down in the deliciously warm water to watch him disrobe. It was a sight she would never tire of seeing. When all his clothes were gone, her intimate muscles clenched at the sight of him, his hard length vibrating with each step that brought him closer to her.

He moved into the tub behind her, his knees on either side of hers as he pulled her back to him. She thought of the foolish child she had been the first time they had been there and how she had wanted him even then. Wanting to touch him, she lightly laid her hands on his muscled thighs, the coarse hairs tickling her palms. He stiffened at first, but a thrill of victory buoyed her when he relaxed and allowed her that small touch.

They stayed that way for a while, letting the warm water relax their tired muscles while savouring the feel of slick skin against slick skin. But he was hard against the small of her back the entire time, and the ache between her thighs had only become more noticeable. It only worsened when he reached over to a bucket beside the tub for a handful of what she assumed to be soap. It was a thick liquid that was already warm when he dribbled it on her chest and used both hands to slowly work it into her breasts. His hands didn't stop there, though. They worked down her arms, her stomach, her legs, until he hooked his feet around her ankles to open her thighs wide so he could wash her there.

She gasped as his strong fingers caressed the swollen tissue, made even slicker by the soap, teasing and tormenting her until she was moving to find release. But he only placed a soft bite on her neck before taking his fingers away, leaving her aching and wanting.

'Not yet,' he admonished firmly when she started to turn around. 'I'm not finished bathing you. I haven't washed your hair.' He surprised her by angling her head back slightly and scooping handfuls of warm water over her hair until it was wet, and then adding the soap. He introduced her to a completely new pleasure when he massaged her scalp with his fingers and lingered over the task until her entire scalp tingled with vigour and her entire body pulsed with arousal.

When he had rinsed the soap away, she pulled away abruptly without giving him the chance to stop her. 'Now. I want you now.'

He chuckled, but it was a husky thing filled with desire, and there was no denying his haste when his hands grabbed her hips to position her so he could mount her from behind.

'Nay, not like this.'

His hands fumbled, and she looked at him over her shoulder, to see that he was clearly confused. 'I want *you*, Eirik. Please.'

A look of wariness temporarily displaced the passion on his features, but he sat back down and gave her a barely perceptible nod. She smiled, triumphant once again, and moved slowly to straddle his thighs. 'I'll keep my hands on your shoulders, or the rim of the tub if you prefer.'

'You can touch me.' He swallowed once and seemed to be mentally preparing himself. It disturbed her so much that she almost gave in and backed down, but it had become important. She needed to do this, and she sensed that he needed her to do it.

She moved over him, while his hands came up to

settle on her hips. She couldn't resist the urge to let her fingers trace the hard muscles of his chest. But he stiffened and sucked in a breath, so she moved them back to the safety of his shoulders.

'Why don't you want me to touch you?'

'I want you to touch me, Merewyn. But—' His voice stopped abruptly and he closed his eyes.

She kissed him, and he quickly took control of the kiss and moved his hips so he found her entrance. Then he pressed upwards as she pushed downwards, and they both groaned aloud as he filled her.

After a moment to savour the connection, she moved experimentally up and then back down, her hips moving in a circular motion that made her grind on the way down. The friction that that movement caused was amazing. She loved the way her overly sensitive nipples raked across his chest as she moved, but she loved it even more when he took a nipple into the wet heat of his mouth as she rode him. Each suckle sent a white-hot shard of excitement down to where she gripped him.

Water splashed over the edge of the tub unnoticed. Her chest bowed into him and his hands held her hips, squeezing and guiding as she moved. It meant that he was still in control, but she didn't care. She was still euphoric that he'd let her take the lead, and the thrill of making those erotic, husky sounds come from his throat was heady. She wanted to watch him, to see his face as he released into her, but all too soon the delicate muscles deep inside her began to clench and contract around the iron of his shaft. He knew, because his hands tightened on her hips and he took over, pumping her up and down on him while raising his own hips to take her hard. She cried out, and her fingernails bit into his shoulders when her release found her. His head fell back, the cords of his neck standing out with the strain as his seed filled her.

The room went fuzzy, and she fell heavily against his chest, unconscious of the fact that her hand rested over his heart, until precious moments later when she finally came back to herself. She was afraid to move, afraid to disturb him so that he, too, realised it. The precious organ pounded in a frenzy beneath her palm, until its pace finally returned to normal. But after a while, her fingertips moved of their own accord in the dusting of soft hair beneath them, indulging in the rare opportunity to touch him. He inhaled sharply, but didn't move. She wanted to look at him, but was afraid she'd see that he was just tolerating her touch, and she thought it might just kill her to see that.

Still, the need to know was too great, and after a moment she dared to look up. He was watching her fingers, but his gaze moved to meet hers, and what she saw there filled her heart with warmth. He was wary, but hopeful.

'Don't ever think I don't *want* your touch.' He captured her hand and brought it to his mouth for a kiss. Then he smiled and caught her chin to hold her steady so his lips could brush across hers. 'I like you in the bath. I think I'll let you do this again.'

'Only if I get to wash your hair.'

He nodded his agreement, and she sat straddling his thighs to wash his hair as tenderly as he had washed hers. She loved to watch his eyes close to savour her touch and the sigh of pleasure that came from his lips. Her gaze flicked with longing to his chest, imagining how it would feel to rub the soap over the sculptured planes and even lower.

Once the bath was finished, he stepped out and grabbed a length of linen before turning to her and beckoning her out of the tub. She felt safe and treasured when he brought it around her shoulders and dried her. When he was done, he surprised her by bringing her cloak around her shoulders, instead of allowing her to dress. Her questioning only caused him to smile wickedly as he pulled on his trousers and boots and then swung her up into his arms.

'Eirik, it's snowing! You'll freeze.' She looked pointedly at his bare chest and damp hair.

'It's just a few steps, and I'll only undress again in our chamber,' he teased and kissed her before walking out the door, leaving their clothing behind to be picked up by a servant.

She tried to hide her laughter against his shoulder when he cursed in response to the frigid wind that buffeted them on their way to the house. She was still laughing quietly when they entered through the back way to reach their chamber and he dropped her on the bed and began to remove his boots.

'You dare to laugh at your master?' Though the tone was harsh, his eyes were teasing.

She smiled and quickly took off the hated woollen cloak, her skin already itchy from it. 'I do when he doesn't have better sense than to go around half-naked in a snowstorm.'

'Then you will pay for your disrespect.' He'd not taken the time to fasten his trousers, as it was late and by using the back door they were sure not to meet anyone. He quickly pushed them down, and she squealed when he tackled her.

'Dear God, you're cold!' His chest was like ice.

'You're not.' He smiled and made a show of rubbing himself against her.

She squealed again and tried to fight him off, but he was too strong. He grabbed her arms and held them tight to the bed while his hips worked between her thrashing legs. Goose bumps prickled her skin, but she was already beginning to warm from her seemingly unquenchable desire for him.

'Don't worry, my sweet girl. I'll keep you warm all night.' His voice had lost its teasing quality and was husky with want and need. He looked down at her with those intense blue eyes that made her weak no matter where they were.

He made love to her slowly, his thrusts long and deep, but unhurried. When it was over, he stayed entwined with her, and they both fell into an exhausted sleep. Morning would come soon, bringing with it all the uncertainty they had managed to hold at bay for one more night. But for now, it was still just the two of them.

Chapter Twenty-Four

They made love again early the next morning and lay quietly afterwards. The playfulness of the previous night had gone, to be replaced by a fear that neither of them was willing to voice. She lay with her head on his chest, listening to its steady beat beneath her ear as the darkness gave way to streaks of grey that found them through the small smoke hole tucked high beneath the roof. She shivered in foreboding, but he mistook it for cold and pulled the fur tighter around her shoulder. She snuggled into him, hiding her face from the reality of the day ahead.

He gave her a few more minutes, and then kissed her head and gently disentangled himself from her to light candles. At some point that morning, someone had discreetly opened the door and placed a hot pitcher of water just inside. She watched as he retrieved it and took it to the basin, where he trimmed his beard and shaved the bristles that had strayed down his neck. Then he quickly washed and dressed. But he stilled, his back to her and his shoulders heavy as he stood in deep contemplation.

Merewyn rose up on an elbow, a brow arched in question. She had just opened her mouth to ask if everything was all right when he turned and strode back to her in determination.

'Come here.' He tried to gentle his voice, but it was laced with anxiety and somewhat sharp because of it.

'What's wrong?' She rose to her knees before him on the bed, making sure to keep the fur tucked around her for warmth.

'Turn around.' His eyes were closed off to her, and she wondered at the change in him, but didn't question it as she did as bidden.

She gasped aloud when he moved her hair to the side and placed something that seemed suspiciously like a slave collar around her neck. Her hand automatically reached up to grab it, but it was already tied snugly around her neck, so she fingered the wooden disk and discerned a rune carved into it. Before she could find her voice, he pulled her back against his chest, his arms tight around her waist.

'I had it made at Jarl Leif's. If it is clear that you

are mine, you won't be in danger from assault here like you were there. I should have had one made for you when we first arrived. If I had, that ugly event might not have happened.' He buried his face in her neck so his next words came out muffled. 'I would kill whoever harms you.'

Her body stiffened with anger and hurt. Had everything that had transpired between them meant nothing? How was it possible that he could still collar her like some common slave? Some part deep inside of her had been hoping for marriage. Marriage would assure everyone that she was under his protection. But instead, he'd given her a collar, as though her worth was only in the fact that he owned her. She was a possession to be labelled and not a lover to be cherished.

She twisted out of his grasp and turned to glare at him, her hurt making her eyes ache with unshed tears. He groaned and pulled her back to him, his mouth crushing hers in a bruising kiss that simultaneously claimed her as it attempted to soothe her. When she refused to respond, he pulled back and cupped her face, his thumbs caressing her cheekbones. 'I have to go. I'll see you later this evening.'

He gave her one last look of regret before he turned and left.

* * *

Hilla came to retrieve her later that morning and, with no immediate options available to her, she had to go along. She needed time to think, to reconcile her new life with what she had hoped it would be. And just what had she thought? Merewyn wasn't sure now. Had there ever really been the possibility that they could shut themselves off from the world around them for very long? Had it ever been possible that she would escape her place as his slave? Her own family had given her to him; it seemed that she was destined to be his slave no matter what she did.

Hilla had brought clothes: the usual nondescript underdress with a dull, woollen apron dress. But Merewyn insisted on the leggings Kadlin—the only person in the accursed land who had dared to treat her as an equal—had given her and dug them out of Eirik's chest to put them on. Then, despondent and uncertain, she followed the woman out of the safety of the chamber.

She was led to a far corner of the main room. Somehow she avoided looking at the dais, even though she could hear voices coming from there and could pick out the steady timbre of Eirik's. Hilla led her behind a partition she hadn't noticed.

It was open at each end, but did a fairly good job of separating the slaves from everyone else. The snow must have driven everyone inside. There were women sitting around sewing and weaving, but they stopped to look her over.

A young girl, Mardoll, whom she remembered as helping her bathe on her first day there, brought her a bowl of that horrid, watery porridge. If it was possible, her spirits sank even more. At the farm they had eaten porridge made creamy with sheep's milk and sweetened with honey that the caretaker had brought for them. But here she was a slave and would be given no special food. She wanted to throw it into the fire, to run out the door and into the snow screaming her fury, screaming that she was a noblewoman and should be treated with respect, but it would get her nowhere. That wasn't even the real reason she was so upset. It was that she wanted to mean something more to Eirik. But, apparently, she didn't.

So she nodded her thanks and took a seat near the small hearth. The women there reluctantly made room for her, and Merewyn realised there was a hierarchy at work here that she had no knowledge of. Except for Hilla and Mardoll, the glances cast her way were filled with distrust. She would find no allies among them.

The day passed in a slow crawl that was made even worse by her sadness. She was put to work helping to weave reed for rushes, a job that was tedious in its simplicity. From her seat on the floor, she had a clear view of her tormentor and couldn't stop herself from looking to him from time to time. He stayed at the dais with his father, Sweyn and a few others she couldn't name for most of the day. Gunnar was not to be seen. They appeared to be in deep discussion about something, perhaps war or raiding, if there was even a difference between the two, because they had maps spread out on the table and sometimes raised their voices in disagreement.

Sometime after noon, the snow stopped and the sun came out, turning the powder into a shining mass of white ice. But that didn't stop them from venturing outside. Merewyn reluctantly retrieved her hated woollen cloak and joined the other slaves at the outdoor fire to begin to prepare the evening meal. As cold as it was, the men shed their tunics and shirts and began sparring, as if needing a release from the pent-up energy of being forced inside for the morning. She shivered as she watched them and bemoaned anew the loss of her precious mother's cloak.

Her gaze was pulled to Eirik's bare chest. Was it just last night he had let her sit astride him in the bath? Was it only this morning that he had loved her so intensely and then held her afterwards? He didn't even look her way once.

Her fingers went up to the disk at her neck, and shame flooded her when she actually found some reassurance there. It said that she was his, but nothing proclaimed that he was hers. She was no one there and would probably never know the privilege of claiming him as her own. The knowledge wrung at her heart and made her look away to fight the tears of anger that sprung to her eyes.

Later that evening, after the sun had set, she walked back to the great room carrying a platter of roasted root vegetables. She climbed the dais and sat it down on the table and made to turn when Eirik called her name. It was his only acknowledgement of her that day. He raised his hand to beckon her around the table to him. She took a deep breath and held her hands stiffly at her sides as she approached him, but he surprised her by reaching out and capturing one of them in his. His thumb traced gently along her wrist.

'Sit and eat.' He didn't smile, but his eyes were gentle as they caressed her face. He nodded to a cushion that had been placed on the floor behind his chair.

'But Hilla said that I should—'

'Eat your fill and then take your rest in our chamber. You've worked enough today.' He cut her off and gave her arm a gentle tug.

Our chamber. The simple phrase shouldn't please her so much, but it did. Unreasonably, it did. She was like a mongrel lapping up any scrap of affection from her master. She nodded and sat down. He fixed a bowl of food for her and she accepted it with a tight nod of thanks. Like that first night, it was filled with the choicest pieces of meat and, this time, a sampling of the carrots and parsnips. He also gave her a tankard of mead. Not the ale and water given to everyone else, but the mead reserved for the jarl's table.

After dinner, she returned to their chamber and immediately fell across the bed. The physical exhaustion of the ride of the previous day, and the late night coupled with the emotional turmoil of the day had left her drained. She barely roused herself enough to shed her clothing before climbing under the fur and letting oblivion claim her.

Eirik came in much later and slipped into bed with her. She didn't open her eyes when he pulled her back against him, his arms wrapping around her from behind. But she laced her fingers with his and fell back asleep.

She awoke the next morning to his fingers stroking her and his body rigid behind her.

'I didn't want to wake you last night, but I can't leave without having you.' His husky voice against her ear penetrated her half dream state. This was the man she'd come to love.

'Don't ever leave without having me. You're not allowed to.' She turned in his arms and draped her leg across his thigh.

He growled and put his arm under her knee to angle her hips to accept his rapid invasion. She cried out in surprise at the sudden thrust, but her body was more than ready for him. She wanted him with the same desperate need, and buried her fingers in his hair to hold him close. He took her so hard, the headboard knocked against the wall, but she didn't care. She didn't care if everyone knew they made love. She didn't care if the walls fell down and the world saw them. He was hers and, despite her best efforts, she was his. Always his. She'd claim him the only way she could.

Afterwards, they stayed in bed for as long as they dared before rising to wash and dress each other. He gave her one last irresistible smile and left. She took a few moments more to braid her hair and make the bed before she followed him.

Hilla was just opening the door of the jarl's personal chamber when Merewyn stepped into the hallway. She quickly averted her eyes when she realised Hilla had stopped to adjust the brooches on her dress. The realisation dawned on her suddenly that the woman must service the jarl in more intimate ways. In the same ways that she herself had just serviced Eirik.

Was there a difference? Her hand went to the collar at her throat. The reminder effectively diffused the euphoria that always followed when they made love and pushed her back to reality.

There was a difference. Eirik didn't make her service him, the logical part of her mind insisted. She made love with him because she wanted to, because she had chosen to. What if the jarl or Gunnar had taken her? She wouldn't have been given a choice.

Was Hilla forced to perform acts that no woman should ever have forced upon her? The thought left her faintly nauseated.

The feeling refused to leave her all through the morning and lingered until the afternoon when she was outside near the large fire, chopping carrots. Hilla worked along beside her, directing the younger women, all slaves, with the authority of a chieftain. No doubt the skill had been learned from many years of cooking meals and being responsible for all the work that went into running a large household. Merewyn wondered how she felt about also being required to make her body available to the jarl. As if the workload she shouldered wasn't already monumental.

'How do you stand it, Hilla? How can you serve him?' The question burst out of her with all the strength she had used to suppress it the entire day. It was none of her business, but that didn't seem to matter.

Hilla didn't seem surprised by the question. 'It's not so bad.' She shrugged. 'They only want servants. It's no different from when I served my master back home.'

'But it is! You have no choice here where we're

collared like animals. You were a free woman back home, weren't you?'

'Nay, I was born to my mother, who served on our master's farm. Never even knew a father. What choice did I have? Where could I have gone to? He sold me, and eventually Jarl Hegard took me. It was just exchanging masters.' She stopped her work to look at Merewyn closely and nodded as if she'd come to some profound conclusion. 'You suffer because you didn't serve in your home.'

'I did serve. I watched the children, gathered herbs, helped with weaving.'

'And did you have a choice in that?'

Nay, Merewyn realised, she hadn't had a choice. The duties had always been there, and she'd never thought to not do them. But it had been a duty to her family, which was different than a duty to these people. Well, everyone except Eirik. She wanted to take care of him. 'I suppose I didn't, but that's different. Besides, I suppose I meant how do you serve the jarl?' Her voice lowered as she tried to get the words out. 'You know, as a wife would serve him?'

'Ah…' Hilla gave her a suggestive smile. 'It's *those* duties you speak of, then. The ones that let your lusty man take his pleasure betwixt your thighs.' She pointed with her bone-handled chopping knife to the group of men wrestling in the snow across the clearing.

Merewyn blushed, but couldn't stop herself from seeking out Eirik with her eyes. He was without tunic or shirt again, currently battling an opponent who gripped him in a bear hug. She shook her head and wondered at their sanity in their insistence on going about half-clothed in this temperature. Even there near the fire, her hands were cold as she worked.

'I had a choice in that, and I don't consider that my duty,' Merewyn clarified.

'That's good to know. It helps if you can enjoy it.'

Hilla seemed to speak in all sincerity, but Merewyn's blush deepened all the same.

'Jarl Hegard doesn't force me, girl. I was here two winters afore he asked. Unlike my old master, who took me first in the fields and then his wife died and he took me into his bed thereafter. I was his favourite because I bore no children. There wasn't any choice there.'

The picture Hilla painted made her blanch. Instantly, she felt shame for lamenting her loss of freedom when others clearly had a fate worse than her own. 'I'm sorry, Hilla.'

'Don't be sorry for me, girl. I'm happy here. Be

sorry for yourself, if you can't find happiness with that man who shows you kindness. I've known him since he was a child. He's got a good heart and since what happened to him…' She shook her head as if to rid that particular line of thought from her mind. 'Well, he understands more than most what cruelty does to a person. And I can tell from the way you look at him that he pleases you well.'

'What happened to him?' Merewyn jumped at the chance to learn more about the past that tormented him and gave him nightmares. But Hilla refused to elaborate and held up her hand, unwilling to even address the question.

'Perhaps it would have been better for you had you been married before he took you. Then you would know the burden of wife. Duties you have no choice in, a man who only takes his pleasure to get children on you that he can send away at his will and you get no say. Slave or wife, Merewyn. There's very little difference to most men.'

Merewyn didn't know what to say to that. There was some truth in Hilla's words, but Merewyn couldn't get past the idea of children. She could be carrying Eirik's child now. She gripped the bone handle of the blade tightly to keep her hand from covering her belly. What would it mean for her if she bore his child? More important, what would it mean for her child? Would the baby be free or a slave? Would she know the joy of being its mother, or would that be taken from her? She didn't know and couldn't allow herself to think of that eventuality just yet.

Chapter Twenty-Five

Eirik sat back from the table and allowed his attention to wander from the heated discussion. There had been a time when talk of war and strategy filled him with excitement, but now it was less than appealing. The invasion planned for spring would happen without the constant bickering and disagreement. He knew what to do and could clearly see it happening in his mind. Any discussion to belabour the attack was stifling.

As his gaze found and settled on Merewyn, he almost smiled as he admitted to himself that there might be another reason for his sudden lack of interest in a subject that had once stimulated him. It had been a fortnight since their return and he'd had almost no time alone with her. He missed their time together, and their evening talks. She was almost always asleep when he came to their chamber late at night.

Merewyn was working with one of the younger girls, he thought her name was Mardoll, demonstrating a complex weave the girl was struggling to master. His gaze went to the slave collar around her neck and fixed there as he marvelled at how well she had adjusted to her new place. Her strength amazed him. He couldn't imagine accepting a similar fate for himself so gracefully. Then again, he'd never imagined asking someone to accept this fate for themselves. If he lingered on the thought, a tiny thread of guilt would nag at him and give rise to something buried even deeper. To the darkness that he kept hidden within him.

It kept telling him that she would never accept him if she knew the truth. That it didn't matter if she was a slave; one day she would find out what had happened and ask to leave him. He couldn't imagine a scenario that would keep her with him then. He couldn't, *wouldn't*, force her to stay. He couldn't bear to see the look that would surely cloud her eyes every time she saw him.

His thoughts turned to marriage. He could imagine no one else that he wanted to be his wife. She was everything that he had always imagined that a wife should be. In his weaker moments, he thought about taking her to the farm and living with her there until they grew old and died together. It was a disgraceful thought for a warrior, but he didn't care. To die in battle paled considerably in comparison to spending his life with her. It was only a thought he allowed to be indulged in his weaker moments. He knew the truth. Even if he could give up his future as jarl, he simply wasn't good enough to be her husband. In his heart, he knew that he could never make her happy, so he was resigned to enjoy the little time they had together.

Every morning he woke up wrapped around her, his arms holding her as if he was afraid she would leave him in his sleep. And every morning he was afraid that she would look deep into his eyes and see that for the weakness that it was. In such a short time, he'd come to physically *need* her in a way he couldn't understand. She kept the nightmares away. But so far she seemed to be pleased to wake up in his arms.

'Eirik?' His father's harsh voice cut through his reverie.

'Aye?'

'You'll go, if there is a need?'

Eirik had been faintly aware of the discussion about two jarls to the south-east who had held out on committing men to the battle. His father was beseeching him to go and personally request their assistance in the invasion. But he knew that it would mean leaving Merewyn behind, and he was reluctant given his father's bitterness about his refusal to marry Kadlin. He wouldn't risk taking her out in winter. The danger was too high.

'Why don't you send Gunnar?'

'Gunnar hasn't seen fit to return home. Besides, they'll listen to you. They trust you.'

Eirik glanced back to Merewyn before addressing his father again. 'Aye, they trust me. But I won't leave the girl unless I know that she's safe.'

The jarl followed his glance to the girl and was quiet for a long while before coming to a decision and finally nodding. 'You have my word that she'll be kept safe while you're gone.'

'You've changed your mind about her, then?' Eirik pressed.

His father slowly shook his head. 'I've never held any ill will towards the slave. I only seek to ensure your future. This trip will help you do that.'

'Then, I'll go if there's a need.'

'Agreed. If we haven't heard before winter's end, you'll go.'

Eirik nodded and bid them all goodnight. Then he headed over to Merewyn and knelt behind her, his need for her far outweighing his need to please his father. The back of his finger caressed the sensitive skin at the nape of her neck. 'Come to the bath with me,' he whispered into her ear. She blushed, but nodded and gave him a sweet glance. He waited for her to say something to Mardoll and then wrapped his cloak around her before leading her to the bath.

He cleared the room and filled the tub with steaming water before bringing her inside. It was already steamy, but he poured more water over the stones to heat the room even more. Just as he finished, she walked up behind him. He instinctively knew her intention a moment before her hand ran lightly up his back. Even though he knew it was she, even though he knew that her touch came from a place of tenderness, even though his body hardened in response, he stiffened and the familiar anxiety burned in his stomach.

'You said I could touch you.' She smiled when he turned to face her.

'Aye, I did.' He was surprised to see that she'd already disrobed, and his eyes drank in the sight of her. It was impossible to explain his reaction to her touch. He'd spent his adult life avoiding any touch that brought him pleasure. After what had happened, it seemed easier, safer, to deny that part of him existed. The response was involuntary.

She moved to put her hand on his chest, but he shifted away just enough to make her stop. The moment the hurt crossed her eyes, he wanted to take it back. So he did the only thing he thought might help, and grabbed her hands and put them both on his chest. 'Touch me as you want, Merewyn.'

'I don't want to make you uncomfortable,' she whispered.

'It's not you. It's just that…' There really was no way to explain. The truth would lead to too many questions.

'Does it have anything to do with what Hilla said happened to you?'

Terror knifed through his chest. 'What did she tell you?'

'Nothing. She only mentioned that *something* had happened. That you had known cruelty. Is it true?' The look of genuine concern on her face wrenched his heart, but it also relieved him. She didn't know, or that look would have been disgust.

'Aye,' he whispered.

As she spoke, her hands moved in gentle strokes across the breadth of his chest and up to his shoulders, only to come back down again. Her fingertips caressed the small scars that crossed his chest. 'Do you mean these?'

Those were only scars from the many scrapes of battle. He shook his head and closed his eyes to savour the caress that had seemed terrifying only moments ago. She moved close until the length of her body was pressed against him. One of her hands moved up to his shoulder and then down his back until she just barely grazed the scars that Hilla had been referring to.

'What about these?' she whispered.

He nodded. Those were the ones he tried so hard to forget existed. He couldn't help but flinch at her caress, because acknowledging them opened the door to the memory, and he couldn't let that come over him now. But she must have felt his reticence, because she laid her head against his chest and moved her fingers to lace with his.

'What about your broken nose?'

As if her words had conjured it, the memory of the blow to his face and the shattering pain turned the black behind his eyelids to the red of that day. There had been so much blood. It had felt as though he'd been drowning in his own blood.

She raised her head to look up at him. 'I'd like for you to tell me one day.'

He took in a deep breath and opened his eyes to look down at her. Never. He never wanted to let her know how weak he'd been. She was smiling at him and pulled his head down for a kiss.

'But not tonight.' Her hand tugged him along as she moved towards the tub. 'I want to bathe you again. Will you let me?'

'Aye.' His voice was hoarse from the unshed emotion building within him. He was at a loss to understand how she so easily unmanned him. He'd been set on there being no tenderness or intimacy between them at all. But he'd been a fool, because having her meant letting her inside, and he had no control over it.

As the days settled into a routine of work during the day and time alone with Eirik at night, Hilla's words haunted her. Though it was still difficult to accept the collar, Merewyn began to realise that she was right. Her duties were largely the duties any wife would perform for her husband. See to the meals, the mending of clothes, and once Hilla knew of her skill at weaving, she was given that to do in the evenings when all other duties had been finished. She began to pay particular attention to the women who weren't slaves. The fishermen's wives and those who tended the animals. The only real difference between them and the female slaves, at least on the outside, was the collar. They all worked very hard.

As midwinter set in and drove them all inside, she had even more time with Eirik. They spent many hours in their chamber, where he would spend time teaching her some words from his language. He told her tales of his travels and kept a map set atop a chest so he could point to each place he'd gone. Sometimes he'd even show her the treasures he'd brought back, eager to share them with her.

One night, he gave her a small silver chest he'd said had once belonged to a princess. When she'd opened it to find a rope of gold set with large rubies, he'd set it around her neck so it hung heavy across her breasts. Then he'd made love to her. The necklace was soon joined by more baubles in gold and silver with sapphires, emeralds, amber and even more rubies. Every night she picked a different one to wear, but only in their chamber, where she could pretend that everything was possible.

The collar didn't matter when they were alone. As long as they were together, the world faded away and she belonged to Eirik, though not because she was a slave. He had captured her body and soul, and she feared that he would always own her, even if one day she found herself free.

In her mind, there was no room for thoughts of anyone else holding her, knowing her so intimately. Even in her dreams when she would imagine standing on the shores of her home again, Eirik was there with her. In the cold light of day, when she would tell herself how irrational that thought was, she would remember that the jarl seemed to disapprove of her intimacy with his son. Not so much the sexual aspect, but the other things. Even though Eirik was careful to maintain an impassive demeanour with her, at least in the hall with everyone around, there were small tells. He always made sure she never worked too long, and at the evening meal he carefully selected her food. At night when he would tenderly touch her arm to beckon her to bed or the baths as he walked by, she would occasionally look up to see the jarl frowning at her.

And there were times when Eirik wasn't even in the hall, but she would catch the jarl's eye. He was always frowning, always unhappy with her. He never addressed her directly, never approached her, but he watched. She knew his censure as surely as if he had voiced his displeasure to her. Whether it was true or not, in his mind she had usurped

Kadlin's place in Eirik's life. Merewyn feared that he would never accept her, even if they someday married.

She didn't know how it would be possible to live there and marry Eirik. The jarl would make it unbearable. She didn't know how it would be possible to return home and marry Eirik. Alfred would make that impossible. The only thing she did know was that she loved him and it would be impossible for her to live apart from him. Even if it meant hiding themselves away at his farm. The only problem with that plan was that spring was looming and she knew that he planned to leave her then to join the invasion of her homeland. She was afraid if he did that she might never see him again.

They needed more time, but time was not on their side.

Chapter Twenty-Six

The long weeks of the usually bleak winter passed in the blink of an eye for Eirik. He couldn't remember a time he'd felt so happy, for the lack of a better word. His days were filled with strategy and mead, while his nights were filled with Merewyn. It should bother him that he was going soft, but it didn't. It should bother him that he longed for her company more than the brotherhood of his warriors, but it didn't. His craving for her was deeper than the flesh. She was a salve to his wounds. The closer the time came to leave for battle, the more he actually dreaded leaving.

For the first time in his life, he imagined a future for himself that didn't include battle and sitting at his father's table, eventually taking his place. Aye, he'd always had the dream of living on his farm, but that dream had always been a temporary respite from fighting. A few short weeks of rest at a time to recover and then return to his real life. It had never been a plan that was meant to be permanent. Now it was the only way he could think that would enable him to keep Merewyn. But even that was fantasy, because his father would never allow that to happen. Eirik knew, too, that he couldn't turn his back on the people who depended on him. There seemed to be no answer.

He assumed that was why he craved to spend every waking moment with her. Their future together was so tenuous he wanted to soak up every bit of her while he had the chance. Unfortunately, it also meant that the nightmares had come back to torment him. Except they had changed. While he sometimes still dreamed of what had happened, he usually dreamed of what would happen when she found out. The way she would look at him. That was the nightmare that had awoken him just now. Someone had told her and she had turned from him. In that way, loving her was a curse. But he was willing to live with it if it meant having her.

Especially if it meant waking up from them next to her. It was late and there he sat in bed, trembling like a newborn lamb on weak legs from the aftereffects. She turned towards his warmth, her thigh draping across his and her arm finding his waist. Even then, even with the memory of the terror flowing through him, he wanted to turn to her and bury himself in her warmth, to hide his face in her neck and find oblivion with her. But he couldn't wake her; it would bring forth too many questions. It would mean she would see him as vulnerable as she had that one night and he couldn't let that happen.

So after running his palm along the firm length of her thigh, he gently pulled a blanket over her and slipped away before making his way to the fur rug. His intent was to go to the small fire and add wood, but he was too pathetic to go that far just yet. Instead, he collapsed and took deep breaths until he could regain some measure of his former strength.

'Eirik?'

He closed his eyes as her voice reached him through the mellow darkness. 'Go back to sleep.' Even to his own ears, his voice sounded weak. He silently cursed the demon that drained him.

But it was too late. The blankets rustled as she moved to her feet and soon her hand was on his shoulder. She didn't speak, but pulled a blanket over them and put her arms around him. They stayed that way for a while until his shaking had stopped and his heartbeat returned to normal.

'Why haven't you told me the nightmares still plague you?' she whispered against his back.

'They always plague me. It's not your problem.'

'Oh, Eirik.' She tugged his shoulder and moved over him so that he could see the outline of her face in the meagre light. 'Why do you shut me out? I don't care what happened to you, except that it still bothers you.'

He wanted to laugh, but he didn't because it would have hurt her. No matter her intentions, she *would* care once she knew the truth. There was no way she couldn't. He wouldn't even blame her for caring. The truth was, he was starting to feel guilty for not telling her, for making her believe that he was someone he wasn't. She deserved to know the truth about the man she was spending her life with. He knew he didn't deserve her.

He rubbed his knuckles across her shadowed cheekbone and imagined the concern he would see in her expressive eyes. 'Trust me, Merewyn. It's better that you don't know.'

'Better for you?' There was a bit of pique in her voice.

He swallowed. Aye, that was exactly what he meant. He couldn't bear that moment, that look that would cross her face.

'You want to keep me away from you.'

'It's for your own good, sweet girl. Please believe me.'

'Nay, I don't believe you. You're leaving in the morning and you haven't even told me yet. Is that better for me or better for you?'

He was surprised she knew, but assumed Hilla must have mentioned it. It seemed the jarls to the south-east needed convincing, and with only a month until they set sail, he needed to go convince them. 'I didn't want to concern you. What's the difference if you spend the days before I leave dreading my departure or if I tell you in the morning? I still leave either way.'

'It matters because you…because we…I thought that…I thought that I meant something more to you than just a slave, just a plaything to fill your evenings with amusement.'

He changed their positions so fast that she gasped in surprise. He sat up and pulled her into his lap, one arm holding her tight while the fingers of his other one twined in the silk of her hair. 'You do matter to me. Your happiness is all that I want.'

'But not if it means giving yourself to me.'

'I am yours in more ways than you will ever know.' It hurt him that she would never know because he could never tell her. What good did it do to tell her that he longed to have her as his wife when it was impossible? What good did it do to tell her that Kadlin's bizarre notions of love were suddenly beginning to make sense to him? It would do no good at all. Eventually, what was between them would end, because there was no great future for a jarl and his slave. This was it for them. He knew her well enough now to know that she wouldn't be able to accept what he could offer her. For now, aye, but not for ever.

'Are you?' Then she deflated. Her breath came out in a rush and she wrapped her arms around him. 'I have dreams that we are married and living on the farm,' she confessed after a moment.

His forehead touched hers and he stroked her back. 'I have those same dreams.' It came out before he could stifle it, but it felt right to say it out loud and let her know.

'I want to marry you, Eirik.' Her breath caressed his cheek as she spoke.

He almost shivered at the pleasure the words evoked in him. Their marriage couldn't happen, but he was pleased that she wanted it as much as he did. His lips brushed hers in a soft kiss of atonement for what could never be. 'I promise to take care of you for as long as you'll have me.'

'We can't marry.' The words came out a bit stilted, evidence of her pain, followed by a solitary tear that fell to his chest from her cheek. 'Ever.'

He took a deep breath and said the words that he'd never wanted to say. 'My duty is to my people. I am the next jarl. Even if I set you free, our marriage is not a choice I'm free to make.' His fingers still trembled against her skin, but he wasn't sure if it was because of his dream or the emotion coursing through him now.

'What of your wants and needs, Eirik?'

He stroked her back and pulled her closer. 'You are what I want and need. I think I knew it even then, when I first saw you on the beach.'

'Will you set me free?'

His breath caught at the pain of those words. He'd always expected to hear them at some point, but always further in the future. 'Do you want to be free of me? Would you choose your family over me now…still?'

'Nay, Eirik.' Her forehead pressed against his and her breath rushed over his cheek. 'But I can't be a slave.'

'Merewyn, please understand that your collar is

the only means I have of protecting you when I'm not around. You're not a slave to me. I just don't have another option right now.'

She shook her head and drew away from him, but he held her tight. 'Nay, Eirik.' She struggled against him and pushed his chest. 'I can't accept that from you. What happens when you leave? Despite how you feel, everyone else sees me as a slave. How do you think I'll be treated when you leave? Do you suppose Eirik's slave will be given special treatment?'

'I do think that. They know you are mine, and even when I'm not here, my word will be respected.'

'You're deceiving yourself. You are not jarl yet and your father is. He doesn't want me here.' She pulled and he finally let her go.

'He's already promised to keep you safe, Merewyn. It's not a problem.' He wanted to hold her, to stroke her and assure her that everything would be fine, but she wouldn't listen now. Morning was fast approaching, and he didn't want to leave things between them like this, but she was being unreasonable. He grabbed the fur and pulled it around his waist as he rose to his feet. He wanted to pace, but still felt a bit weak, so he sat with one hip on the edge of the bed. 'I'm not sure what you want from me.'

She was silent as she grabbed another fur from the bed and walked to add more wood to the fire. In its glow, he admired her noble profile. She stood staring into the flames, her back rigid with anger and the fur tight around her shoulders.

After a moment, she spoke. Her voice was calm with a thread of anger underneath. 'I want you to understand that while you ask everything of me, you hold back from me.' When he opened his mouth to rebuke that, she held up her hand to hold him off. 'It's true. I'm to give up my life—I'll admit, it wasn't a very complete life—to accept a life as your slave. You say there can't be marriage, and I suppose I understand that. But there is a part of you that you hold back from me. I can't know you, really know you, without understanding you and what happened.'

He staggered from the blow. 'Merewyn, you don't know what you ask of me.'

'Nay, I don't know.' When she turned to face him, he could tell the anger had drained from her face and shoulders. 'But I know that your nightmares plague you almost nightly. I know that whatever it is, it's tearing you apart inside. I know that you fear telling me. I could understand that, except I feel that you don't want to tell me because you don't trust me to know. I love you, Eirik, more than I've ever loved anyone. It frightens me that you don't trust me. It frightens me that my feelings for you are deeper than yours are for me. It frightens me to know that you will be in battle soon and we may never have a chance to—'

He crossed to her and pulled her into his arms, unable to bear the pain of her words. He buried his nose in the silk of her hair and breathed her in. When he could finally speak, he didn't recognise his own voice. 'Don't be afraid. I'm as lost as you are, Merewyn, I swear it. I'd be a broken man without you.' She trembled against him, so he held her tighter and came to a resolution. He couldn't offer her marriage, couldn't offer her any more of himself than he already had. But he could give her this. If she turned away from him, it would crush him as nothing else ever could, but he could give her this choice. 'I'll tell you.'

'Eirik…' She kept her arms tight around his waist. 'You don't have to tell me now. That's not what I want. I don't want to force it from you. I just want to know that someday you will feel that you can.' Now that her anger had drained, she felt guilty for pushing him into something that so obviously made him uncomfortable. It wasn't right.

His hands rubbed small circles on her back. 'I know what you want, Merewyn. I want it, too, but I can't give it to you. This is what I can do now.'

She looked up at his beloved features in the firelight and noted the shadows under his eyes. She couldn't resist touching his lips, and smiled when he kissed her fingertips. 'You don't have to. I can wait until you're ready.'

He leaned down and placed a gentle kiss on her lips, but he wasn't smiling, even when he pulled back to meet her gaze. 'You deserve to know. You're right. I've been keeping it from you because I've been afraid it would push you away from me. But that should be your choice. Besides, sooner or later you'll hear tales from someone else. I'd rather you know the truth from me.'

'Are you sure?'

'Aye.' He dropped his arms to take her hand and lead her back to the bed. Once inside, he pulled the bed curtains so it was dark and only a hint of the firelight could be seen. 'I do have a request.' His voice reached her through the darkness.

'Anything.'

She wasn't sure if she only imagined the faint tremor of his voice when he spoke. 'I want you to promise to stay the rest of the night and don't say anything. Whatever I tell you, please don't say anything.'

She nodded, but then realised that he couldn't see her, so she found her voice. 'I won't say anything.' Her skin prickled with the awareness that something was about to happen that would change everything.

'Then come lie with me.' His hands took hers and pulled her down so that she was lying on her side with her back to his front. He pulled the furs over them and wrapped his arms around her. It was a while longer before he began to speak. His voice was strong and, even now, betrayed no emotion.

'My father's punishment for stealing is to take a finger. One fast slice of his blade through the joint.' He ran his forefinger lightly across hers to demonstrate the motion. 'It's harsh, but it's a clean cut that heals and doesn't usually fester. Not on the surface, at least. It festers in the brain instead.

'There were three men who received this particular punishment for stealing his sheep. I don't know why they did it and I didn't know them before the day they found Gunnar and I out fishing. We were just boys. They jumped us from behind before we even had a chance to fight them off. Before we knew it, we were bound while the bastards built a fire and cooked our fish. They laughed the whole time about how they would cook us next.

'I still don't know how I managed to do it, but I found a rock with an edge just jagged enough to cut the binding on my wrists while they gorged themselves. By the time I had cut Gunnar loose, one of them saw us and I fell along the rocks as we ran. They got me, but Gunnar got away to get help.'

Merewyn closed her eyes, unwilling to hear what happened next, but unable to tell him to stop. She saw the scars on his otherwise perfect back and could only imagine how they had been put there. Suddenly, she didn't want to know or imagine his pain. She bit her lip to keep herself quiet, but she couldn't stop the slight trembling of her body as she listened. He felt it and tightened his grip around her.

'One of them threw a rock and hit me in the head. It kept me down until they could get to me and bash me across the face.' His voice trailed off as he re-lived the memory.

'Eirik, please—' But his fingers covered her lips.

'Shh. No words now.' Then he took a deep breath and continued. She sensed then that it had become something that he needed to tell her, so she snuggled back against him and laced her fingers with his. 'I was bound when I awoke and strapped to a log. They had taken my clothes. One of them had a knife and boasted that they would carve their names into my back. You've seen it, but it's not their names anymore.'

She frowned and opened her mouth to ask what he meant when she remembered her vow of silence. But he knew her confusion. 'Aye, I wanted it gone, so we obscured it.'

With more scars. The words hung in the silence between them. She couldn't imagine what it had taken to submit himself to that pain all over again so their marks could be erased from his body for ever. Tears seeped silently down her face.

'After they carved their names…' He paused and took a deep breath. His trembling matched her own. When he spoke again, his voice was softer. 'They violated me. One after the other, and I was too weak to stop them.' He buried his face in her hair so the next part was muffled. 'My father came later, but too late to stop them.'

She couldn't stop her tears from coming harder as she imagined the boy Eirik had been, subjected to such torture. It made her physically ill to imagine him in such pain. He must have felt so hopeless, so utterly abandoned to them and their horror. Now he must feel that she'd think less of him because of what had happened. She wanted to tell him how brave she thought he was, how his pain hurt her, how she wanted to hold him and keep him safe so that he never had to experience pain again. She turned to do that, but he raised his head to look down at her. Even in the shadows of the dark, she could see that his face was tortured.

'Please, Merewyn, you promised.'

So instead of talking, she pulled him down into her embrace. He made a sound, but stifled it as he pressed his face to her neck. It was only then that she felt the heat of his tears against her skin. It made hers come all the harder.

She thought back to his own capture of her and realised exactly how gentle he'd been. Dear God, it could have been so much worse for her. But he was too kind, too good to want anyone to live through what had happened to him. Even that first day on his boat, he'd tended to the scrapes the ropes had left behind because he couldn't bear to see her hurt. She was so lucky that he had found her. She wanted to tell him that, and vowed that she would in the morning before he left.

But when she awoke the next morning, he was gone.

Chapter Twenty-Seven

Merewyn didn't take her supper on the dais anymore. In fact, she avoided it at all costs, even pleading with Hilla to have her do something else besides serve there. The jarl had set a precedent of ignoring her, and she felt it best to honour his disposition. She kept to herself, helping with the cooking and weaving and doing her best to not think of Eirik and their words from that last night. But he was everywhere, especially in their chamber, where his scent still lingered, and she wondered if he was warm enough or missing her as much as she missed him.

She couldn't wait to see him again and assure him of how much she loved him. Though she still didn't know what their future would bring. When he was around she could almost pretend that their relationship was sustainable, but when he was gone there was nothing to give her the illusion that her station had been elevated. The slave's food and clothing, not to mention the collar, reminded her. How much worse would that be when he left in the spring to invade her homeland? She could hardly stomach the thought, the senseless slaughter that would surely erupt. And to be left behind, to be left to the whims of his father and perhaps even his brother, made the situation infinitely worse. So she tried her best not to think beyond their time together.

Gunnar, who had been absent the whole winter, returned at the beginning of the third week of Eirik's absence. He simply walked in during the evening meal. He was dirty and unkempt, and his hair looked as though it hadn't been cut since she'd last seen him. Then, the hair on the sides of his head above his ears had been shaved, but that had grown in to make him look almost feral.

From her vantage point behind the slaves' partition, she hadn't seen Gunnar until he'd reached the dais. She didn't see the men he'd brought in with him until they walked farther into the house, perhaps on their way to leave the numerous packs they'd brought in with them before the jarl. She'd never seen the men before and wondered if they belonged there or were simply visiting. Their presence probably had something to do with the upcoming invasion, so she looked back to her work and tried to ignore them. Thoughts of the war only filled her with melancholy and anger.

Unfortunately, her presence hadn't been forgotten. About an hour later the jarl called for her. His voice rose up over all the others in the room as he called her. He didn't call her by name, he simply called out 'slave', but there was no doubt to anyone that he meant her. All eyes turned to watch her. As she stood and smoothed her skirt, she noticed her hands were shaking, so she put them into fists at her sides and approached the dais.

Gunnar and the two men he'd brought along had joined the jarl at his table. One of them had taken Eirik's place. Vidar appeared to have gone to bed. Sweyn had gone with Eirik, so she was alone with no allies, except for maybe Hilla. But she doubted the woman's willingness to go up against the jarl.

Jarl Hegard spoke an order, and by now, though her spoken Norse wasn't as good, she could comprehend the meaning of his words, even if she didn't understand every one of them. 'Serve our guests, slave.'

Gunnar translated to be sure there was no doubt she understood. 'He would have a noble serve our guests.' He wasn't smiling, but she could see that a smile lurked in the depths of his amber eyes. 'Not to worry, fair noblewoman, they lack any discernible manners, so simply place the platters of food close enough and your job is done. It's the same principle for feeding mongrels.'

She took a deep breath and wished she hadn't. The smell coming from the two newcomers was horrid. Gunnar, though, appeared to have visited the bathhouse before the meal. His hair was still unkempt, but his person was clean and he'd donned fresh clothing. She nodded and tried not to breathe when she got close to them. Gunnar was right. Their table manners were atrocious, so she didn't watch them as she stood by, waiting to be summoned for more mead. Halfway through, Gunnar indicated that she switch them to ale, and the men didn't seem to notice.

He did notice her, though, and kept a watchful eye on her as he ate. When he finished, he sat back and looked at her. 'They can't understand us, so I'd have the truth from you, girl.'

'Why should I tell you anything?'

He smiled. 'You don't have to. But I've heard that my brother has a fondness for you, and I'd like to know if it's true.'

She supposed it wasn't surprising that people had talked of her and Eirik. He had never taken another woman to his bed before, but it was still disturbing to be talked about. Also, she wasn't completely sure what Gunnar would gain from knowing the truth about them.

When she was silent, he shrugged. 'Tell me this, then—do you still want to return home?'

She didn't know the answer to that question. It had been one that she'd been struggling with ever since Eirik had left. She didn't want to leave him, but she could see no future with him at his home. 'I want to be with Eirik,' she stated softly.

He didn't say anything else, and the other men continued eating even after the hall had quieted and most people had sought their sleep. Her own eyelids were starting to droop, and the conversation at the dais faded to a steady drone that she couldn't be bothered to struggle to interpret anymore. She began to fervently hope the meal would end soon; her only wish was to go to bed and dream of Eirik. It still smelled like him and helped to keep her feeling close to him. But before she could go to it, she was called to refill their ale. This time a hand on her wrist stopped her from moving away when she'd finished.

Enslaved by the Viking

Their glances had grown more lascivious as the night had progressed, but now the man who held her arm looked at her with open lust on his face. The idea was sickening, and she became frightened when the jarl laughed at the man's impertinence. The hand tightened on her wrist while his other hand went to her hip. She was thrown momentarily off balance when the man pulled her close, forcing her to lean into him to keep upright. His hand moved from her hip to cup a buttock.

Merewyn dropped the pitcher of ale and pressed firmly against his shoulders, but the man didn't budge. The resistance seemed like a game to him that made him laugh and bury his face in her breasts. His fingers pressed into her, and the only thing stopping his invasion of her body was the thick wool of her dress.

'Nay, please, I belong to Lord Eirik!' Then in his language she cried out, 'I'm Eirik's slave!' The words made a few people raise their heads to look at her, but no one moved to stop the man. Even the jarl didn't seem fazed by it. She looked to Gunnar, her plea in her eyes, but he only watched, his expression bored and unchanged from just moments before. She looked to Jarl Hegard. 'Eirik would not want this!'

But the other guest wasn't to be left out, and he reached for her other arm. His hand was like a vise around her forearm as he pulled her towards him. He spoke angry words to the jarl, something about how she should be given to him first, and then moved his hand to grab a fistful of her hair. Dear Lord, he was demanding her for himself! She felt like a toy being pulled between two boys.

'Father!' Her gaze jerked to Gunnar, who had spoken. 'If the slave is to be enjoyed by anyone, then it should be me.'

'Let our guests have her.' Jarl Hegard smiled without looking away from the spectacle. His gaze caught hers and she saw the triumph shining in their depths. He'd wanted this to happen, had intended for it to happen when he'd had her serve the mongrels.

'I want her! I found her in that cellar. She should be mine. I'll not have this filth ruin her first.'

The filth in question seemed too busy fighting over their new bone to take offence at his words. But she had heard them and understood them and honestly didn't know if he would be worse than them. She didn't want any of them. She wanted to be Eirik's wife so none of this would happen. She wanted to live somewhere she didn't have to worry about being taken away from him. In complete despair, she fought them. Somehow she wrenched her arms away and began scratching and pounding until she was let go. The freedom didn't last long, however.

She wanted to kick and scream and fight until they all lay there broken and unable to torment her, but just as she raised her foot, someone picked her up from a great height. Almost immediately she realised it was Gunnar. He turned her so she was lying over his shoulder, exactly as she had been on their first meeting. So she fought him again, just as she had then.

The jarl stood. 'Gunnar!'

'Would you deny me my due? Again, Father? I take enough seconds around here. I will not take seconds from them.' He waved his hand at the two men in disgust. 'Let them have whatever is left of her.'

'But Eirik. Think of your brother.'

'*Now* you think of him? Think you he would be pleased you give her to them?' Gunnar nodded to the two men, who were looking at him with murder in their eyes, but given how they swayed on their feet, she wasn't sure they'd be much trouble for him.

'I don't care if he kills *them*, but I won't have that slave come between you. She's caused enough trouble.'

Gunnar laughed. 'He would kill them, aye, but you wouldn't go unscathed. You've lost your own game and you don't even know it.'

The jarl said nothing and no one intervened as he took her to his chamber and locked the door.

Chapter Twenty-Eight

She screamed when Gunnar slung her off his shoulder so that she landed with a thump on his bed. She prepared herself for the inevitable fight, but was taken aback when he simply stood there smirking down at her, mischief lighting the amber in his eyes so that they seemed to glow.

'You've lost your mind,' she concluded. 'Eirik will kill you.'

His gaze travelled the length of her body, his cheek smarting red where she'd landed a blow with her elbow as she struggled. Good. It served him right.

'He might try, but he'll be glad you're safe. Unless he left you for the use of our guests?' His brow rose on that.

'Nay, the jarl betrayed his trust.'

'The jarl.' He laughed without mirth and shook his head. 'The jarl has a bad habit of meddling.

He chose that demonstration so you'd know your place. Eirik places too much faith in fools.'

Merewyn took a deep breath to try to slow the beating of heart. Her body was still tensed for a fight, but it looked as if Gunnar wasn't after a fight. Was he? She knew what he said was true. Jarl Hegard had looked at her with such triumph, there was no doubt that he had orchestrated the entire situation so that she would know she had no place there as anything other than a slave. How did he know that what she wanted above anything else was to be Eirik's wife? How did he know just how to hurt her? There was no doubt left that he would stand in the way of any marriage between Eirik and herself.

'Is my desire to be more to Eirik so obvious?' She hadn't been aware she'd spoken the despairing question aloud until he answered her.

'I wouldn't know. I've only just arrived. But you're a noblewoman. It's not a surprise that you'd not want to settle for being his slave, his pleasure slave at that, unless I've misread the situation.'

She blushed and looked away, unwilling to discuss her intimacy with Eirik.

He laughed again, a short bark of laughter that raked across her, unsettling her. 'So the truth comes out. He is bedding you, which means my debt is finally paid. Move over.'

She barely had time to move out of the way before he flopped down on to his back beside her. She immediately scrambled to the foot of the bed, her legs protectively curled to her chest. He rubbed his hands over his face, as though he was suddenly very weary, and when he dropped them he regarded her with a heavy-lidded gaze. 'Don't worry, little slave. I won't touch you, even though I'm sure I'd enjoy it very much. Unless you want me to. I can promise you'd enjoy it, too.' That smirk was back in his eyes, baiting her.

'Eirik would kill you.'

'I won't tell if you won't.'

She looked away. She'd never known him to tease her before and didn't know how to react to this side of him.

By the light of the single candle in the room she could see that the chamber was similar to Eirik's. There were treasures displayed on the few wooden shelves and chests that she didn't doubt held even more. But there weren't as many. Perhaps that was a reflection of his status as a younger son or bastard son. Eirik had explained his parentage and she had to wonder if that accounted for his foul mood most of the time.

Now that the initial heat of the confrontation was beginning to fade, her body shook a bit. She wrapped her arms tighter about her legs to hold the shaking at bay. The realisation of just how close she'd come to being given to those horrible men was nearly overwhelming. She couldn't exist here as a slave. She couldn't.

'He won't marry you, if that is what you want.'

His voice cut through her thoughts, as sharp as a blade cutting fat from the flesh. She flinched—she couldn't stop her reaction any more than she could stop the complete hopelessness that settled over her. Though Eirik had already told her as much, she'd still held out hope that she could make him see how good things could be if she was his wife.

'You're cruel.' She refused to look at him, and kept her head down on her knees.

'I'm sorry. I don't say it to be cruel. But you have to know what's at stake for him. Eirik wants to be jarl. Hegard wants Eirik to be jarl. A jarl cannot wed a slave.'

'I am a noblewoman. I would be his equal back home.' She despised the tremble of her voice.

'But you're not home, little slave. You are here,

and here you are a slave. Even if he frees you, your status would be too low for a jarl's wife. Though, I grant, you'd be an excellent mistress.'

Merewyn closed her eyes against the pain the truth of those words caused. Was that her lot, to accept being a mistress when he took a wife? She couldn't share him, couldn't know that he took his pleasure with another, or that another gave him pleasure. He would have children with a wife, and what of her own children? Would they be like Gunnar? Reduced to second best with little hope of having their father's endorsement?

'Wouldn't he be jarl no matter who he weds? He is the heir, is he not?' She did look at him then, not caring if her words were harsh.

'He is not. Sometimes the jarldom passes to the eldest, like with the farms, but sometimes there is bloodshed if someone else has a claim or wants it enough and has the warriors to support him. Eirik wants to be jarl. It's the only thing he's ever wanted his entire life. He won't risk men not endorsing his claim because he married his pleasure slave, noble as she may be.'

She had to pause before she spoke to fight the painful lump that had swollen in her throat. Nay, Eirik would not marry her if it meant he would lose his place. He'd spent his entire life preparing to be jarl. 'Do you want to be jarl, Gunnar? Don't you have a claim?'

'Of course I do, and I'd like it very much.'

'How much? Enough for bloodshed?'

'Perhaps.'

She stifled her gasp of surprise and outrage. He spoke so calmly, as if they were discussing something besides the death of his brother. 'Then why save me from those men if you hate Eirik so much?'

'I never said that I hated my brother, only that I want to be jarl. I don't harbor ill will for him. But that has nothing to do with saving your virtue. I owed him a debt and now it's repaid.'

She took a deep breath and broached a subject she was almost certain she shouldn't be discussing with him. 'Do you mean that you owe him a debt because you left him that day?'

'He told you?' She couldn't have shocked him more if she had sprouted a horn on top of her head.

She nodded, unsure of his thoughts and if she should have mentioned it.

His demeanour changed from lazy indifference to hot anger, though if it was anger at himself or her, she couldn't tell. He sat up, eyes blazing as he pinned her with his gaze. 'Aye, because I did nothing. I did nothing and he suffered. Go to sleep. If you know what's good for you, you'll stay here in this chamber until he returns. If you do go out, limp a little so it'll seem authentic. As a matter of fact, you haven't screamed in a while.' He lunged for her, and she did scream as she jumped away, falling over the edge of the bed to the floor.

He poised above her on the bed, knees spread wide. In that moment, she realised that he was every bit as powerful as Eirik, his frame large and exuding strength. His eyes were fierce and bold as they touched her. 'I told you I wouldn't touch you. I'm not quite the villain you seem to think I am, but the scream sounded convincing.' He smirked as he turned, but she couldn't help but feel that she'd let him down.

'I didn't mean that I agreed with you. That you owed him a debt.'

'Of course I do. He yelled for me to run and I didn't even look back. What could one eleven-year-old boy do but run? I ran. It seemed like hours before I found a washerwoman downriver. She sent her boy to find Father and I ran back to help Eirik, but I could do nothing. Nothing but hide and listen to his screams as they beat him.' He took a deep breath, his voice almost shaking with fury when he spoke next. 'I could only…only listen and do nothing.'

'You were only eleven.'

'Well, my father thinks I should have died to help him. Perhaps I do, too.'

'You didn't—'

'Just go to sleep. This isn't open for discussion.'

The stir of pity in her chest surprised her. Gunnar was a hardened, cynical man, but her heart ached for the guilt-ridden boy. As he settled down to sleep, Merewyn stayed huddled on the floor at the foot of the bed, and her thoughts turned inwards. Eirik would never be hers here. Gunnar's words had driven the point home. They were doomed to part. She had always feared it, known it somewhere deep down to be true, but now it was confirmed.

A trembling hand went to her belly. Her menses were only two weeks late, not nearly late enough to be sure, but she *knew* a tiny life grew inside her. Her breasts ached constantly, and there was a heaviness in her middle, a strange fullness that she'd never felt before. It was time to think about her child. If she stayed, he or she could grow up like Gunnar. Bitter and resentful, especially if—*when*—Eirik married and had children with a wife.

She closed her eyes at the mere thought and pushed it away.

She curled into a ball as her emotions warred within herself for dominance. There was no easy answer, but she knew that the same man who cared for her so tenderly wouldn't treat his children with the cold callousness of the jarl. She couldn't leave him. But neither could she stay. The jarl had made sure of it.

Merewyn awoke a split second before the door splintered and broke away from the wooden hinges that held it in its frame. The fire was banked in the hearth, but it gave off enough of a glow that she could see Eirik standing there. Her heart gave a little jolt when she realised her wait was over. She'd spent the past five nights in Gunnar's room waiting for the two men to leave so they wouldn't dare think they would deserve time with her.

But her eyes narrowed as she came to the realisation that there was no happiness on his face. He was not in the least pleased to see her. In fact, she wondered if he'd even seen her, as the focus of his sole attention was Gunnar, who was just stirring in bed. He came to his room every night inebriated to the point of oblivion and barely paid her any mind as she slept on a pallet on the floor.

Her cry of warning was the only thing that roused his attention, just before Eirik roared an oath and ran towards his brother, sword held high over his head. The look on his face was reminiscent of that night he'd beaten the man who had assaulted her at Kadlin's. There was no trace of pity or mercy in the hard features. She blanched and watched in stunned helplessness as the sword swooped down skilfully to find its mark.

Gunnar came to just in time to dodge the blow and launch himself to the far side of the bed. He came up looking a bit dazed, but his face cleared quickly enough when Eirik swung at him again. Gunnar jumped away, causing the sword to crash through one of the bedposts. There was a spray of splinters as the weight of the bed curtains pulled the supporting wood beams down at the corner. As Eirik fought the heavy fabric, Gunnar ran to where his own sword rested in its place on the wall between the bed and the door.

Eirik pulled free just as Gunnar got his hands around the grip and yanked it down. The two blades met with a deafening clang. As they moved, she saw very clearly how the two brothers were vastly different. Eirik was strong and steady, striking with precision and control for all that he was angry, where Gunnar was fast and unpredictable, almost wild in his strikes. Despite their differences, they were a good match, neither of them giving nor gaining ground for long.

'Stop fighting him, Eirik. It's not what you think. He saved me.' Her words didn't seem to get through. 'Gunnar saved me!' she yelled louder, to no effect. Just when she was figuring out how to insert herself into the fray, Jarl Hegard came in, followed by Sweyn, each bearing his own sword.

She had an insane vision of the three of them fighting to the death when the older man ran between them. But Eirik seemed to come to his senses and backed away to allow room for the jarl, though he still held his sword as if ready to swing it. His powerful forearms flexed beneath his sleeves, and his shoulders were tense, ready to strike. Gunnar was shirtless and already his torso was soaked in a sheen of sweat. He, too, was tense, not trusting the interruption to be more than temporary.

'I will kill you for touching her!' Eirik's voice was clear and steady above the jarl's softer murmur.

'Are you sure she's still yours?' Gunnar's taunt landed, and then the shouting began.

Eirik lunged, but his father's bulky frame held him at bay. The jarl urged them both to calm themselves and wanted them to go to the hall to talk. Eirik was on the cusp of disregarding his father and laying into Gunnar. She saw it in the way his fingers flexed around the grip of the sword, so she rushed forward and grabbed his arm. 'Eirik, I am unharmed. Gunnar saved me.'

His gaze jerked to her as if he had forgotten her presence. The rage and momentary blankness in his stare made her step back in befuddlement. This was not the tender lover who had left her just weeks ago. This was the Viking, tortured and controlled, who had enslaved her.

'Gunnar saved me. Your father was going to give me to two men who were visiting and Gunnar brought me to his room and I've stayed here since. He protected me.'

Eirik looked first to Gunnar, who stared back at him with fury blazing in his eyes, and then to the jarl, who had the grace to look chastened. 'You would give her away? You vowed to keep her safe.' His voice was so calm it sent a ripple of terror down her spine.

The jarl stared back at him before answering, 'She has no place here. My first duty is to your future.'

Those few words made the tension in Eirik's shoulders drain away, so that when he took a few steps back, the sword hung down at his side. He looked as if the air had been knocked out of him, but in moments he'd recovered and his face was hard, resolute.

'Come.' He grabbed her arm and pulled her with him as he walked towards their chamber.

'You cannot keep her!' The jarl's voice followed them, bringing Eirik to a stop just before walking out the door.

'I will keep her.' Eirik glared at him.

'You will *marry*. If not Kadlin, then someone else worthy of you, not this slave.'

'She is a noblewoman.' The continued calm of Eirik's voice made her uneasy.

'She is nothing here. She will never be anything here. You will never be anything here if you keep her.'

Eirik's jaw worked as he watched his father. She wanted to intervene, to offer some solution, but could only watch in horror at the drama playing out before her. Then Eirik's gaze shot to his brother and he spoke, addressing Gunnar and then Sweyn. 'We leave for Northumbria in three days. Start loading the boats.'

Chapter Twenty-Nine

Eirik grabbed her arm and pulled her to their chamber. Once there he let her go, slammed the door and sheathed his sword before throwing it across the room so that it knocked down an entire shelf. Its contents went clattering across the floor. She jumped, but didn't take her eyes from him. Outwardly, he looked calm, deathly calm, and that frightened her. She wanted to hold him, to assure him that things would be fine, but she couldn't. She didn't know that anything would be fine.

Giving him a moment to calm himself, she went around the room lighting candles before coming to stand before him. 'Eirik, I know what you must have thought. You left that morning before you let me talk to you.'

He closed his eyes, and her gaze caught on his throat as he swallowed hard. When he opened them, he seemed to do so with new resolve, and he looked at her, but she wasn't sure that he was actually seeing her. It made her chest ache to know that he expected her to reject him, or that maybe he had thought she had chosen Gunnar over him.

'I still love you. Nothing that happened in your past could ever change that. I love the man you are now...the one who stole me from my home, but gave me so much more than I had before.' She approached him as she spoke, but was still hesitant to touch him. He seemed almost like a stranger to her, this new person who stood before her with all of his secrets finally bared. But not as foreign as she had imagined when they had first stood together in this very chamber. He was the Eirik she loved, only better because now she really knew him. There was suddenly so much more to explore together.

That thought gave her the courage to touch his chest, her hands moving slowly but with purpose up to his shoulders. 'There will never be another man I choose over you. Never.'

He shuddered beneath her palms and watched her warily. 'How can you say that when I am so weak?'

'Not weak. You had no choice. You survived, and you're even stronger for it.'

But he shook his head. 'I did survive, but not without damage. I don't know if I'll ever be whole again. Do you know that the entire time I was gone I didn't have a single nightmare, but I still couldn't sleep because I needed you? What kind of warrior am I?'

She wanted to smile, but kept the way her heart flipped in her chest to herself. 'A warrior in love.' Certain of her place now, she slowly stroked a hand down the broad expanse of his chest and over his flat stomach. 'I love you. Please let me show you that you're worthy of love, of pleasure.'

He didn't move, and his breath came heavy above her ear. For a moment they simply stood locked in an embrace, but when he didn't resist, she moved her hand lower until she cupped him. He hardened and lengthened beneath her touch. He wanted her touch. When she was certain he wasn't going to push her away, she squeezed gently and moved her hand in a rhythmic stroke against him. His ragged gasp of pleasure made her heart leap in happiness, which made her bold in her eagerness to touch him. She worked her hand in the waistband of his trousers and reached in to grab the hard velvet length of him. She closed her fingers around him, noting that he was hotter than she'd imagined he would be, and moved her palm in smooth, even strokes up and down his length.

His breath grew harsher with every stroke, exciting her, making her hand work faster to bring him to release. His hips moved into the grip of her hand, eager for her stroke, while his hands gripped her hips, holding her tight. When he began thrusting against her, she realised he was close and knew a strange desire to taste him as he had tasted her. She stopped caressing him and pushed against his embrace to move to her knees before him. When her eyes met his, she didn't even have to voice her request. His eyes were like flames burning into her.

The fingers of one hand tangled in her hair to hold her steady. It was the small bit of control he would always maintain, but she didn't care. Even that excited her. His thumb stroked her bottom lip and then pressed so that she opened to let it inside. She sucked it while his other hand worked the fastenings on his trousers until he freed his length and pressed the head to her lips, replacing his thumb. Greedy for him, she let him inside and held tight to his hips as he thrust in short, shallow pumps until the saltwater taste of him bathed her tongue and his groans filled the room.

He let her go and pressed his hands heavily against the door to support himself. His legs trembled, and she wondered briefly if he might wish for her to not touch him now, but she couldn't stop. Her hands moved up his hips, over his stomach and up to his shoulders as she stood. Before he could say anything, she kissed him, her hands meeting behind his neck to hold him close. Much to her delight, he caressed her back as he pulled her close. His entire body shook against hers, but instead of hiding it, or pushing her away, he held her tighter.

She squeezed her eyes shut to block the tears of joy that had come to them.

His lips trailed kisses across her cheekbone and down her neck. 'Thank you,' he whispered against her ear as he lifted her, so that she put her legs around his waist, and walked them to bed.

There he took his time and undressed her, kissing each part of her that he revealed, until he was ready for her again. She cried when he joined with her, because it was so perfect and beautiful and everything she knew couldn't last.

The morning beckoned, but Eirik couldn't summon the strength to leave her just yet. He'd kissed her tears away and loved her until they both lay exhausted, but still they hadn't slept. He was exhausted from spending every waking moment of the past month trying to figure out a way to keep her, to make her understand that he could be worthy of her. But it seemed that hadn't been a problem after all.

The problem was the life he had planned for himself. It was keeping them apart. If he went on to become jarl, then he would lose her. It was as simple as that. He would eventually have to marry, and he couldn't expect her to accept that. The mere thought of another man laying claim to her, if the situation were reversed, was enough to drive him mad with anger. He couldn't assume she would be happy to live that way. A wife would see her as a threat, even if he did install her at the farm. What wife would want a husband who was obsessed with his slave? It wouldn't work. He didn't even want to imagine it.

Then there was the betrayal by his father to consider. It shouldn't surprise him, but it did. Eirik knew the man's only goal was to see him installed as jarl. He just had never thought his father would stoop to lying to him to achieve it. It left him questioning how he could continue to serve the man, and if he even wanted to be jarl. But what was there for him if he wasn't jarl?

Merewyn. The answer came through like a shard of light after a storm. Merewyn could be his, but only if he gave up his destiny. Even if he could, what would there be for them?

'What will happen to us?'

He raised his head from her belly to look down at her. His gaze raked upwards from her narrow waist to the perfect mounds of her breasts, tipped with plump nipples, swollen now from his attention, and up to the slave collar at her neck. He touched it and looked up to her deep doe eyes. 'I'm not sure. But it's clear you can't stay here.'

'I could wait at the farm with Harold. I'm sure he'd keep me with food.'

He was already shaking his head before she even finished. 'My father can't be trusted. I'm sorry that I thought he could. You'll have to leave with us.'

'For Northumbria?' She sat up in shock. 'You're not taking me home, are you?'

He didn't know. He honestly didn't know what the future held for them. If the battle was bad, he'd have to return her to ensure her safety. Their camp would be no place for her. Instead of answering, he rose to his feet and dressed quickly.

'Eirik? Tell me what you're thinking.'

He only shook his head and gathered his armour and sword. Maybe her home would be better than the life that was ahead of him. There was only one way that he could even remotely consider it working out, and it was almost not worth considering. It would be unfair to give her hope when he had no idea what could happen. He needed to talk to his uncle before he knew for certain.

'I don't know, Merewyn,' he finally answered when she rose to her knees and perched on the edge of the bed. 'I only know that there is no future for us here. We leave in three days.'

Gunnar came for her before dawn on the third day. A short rap on the door was her only warning before it swung open and he stood in the frame, a shadow in the cold night.

'It's time to go home.'

She sat up fully clothed, because she'd been expecting someone to come get her very early. Though she'd hoped it would be Eirik. 'Where is Eirik?'

'On his boat.'

She took a deep breath and let it out slowly. 'Do you know what he's planning? Is he returning me to my family?' Of course he was, but she needed the confirmation. There was nothing else for him to do. She couldn't follow him into battle.

'He'll negotiate with your brother. Come, we have to go.'

The confirmation was more painful than she'd thought it would be, and she took a moment to gather her strength before swinging her legs over the edge of the bed. Eirik was returning her of his own free will. He could have taken her to the farm. What did the jarl care about him keeping a slave there? She turned to grab the fur she'd slept with, the only thing left in the room. Sweyn and another man had come to empty the chamber the day before, and had taken everything except the bed and tables. Even the silver chest filled with the presents Eirik had given her. She had voiced her displeasure at that, but Sweyn had only looked at her with enough pity in his eyes that she'd felt ashamed without even knowing why.

Pulling the fur around her, she followed Gunnar along the path to the river. Spring hadn't yet made its appearance, but winter was losing its death grip on the land. The snow had melted along the banks of the river. She felt an odd melancholy to be leaving. The place had only been her home for a short while, but it was where she'd found love with her Northman. She regretted that she'd never see the farm again. Truth be known, the farm felt more like home to her than anywhere. She blinked back a tear and swallowed back the ache in her throat.

She was surprised when Gunnar led her to a boat and followed her on board. She looked for Sweyn, who had crossed with her on Eirik's boat, but she didn't see him. None of the men looked familiar to her. This was Gunnar's boat. Eirik was nowhere in sight. He wasn't even returning her himself. She strained her neck to find him on his boat, but she wasn't sure which one it was. The figureheads had all been taken from the prows, so she was at a loss to identify the one with the terrifying dragon she remembered. There were more boats than she remembered, too. At least double the number now than on that trip. They already stretched in a line down river on their way to the fjord.

It wasn't until later when they were on the open water and the sun was up that she was able to pick him out. She recognised the sail when it was raised, and then the blond head of the giant helping to raise it. Her belly gave that little flip as it always did when she saw him after an absence, prompting her to put her hand there and think of the life that it sheltered. If she told him about the child, would it change his mind so that he would keep her? He must know that a baby was a possibility. He must know and not care because he hadn't bothered to ask.

She turned away in misery and looked back towards the shoreline that had long since disappeared. Her life had changed so much in the brief time since she'd known him, but now it seemed that nothing had really changed at all. She was still unwanted by those she loved. She closed her eyes and took a deep breath, vowing not to cry.

Chapter Thirty

She was able to keep that vow all the way up until the moment she saw Eirik. The seasickness had claimed her again, only this time the recovery had been slower, probably due to the baby that she was now certain she carried. By the time she had disembarked, she'd been so weak that she'd leaned heavily on Vidar as he led her to a tent. There were hundreds of them set up just past the stretch of sand that was the beach. Eirik came by the morning after they were settled, standing outside the open flap of the tent and dipping his head just enough to look her over where she lay on a pallet.

She sat up immediately, but he turned his attention to Vidar and the few men who stood outside near the fire. Their voices were too low to make out what they were saying, but there was no mistaking that he was ignoring her. She blinked back tears and got to her feet to go to him, but he took pity on her and came inside, closing the flap behind him.

'How are you feeling? You're still pale.'

She nodded, unwilling to spend the few precious moments she might have with him discussing her health. 'I'm fine. Tell me what's happening.'

He held himself still, but then the tension drained from him and he drew her into his arms. She gripped his shirt tight and buried her face in his familiar warmth. 'Whatever it is, tell me, unless you mean to leave me, and if that's the case then you must know that I won't stay. I'll come looking for you.'

He laughed and held her tighter. 'I've spoken to Uncle Einar and we mean to go talk with your brother.'

'Why?'

'Do you still want to marry me, Merewyn?'

The question caught her off guard so she pulled back to look at him. The uncertainty on his face was enough to make her stomach clench in pain. 'Aye, Eirik,' she rushed to reassure him. 'I want to marry you more than anything.'

'If everything goes well, then we will be married. If it doesn't…I'll have to send you somewhere safe. Away from the fighting.'

She nodded. Part of her wanted to tell him about the baby now, but she didn't want to add to his burden, so she held silent. 'But you will send for me later?'

'Aye, if I can, when it's all over. We leave now and should know more in a day or so. I have to go.' He bent and kissed her, a deep claiming kiss that left no doubt in her mind that he still wanted her. Finally, he reluctantly broke the kiss and pressed his forehead to hers.

'Please be safe.'

'I love you, Merewyn. Never forget that.'

The hardest thing she had ever done was watch him leave.

As far as she knew, he didn't come back, and on their fourth morning there, Vidar was binding her wrists and helping her mount a horse to follow in their direction. She'd protested the bindings, because they were unnecessary. What would she do? Grab a sword and start maiming Vikings? Take off on her pony for home? The only home she wanted to flee to was the farm and it sat across the sea. But Vidar had shrugged and left the bindings so loose they weren't effective.

Most of the other men in camp came along with them. Some on horseback, but most on foot.

* * *

By midday, she recognised the manor's beach and gasped when she saw Alfred on the far side, directly across from Eirik, with almost as many Saxons with him as they had Northmen. It had only been months since she'd last seen him, but her first sight of her brother now was a shock. She remembered him as large, solid, staunch, but the man who dismounted and walked the few steps across the beach to meet Eirik looked old, tired and defeated. He'd yet to glance her way. If that was because he'd failed to see her or because he didn't want to see her, she didn't know. At her gasp, Vidar slanted a harsh glance her way.

He was angry he had to play nursemaid and wasn't out there with his brothers. He'd grumbled as much the entire morning. She couldn't say that she blamed him. Her strength had returned, and neither of them believed that she needed a nursemaid, but he'd been ordered to mind her all the same.

She tugged at her bindings, wary of what was happening despite her brief visit with Eirik. She wasn't entirely certain he hadn't happened upon some misguided, noble scheme to return her, believing her safer with her family than in the middle of a war. If that was the case, she planned to tell Alfred of the child growing in her belly at her first opportunity and knew that he would either demand marriage or would refuse to accept her. Either way, she would not go back to the manor.

Only after her lower back started cramping from sitting on the horse so long did Eirik signal and Sweyn walked to collect her. She stomped her feet to force the blood back into them before she walked with Sweyn to join them exactly in the centre of the two sides. She tried to feign a demeanour as stoic as the men, but couldn't stop herself from letting her gaze linger on Eirik's unresponsive profile before giving Alfred her full attention.

'This is the man who took you?' He indicated Eirik.

Whatever she thought he might say to her, his brusque manner wasn't what she was expecting. Before she could even think to form an answer, Eirik's voice interrupted. Menacing and too controlled. 'Your wife gave her to me.' He said *wife* like a curse.

Alfred ignored him. 'You have been unharmed?' His voice was so cold that it took her a moment to answer.

'Aye' was all that she could manage. This was not the stoic yet gentle brother she remembered.

'Have you been violated?'

She was so shocked by the question, she couldn't answer, which prompted Alfred to ask again. 'Are you intact, Merewyn?'

She shook her head, unable to give voice to the words, unwilling to share that intimacy with this stranger who demanded answers from her. Despite her earlier resolve to tell him of Eirik's child, it seemed too impersonal now, too callous to blurt it out here in front of everyone. To tell him before she'd even had a chance to tell Eirik. But it was as if this stranger knew.

'Do you carry his bastard?'

'Enough, Saxon!' Eirik's voice was so forceful it made her jump.

'It's my right to know.'

'Nay, it's not your right to know. You have no rights here. Your wife gave them away for you. Either we do this now—no more questions—or we go and I'll take your home by morning.'

Merewyn looked between them, certain something was happening of which she had no knowledge. Before either of them could speak again, they were joined by a monk she didn't recognise wearing dark robes and the man she recognised as Alfred's captain of the guard. The monk looked nervous, and as soon as he began to recite the familiar Latin words, she understood why. She'd seen enough babies christened to understand what was happening. Though the setting and bottle of water he uncorked was strange, he was baptising Eirik. The monk wet his fingertip with the water and drew the sign of the cross on Eirik's forehead.

It happened too fast to be valid. She was certain it couldn't be legitimate, but as fast as it had begun, the bottle was tucked away and it seemed it was finished. But then the monk immediately turned to another part of his book and began reading.

'Wait!' Eirik held up his hand and the monk's gaze flicked up, though he seemed too afraid to lift his face from the book. 'Your men should put down their weapons now.'

'Not until it's finished, Dane.' Alfred's gaze flicked to her, starting a hollow deep in the pit of her stomach.

'We'll start with the spearmen,' Eirik continued as if he hadn't dissented.

Alfred relented and waved his hand. One by one the men tossed their spears. As the monk continued reading, it became clear that it was her wedding day and Eirik was her groom. Her blood roared so loud in her ears that she didn't hear a thing until the soothing murmur of Eirik's voice reciting his vows reached her.

Once he finished, more of Alfred's men laid down their weapons. When it was her turn, she hesitated, prompting Eirik's first look at her. She hadn't been expecting warmth in his eyes.

Eirik didn't smile, but she saw approval in his eyes. It mixed with the warmth to fill the hollowness within her. 'I'm sorry it has to happen this way.' He spoke low and in his own language so that Alfred couldn't understand. 'But will you take me as your husband?' She tried not to smile; it didn't seem right to allow Alfred to see how happy they were. But she nodded and didn't take her eyes from his as she repeated the vows. Only when it was finished did all of Alfred's men lay down their arms and Eirik cut the ties binding her wrists.

Gunnar and Sweyn each took a side and ushered Alfred towards the manor, and the Danes followed, even the others who she had thought had been back at camp, could be seen coming from the southwest. Eirik waited until they had been left in relative peace to bring her hands to his lips.

'We've spent the past days negotiating your brother's surrender. He'll help in our campaign to capture his king, in exchange for the safety of his men and family. It only cost a small fortune to pay his men to follow suit, but they all agreed. We'll be staying here, taking over the manor.'

'You won't be jarl now.'

'I'll be jarl here. Now. In my own right, and not because my father decreed it.' He shrugged and pulled her closer. 'Besides, here I get you. I choose you, sweet girl. I'm sorry I doubted that I would, that I made you doubt that I would. Being jarl is meaningless if it means giving you up. I only want you at my table, at my side, in my bed. I could never want any other woman fulfilling that role.'

'Mothering your children?' she asked, prompting him to look down at her.

'Aye, even that.' He took in a deep breath, and his hand went down to her belly as if to feel the life growing there. 'Are you—?'

She nodded and he smiled, his arms sliding around her again to pull her close so that he spoke near her ear. 'This is where I first saw you. I thought you were a siren. My own personal siren. I wanted nothing more than to be here with you, just like this.'

She leaned back just enough to look at him, remembering that first terrifying sight of his deep blue eyes. It seemed so long ago. Her hand moved to rest lightly above his heart. He took a deep breath, but accepted her touch, and she pressed until she thought she could feel its steady, reassuring beat beneath the chain mail. 'If only I'd have known you were my own personal Viking come to free me.'

He smiled that rare, genuine smile that always made her heart leap and claimed her with his kiss.

Epilogue

Merewyn smiled as Eirik roused in bed behind her, and his large hand came around her waist to splay against her now-flat belly. He looked over her shoulder and down at the baby suckling at her breast. The look of utter love and devotion on his face was enough to make her heart clench.

'He grows larger every day,' he whispered in awe. He touched the babe's cheek with his finger, drawing her eye to the wooden disk that rested on her breast. The slave collar was gone, but she'd kept the disk with its rune inscription of his name to wear on a necklace.

'Aye, he's strong like his father.'

'And his mother.' Eirik kissed her shoulder, but a voice calling outside the door drew his attention. 'And his sister,' he added, and smiled as he moved from the bed to pull on his trousers. Then he went to open the door for the toddler, who ran in and gave her a kiss before promptly settling herself in his place on the bed. He thanked Sempa and closed the door before joining them all on the bed, scooping his daughter up to cuddle her against his chest.

The baby had finished his breakfast, so Merewyn held him tight against her breasts as she rolled over to watch them murmuring about the trouble they would get into that day. And then she silently gave thanks that Eirik was with them and not out fighting as much anymore.

The king was being displaced and Alfred had been installed in his court as an intermediary. Dane law was firmly established in Northumbria, and Eirik ruled from Wexbrough Manor while Einar and Gunnar battled to the south. She sometimes wondered what Jarl Hegard thought of his eldest son becoming a powerful jarl in his own right, but they never heard from him directly. She regretted that their marriage had caused strife and hoped the older man would one day accept it. Gunnar had told her once that Kadlin had spoken favorably to Jarl Hegard about them and hoped that her words had helped. Merewyn regretted that she hadn't been able to know Kadlin better.

Eirik caught her eye and smiled. His nightmares weren't completely gone, but he hardly had them anymore, and when he did he was easy to rouse from them. He shifted the toddler to his left arm and brought her into the embrace of his right. She smiled and touched her firstborn's chubby hand where it rested on Eirik's chest and admired her mane of golden hair, so like her father's.

This was what she had wished for on the beach for all those years. Sometimes she still couldn't believe that her wish had come true.

'When is it my turn for breakfast?' her Northman whispered near her ear.

She laughed and snuggled closer to him.

* * * * *